The Apathy Engine

Paul Gallimore

CONTENTS

1 MEETING GONORILLA 1

2 2042 13

3 DAWN AND HER BOY 20

4 THE LEAGUE OF PSYCHOPATHS 26

5 SECRET BUNKER NUMBER 14 37

6 THE PLAN 54

7 THE BIG STRIDE 65

8 MR. WALSINGHAM 77

9 THE AFTERMATH 89

10 THE BIG MATCH 99

11 PLOUTON 111

12 MISSING 123

13 MR. BLOATER 131

14 DUPED 148

15 ENGLAND EXPECTS 163

16 NOBODY REALLY KNOWS 182

ACKNOWLEDGEMENTS 187

OTHER BOOKS BY THE AUTHOR 188

1 MEETING GONORILLA

Lying back, hands behind his head, Cyril Greaves, with a slight shiver became aware at a subconscious level that something was amiss. The details of the irregularity had not yet been reported to the bridge, but at someplace in the distant outreaches of his neural network signals were being passed. They were only elusive and confusing smoke signals at that moment, but he was picking something up right enough.

With an effort Cyril opened his eyes and propped himself halfway up, onto his elbows. He sighed deeply, almost aggressively, yet with unmistakable tones of self-pitying wistfulness. It was a sound he was making more frequently these days, hence the refinement.

Inwardly, he reproached himself and foresaw the onset of a terminal malaise. He scolded himself, 'Is this really the way to conduct a life?' he thought. Then thrust himself all the way up to the sitting position and rested his back against the high arm of the sofa. 'There really, really, has to be more to life than this.'

"Filth," he commanded imperiously.

"German?" the Apartment Management System asked.

"Just get on with it."

The lights in the room dimmed imperceptibly to match the luminosity of Cyril's preferred setting and a huge screen over to his left instantly came to life.

Cyril was a great one for imperceptible settings. The heating in his apartment was supposed to be maintained at 20.71 degrees C, giving rise to much mocking amongst the few who visited him.

The colour and razor-sharp definition of the on-screen picture were superb, you could see every tiny detail of the fleshy terrain of the young actress's face; every square millimetre of creamy skin and all the soft, blonde, downy hairs at the top of her forehead. This screen represented the pinnacle of audio-visual engineering, what used to be described as state-of-the-art.

The camera moved out from its subject, just a fraction, away from the girl's face. There was something brown clamped to both of her ears. Cyril tilted his head to better see what it was, but the camera was still too close in. The picture angle and distance remained static for some while, teasing the viewer into doing exactly what Cyril was doing now; darting his head from side to side like a bemused lizard. Eventually, the focus was pulled back a little enabling Cyril to identify the brown things as a pair of boots; knee length boots, worn by the girl herself.

"Oh no! Typical German—"

"Offen weit," said a man standing at her side, sounding like a dentist. A dentist who had surrendered the pastel-blue plastic apron in return for leather cowboy chaps and nothing else.

"She is offen weit," Cyril shouted back, "you can't get much weiter offen than that. And what the hell is that smell?"

Another German porn star with depilated genitals and wearing just an old-fashioned train driver's cap from the days of steam handed his colleague a bottle of wine.

"Oh my God," Cyril moaned, genuinely dissatisfied, bored, and light years from suffering the dull ache of an erection, "It's just so German! Why can't they get wine racks like everybody else? Football!"

The screen changed to display a powerful Teutonic body strolling nonchalantly across a verdant, immaculately manicured football pitch. It was yet another German; this time, Horst Kaltz. He was rolling the ball beneath the sole of his boot. He looked up and played it forty metres with the outside of his left peg to the Italian, Peppi Mancini, who killed it stone-dead with a single touch from a lazily outstretched leg.

"Not this stuff, real football. And what's that smell? Change the smell for God's sake!"

The screen changed again; to Cyril's preferred setting this time, The English Pub League; football streamed from his own website.

Now two stocky Englishmen were thundering side-by-side along the right flank of a badly worn and furrowed football field, somewhere in Luton. The player in possession of the ball, Eddie Shand, the wily wing wizard of The Dog and Duck, had evidently decided that a suitable opportunity had presented itself to loft a high, sweetly curling cross into his opponent's penalty area. He drew back his leg in readiness for the lofting.

"Go on Eddie my son, fly like the wind! Why not, it's the only thing you're any good at."

Eddie Shand's most immediate opponent, Percy Cooke; fellow thunderer, arch-rival and hatchet man for the poncey new wine bar, The Artificial Intelligence, happened to share the same exquisite sense of timing as his adversary. Uncannily, he had selected that very same moment for brutally hacking Shand's legs from under him, which he proceeded to do with the consummate gracelessness of a master. The ball passed tamely into touch, whilst Eddie Shand went aquaplaning at high speed across an Olympic swimming pool-sized puddle and into an advertising hoarding. The referee waved play-on.

"That's more like it," Cyril grinned. "Hey! Why didn't you put this on in the first place instead of that Euro-cak?"

He sat up, clearly annoyed and not a little puzzled. "And another thing, it's too cold in here? And I've just realised there was a fly in here earlier. When I was dozing a fly flew past my head, didn't it? And it smells like a farmyard in here."

"There are no flies in here Cyril." The computer was quite adamant.

"You put the wrong football programme on, it's too cold, the whole room now stinks of pig's shit, and I definitely felt a fly earlier. What's going on?"

"There's somebody who wants to speak with you."

Cyril looked at the screen to see who the caller was. Instead the screen went black, the holoplayer came to life and Neville Boyle took shape in front of him. Neville was standing in the hallway outside of Cyril's apartment and he had a friend with him; an attractive looking female one.

"Oh yeah, that's another thing. The football, fair enough, that had to be on-screen, too big to be a hologram, but how come the porn video wasn't a floor show?"

"Can I come in Cyril?" asked Neville's hologram before the computer could reply.

"Where are you?"

"I'm outside the door."

"What? My door?"

"Yes, just outside the door."

"Oh, I didn't recognise my own hallway. The hologram's a bit fuzzy, that's probably why." Cyril turned away from Neville's 3D image and barked at the computer, "Open the door! If you can remember how to do it."

"I don't know the code, you never told me."

"Not you Neville, you moron, I'm talking to the computer, it's malfunctioning."

The door hissed slightly, then opened. Neville and his attractive lady friend walked through. Neville now stood next to his own facsimile.

"I don't normally say this to other chaps, but you're a devilishly handsome fellow," he told the hologram, which slowly dissolved.

"This is Gonorilla," Neville told Cyril. "What's that awful smell? Are you unwell?"

"I'm fine, thank you. It's the entertainment system odouriser, it's on the fritz."

Cyril was a bit taken aback by the girl's name, it was way too close to 'gorilla', but if anybody could pull it off, he thought, it was this vision of loveliness before him. He also wondered what she was doing with Neville.

Naming had become ever more unconventional over recent decades. The tipping point was when Seven Beckham became a celebrity in her own right. In the year twenty thirty, Seven was the most popular girl's name in the western world, but it spawned actual mathematical one-upmanship, so that by twenty thirty-one the most popular girl's name was 'Eight', followed the year after by 'Nine' and so on, until some mothers exercised the nuclear option and called their children 'Amillion', 'Abillion' and 'Atrilliana'. There were now even girls called 'Gooji', which was short for 'Googol'; ten raised to the power of one hundred, and 'Plexi'; short for 'Googolplex'; ten raised to the power of Googol.

"Hi. Lovely name, by the way." He smiled at Gonorilla and hoped that his remark didn't come across as sarcasm.

"Thank you for a kind compliment, Cyril" she replied. "You are most thoughtful. I was named after one of the daughters of King Leir, from the play of the same name. My name should not be confused with King Lear's daughter from Shakespeare's play of the same name; the two plays are not the same. In fact, Shakespeare's character was called *Goneril*, not *Gonorilla*, so the comparison is inexact."

Cyril hesitated slightly at the strange formality of her speech, but soon composed himself. "See if you can see a fly Neville."

As Cyril spoke a pencil thin beam of red light flashed briefly and burned a spider that had been sitting on Neville's shoulder.

"Hmmm," said Cyril, sounding unconvinced by what he regarded as the computer's showy attempt to make amends.

Vacuum motors started up from behind the walls and sucked away any residue that might have reached the floor. The motors stopped almost as soon as they began. The Laser fired again and removed another spider from the visitor's leg, then the motors whirred up again.

"Alright then, I give in, where have you been this time?"

"Nowhere," Neville replied slightly defensively, raising his airman's goggles. "Well, just the usual really, walking around on my lonesome from one pyramid to another. There's actually no need for all this cleanliness you know, spiders and flies don't hurt you."

"You were not lonesome today," Gonorilla corrected him. "I accompanied you."

"Yes," Neville agreed, "Gonorilla and I met for the first time yesterday, out striding, and she joined me for part of today's expedition."

"We strode together for a little over one-point-three miles," she pointed out.

"Right," Cyril offered by way of a meaningful response.

Neville had been a stridesman for around five years, ever since he realised that his area of scientific expertise, which happened to be statistical analysis on micro-organisms in the Kent desalination plants, was becoming ever more pointless due to the fact that he was being totally outclassed and outperformed by the technology.

So, Neville gave it all up to cut loose, become a stridesman and spend his time walking in the outlands. At least, he did on three days of the week, weather permitting.

"I never said flies and spiders would hurt me, did I? What's bothering me is that the computer is putting on the wrong TV channels, making the temperature too low, putting stuff on screen when it should be on hologram, producing farmyard smells to accompany porn and telling me there's no fly in here when I know there is. See if you can see a fly."

Neville parted his brown, knee-length, leather coat and planted his hands firmly on his hips and began to survey the walls of Cyril's apartment.

The long coat and the airman's goggles were the hallmark of the stridesmen; the latter-day frontiersmen and women who regularly shunned the demat chambers in favour of the age-old mode of transport made famous by their forebears - walking. In truth they never walked all that far; just a few miles at a time, but it was a few miles more than anybody else. Some of the older folk compared the stridesmen to fresh-water anglers. Such was their aura and mystique.

Now that the demats had emerged as a preferred form of transport; even over short distances, minor roads were being less well maintained and many were completely overgrown. The degree to which the countryside was untended was exacerbated by the irrigation of African, the Australian Outback and some deserts, which thereafter became agriculturally rich, as well as being vast in size. This, coupled with the ability to transport goods across the whole planet in seconds by dematting had meant that many small farms, worldwide, had become less important, often commercially unviable, and, as a result, part of what regular urbanites referred to as 'the outlands'.

"This your design?" Neville asked, nodding at the walls.

Cyril was revolving slowly, anxious to be the first to spot the fly.

"Programmed it last night," he affirmed.

"No wonder you're always so miserable if this is what you inflict on yourself."

"There it is, Nev, up there, right by the motion sensor. Hey, computer! It's right by one of the sensors."

"I have been scanning for insects and running self-diagnostics ever since you first claimed to see a fly, and I have to report that diags are clean and I still do not detect a fly."

"Well, try sensing for sound - buzzing, or whatever they do."

Cyril, Neville and Gonorilla held their breath, in order to give the AMS (Apartment Management System) an even chance of detecting such a tiny noise.

"I am picking up sounds that could well be a small insect. Would you like me to fire the pulsed laser?"

"Course I would, that's what you were built for."

"Only, sound sensing is not nearly as accurate as heat and motion with radar confirmation and library verified molecular identification. I can only guarantee calibration stage-one accuracy."

"Meaning?"

"Meaning," Neville cut in, "that the computer is not promising that it won't shoot your nipples off."

"Forget it, stupid machine. I'll resort to a method taught to me by my grandmother."

Cyril left his visitors in the main accommodation area of the apartment.

"He's just getting something from the kitchen," Neville told Gonorilla, in case she hadn't grasped the situation.

"Yes," she responded "I believe he is consulting with his grandmother."

"No," Neville retorted, "I don't think—"

Cyril burst back into the room. "Duck!"

Neville dived for cover as his host hurled a wet dishcloth across the room at the wall where the fly had come to rest.

"See, look at that. Who needs computers? That method never, ever fails. Wet dishcloth. Too fast for them. My grandmother taught me that."

The cloth slid down the wall leaving a trail of water all the way to the floor. Cyril bent over the cloth and tossed it over to reveal the fly, which was on its back with its legs slightly curled, apparently deceased.

"Vacuum," Cyril commanded.

"No! Wait!" Neville interjected. "Wait."

"What is it," Cyril asked, "did you want to say a few words over the body first?"

"No." Neville replied, untouched by the sarcastic content of Cyril's remark. "No, I thought you might like to have the computer analyse the fly, to try to find out why it was undetectable?"

"How can it analyse the fly when it won't even admit that it exists?"

"Hmmm." Neville hadn't considered that. "Well, at least we could put it under the microscope and have a look ourselves."

Neville carefully picked the fly up by its wings and held it up at eye level. They both peered at the intruder and concluded that it looked like a bluebottle, except that it was grey; slate grey. Neville took it over to the computer interface, which was essentially just more sensors for one thing and another. Part of the sensing equipment was a plastic drawer, which was used to house items requiring visual enlargements; books, maps, foodstuffs, anything that you wanted to have blown-up and displayed on-screen.

"Times two hundred," Neville ordered.

The screen was switched on immediately and the right side of the fly's body filled half of the big display area. The two friends stood back, far enough to take in the detail. The fly's legs looked like thick, chunky, hairy tree trunks.

"Yuck." Cyril cringed. "Let's look at its eyes."

Neville opened the drawer, rotated the fly, then closed it again.

"Eeeaagh, disgusting," was Cyril's reaction to the alternative viewpoint. "Bloody awful looking thing. Chuck it on the floor and let's blow it away."

"Hang on," Neville pleaded, "don't be hasty."

He opened the drawer once more and did something else with the fly, then shut it again.

"Display," he called to the computer.

This time the screen showed a picture of the fly's belly, which to Cyril was every bit as distasteful as the rest of it.

"Get the filthy thing out of my micro-drawer."

"Times five hundred," called Neville.

This time the entire screen was filled by just a portion of the fly's mid-section, such that the head and the other end of the body were out of view completely. They could only see the underside of the creature. They stood back even further this time to try to assimilate the information. As they did so, first Cyril's, then Neville's mouth dropped open. They could make out a marking, etched or grown into the body of the fly:

F-56 BLUEBOTTLE - STEALTH VARIANT

Neither of them spoke for several seconds.

"No wonder the computer couldn't detect it." Neville shook his head admiringly. "But why would they want to make a stealth fly?"

"Tsch!" was Cyril's contemptuous response. "What makes you think it's a they?"

"Well," Neville stepped back defensively, "it's obviously some kind of dastardly corporate invention, isn't it? I mean it's hardly—"

"It's obviously the work of that little pillock, Beeba."

"Beeba?" Isn't that—"

"Yes, it is."

"Wow, that's hugely impressive. You have to admit it, that is totally awesome."

"I told her not to buy him a Junior Scientist Genetic Engineering Set for his birthday, but would she listen? He's only had it a couple of weeks."

Cyril told Neville and Gonorilla to be seated. He wanted to ask them what had brought them to his apartment and to learn more about this beautiful looking woman who had either taken leave of her senses, or, as Cyril suspected, was not even a real person.

It occurred to Cyril that Gonorilla had all the hallmarks of a Botty Bot, one of the new 'All Woman' replicas developed fairly recently by the American corporation IOW Dynamics Inc., a subsidiary of The Bloater Corporation.

Although Cyril was never sure if he had seen one personally, Botty Bots were all the rage and everybody was talking about them.

Botty Bots were all said to be fabulously attractive, like Gonorilla, with what the manufacturer's literature called 'optimal buttock curvature and compression resistance' or 'great arses', as they were referred to colloquially. Physically, Botty Bots were supposed to be irresistibly attractive to heterosexual men and there was no shortage of individuals who boasted that they had had sex with them. Really great, unbelievable, mind-blowing sex, which came with the full range of authentic, ridiculous porn star sex noises included.

The word was that Botty Bots were not truly sentient, but their movement, touch, feel and response programming was reckoned to be uncannily good. Hence, they seemed very authentic, better looking than real people and, it was said, somewhat more boring than almost everybody.

Amongst the tech savvy online community, it was widely known that IOW Dynamics were striving for full sentience for their machines, which many people considered to be a threatening ambition on the part of the company. Meanwhile, it was also known that the latest software update level for the Bots was named, 'Hairdresser'.

Botty Bots were reported to have equally impressive male counterparts; unofficially known as the A-9's. So-called because they were all endowed with a nine-inch penis. Not only that, but the A9's did not complete their sexual performances in the same time that it once took Usain Bolt to complete the one hundred metres sprint. Neither did they simply roll over afterwards and go to sleep. Instead, they would stay awake to make small talk for hours if required, or else select from over fifty reassuring post-coital phrases, including 'I guarantee that I will re-decorate the hall and the kitchen first thing tomorrow morning' and 'I am so looking forward to your friend, Mary's, wedding. We must go and shop for new clothes together, tomorrow.'

The official line from IOW Dynamics was that none of their Bots were currently in public circulation and that none were available for purchase, but public opinion disagreed. It was considered to be common knowledge that the Bots were being trialled amongst the population in a number of countries, including England, where Cyril lived.

What people did not realise was that mass production was hampered for the foreseeable future by the fact that the Bots required substantial quantities of rare earth metals, such as indium, niobium and ruthenium, and these were now largely under Chinese control and, in effect, rationed in western countries; a problem that IOW Dynamics would need to overcome.

"So, Nev, what brought you two over here today?"

"Just happened to be striding in the area, so I thought that I would introduce you to Gonorilla."

"Cool."

"What made you become a strideswoman, Gonorilla?"

"Striding is very good for human blood circulation; it exercises the heart and lungs, fights obesity and is recommended by leading medical practitioners."

"Cool, right. And you just bumped into each other the other day, did you?"

"Yes, that occurred yesterday. The weather was very fair and I independently decided that it was a fine day to stride. My opinion was reinforced by consulting the local weather forecast. I set off from President Alex Jones pyramid - which is named after the forty-seventh president of the United States of America - at ten o'clock and boldly strode into the outlands. After only thirty-seven minutes I enjoyed the good fortune of a chance encounter with our mutual friend, Neville."

"Nice one. So what, you're going to be doing more striding together, are you?"

"Yes, I hope that we shall. Neville is peachy, wonderful,

sensational company."

Cyril glanced over at Neville and wondered how he had managed to miss those qualities during the twenty years that they had known each other; since year-seven at school. Neville returned a blank, non-sensational look; something he had always specialised in.

"I should now like to visit the little girls room if I may? Though, as this is a male's apartment I suppose that it should be called *little boys room*? Or, as some say, bathroom."

"Or toilet," Cyril offered. "Help yourself."

He watched her carefully as she walked out of the room, paying particular attention to her buttocks as she went.

"She has a rather nice bottom, your girlfriend."

"Not really my girlfriend yet, we've only just met."

"You don't suppose she just might happen to be a—"

"Definitely not." Neville cut in, "You just don't know her like I do. She's actually very warm and funny and, you know, really sentient."

"Right, but you could just ask her outright."

"What, ask an attractive woman that I have just met— In fact, the first woman that I have met in—"

"Your whole life."

"In about two years - if she's a robot?"

"No, no. Good lord, no. Just flip the question a little."

"How?"

"Ask her if she's human."

"Really?"

"No, not really, I was joking. But remember the old second world war films? They always flushed out the German spies by asking them questions that only the locals would know the answer to, such as who won the F-A Cup Final last year. That was a favourite."

"Right, well that's not going to work because it's a known fact that all of the Bots are engineered with what spies call a *legend*, built-in. In other words, a backstory; a personal history."

"Worth a try, though."

"Not worth a try. I can't believe that you're pulling apart a woman who is destined to fall in love with me."

"Already has by the sounds of it, you peachy son of a gun."

The toilet cistern could be heard flushing in the near distance and Cyril and Neville commenced to lounge, ostentatiously.

Gonorilla returned to the room and told them how refreshed she was now feeling.

The three of them chatted for a while longer.

"Well," Cyril said at length, "there's things that I have to be doing. I need to sort the F-fifty-six, stealth fly situation out for one thing."

Neville and Gonorilla took the hint and stood up and made ready to leave.

"Oh," Cyril remembered, "don't forget it's Tyler's psycho gig at The Comment tonight. Are you both going?"

"Probably, yes," Neville replied. "I suppose one shouldn't miss an opportunity to be at an event like that." After a short pause he bit the bullet and addressed his new, would-be girlfriend, "Gonorilla, you don't know who won last year's F-A Cup Final, do you?"

"Chelsea beat Tottenham Hotspur three-one in a thrilling encounter. The match was only settled after extra time and penalties," she replied.

"That's what I thought," said Cyril.

2 2042

Alone again, Cyril made himself a nice cup of tea and plonked himself back on his sofa, and when that wasn't bringing him answers he moved over to his dining table and sat on a chair, before finally moving back to the sofa.

It wasn't that he was depressed or anything nasty like that; the truth was that in the year 2042 things were good for Cyril, as with everybody else.

Most people lived in highly advanced societies where everybody was provided with everything that anybody ever really needed. Many worked at least part-time, but only because they wanted to, or because they had some special business idea, or other ambition.

The world's energy problems had been solved a decade previously by the vastly cleaner thorium-based nuclear reactors that the Chinese had been first to crack, along with fifth generation photovoltaics that covered just about any surface that could sneak a peek at the sun. There was even word of the world's first production version of an over-unity generator on the horizon; a perpetual motion machine which would produce electricity with the aid of permanent magnets, with minimal energy input and no polluting by-products.

Food was also plentiful, now that so many vast and barren areas of the planet had been terraformed and made agriculturally productive. Even if they had not been, food could be reconstituted using technology. The nanobots seemed to be able to make anything from anything. They could take mounds of rubbish and convert them to raw materials, or in some cases actual alternative items. Nothing was ever wasted. So much so that even old landfill sites were being excavated for re-usable material. It was a time of untold abundance. Ashes to ashes, dust to dust, molecules to selfie sticks.

Part of the great success of societies in those years was the smooth running of things. In England, as in other countries in what used to be called the Anglosphere, and the western world generally, governance had shifted away from representative democracy to direct democracy. In practice this meant that there were far fewer politicians and those who still operated tended to act as advocates for things and custodians of democracy, whilst ordinary people voted electronically on virtually all issues that came before their governments.

These were the days when President Lincoln's, 'government of the people, by the people, for the people,' leapt out of the Gettysburg address and into public life for the first time ever.

The odd thing was that no matter what issues came before national governments, the people always seemed to arrive at exactly the right decisions. As a result of such a surfeit of voter wisdom, everything in the garden was rosy. Just everything was absolutely hunky-dory.

Yet, not everybody was happy with the new status quo. The order of things chafed against human nature it seemed to Cyril.

Mankind had stopped wandering around looking for food ten thousand years before, when he had invented farming. Thereafter, the first city states were born and then empires. First, there were city empires and then national, financial and business empires, but the thing was this. Whichever kind of empires man chose to build, he did not expect them to be handed to him. That was the problem; men like to strive and fight for what they get, even kill for it, not lie on a couch and wait for feeding time. In 2042, people were living like pampered zoo animals.

Cyril was not working, since he clearly did not need to, and he found no extra purpose on the occasions when he did. Instead he had channelled his energy into his website; EnglishPubLeague.com. The site started as a joke, a roundup of local amateur football (soccer) games; so-called Sunday league matches. The joke was built around the deliberate romanticising of low quality football and footballers in a parody of the high paid and glamorous professionals.

However, what started as a joke rapidly gained traction on social media and the website started receiving video clips from across the country and beyond. Where people would have normally posted their funny, or impressive, soccer related videos directly onto YouTube, they were now often choosing The English Pub League, or EPL as it was known, instead.

What helped matters tremendously was the quality of web hosting that was available by that time. Heavy bandwidth video streaming was available to anybody with a website. In addition, there were local video companies who were erecting temporary builder's scaffold towers to video EPL games. They were providing this service for free in exchange for having credits run during the intros of the EPL's live feeds.

Besides all of this, Cyril was doing interviews with various Sunday league players and using his photographer friend, Tyler Plummer, to take high quality pictures of them in a studio. So they all looked liked stars when they were off the pitch - much less so on it. It didn't take long for a swathe of marriage proposals to arrive for the players, as well as less binding, more prurient ones, to start turning up in the email inbox.

In recent weeks Cyril had started to receive financial inducements to advertise from the English Pub League website. He, along with many of the better-known players, had been offered clothes to wear and brands to promote. The requests to advertise from the website included half-sized cigarettes called 'Half Time', hangover cures, such as 'PintGone', orthotics for flat feet and weight loss products for 'the larger athlete'. The often septuagenarian referees were getting offers to advertise designer spectacles, as well as vitamin pills and potions for the over-fifties.

The games were no longer attended by just one man and his dog, plus the odd girlfriend and a couple of mothers who couldn't let go; there were now usually small crowds at the sides of the pitches. Some matches even had proper fighting amongst the supporters to echo that which occurred on the pitch.

With regard to website traffic, it was difficult to say what the monthly number of unique visitors was; the figure seemed to be rising exponentially. The big news was that there were occasions when a streamed game between Cyril's local pub, The Troll's Comment, and a nearby rival, The King's Hampton, say, could take serious viewing figures away from The European Champions League, or the mighty English Premier League. All of this was bringing attention from on-high. Sometimes unwanted attention.

One of the world's biggest corporations was The Bloater Corporation, which was a holding company for a huge number of subsidiaries that were each famous in their own right, plus hundreds of smaller subsidiary companies in places like Barbados, British Virgin Islands, Jersey, Luxembourg, Monaco, Switzerland and the rest. These countries represented, of course, the so-called, 'secrecy jurisdictions', from where Bloater's large corporations could bill themselves for work that nobody had really done and thereby drastically reduce their legitimate tax burdens. In fairness, this behaviour was not a Bloater Corporation invention, it had been standard large business practise since at least as far back as 1990.

The massive Bloater Corporation, it seemed, was slowly starting to take control of the world. They ran schools, security firms and even police forces in all major countries. They were attempting to acquire more and more newspaper and television companies, as well as film and media production companies; which created game shows, soaps operas and video games.

Bloater Corporation had highly placed representatives in EUFA and FIFA along with top people in other sports. Their manufacturing divisions were impressive, high-tech and growing. It was not just the Bots that were getting people talking, they were building a vast manufacturing base in low-tech as well as high-tech goods, and their products were everywhere. Bloater Corporation's most well-known venture, before the Bots became famous, was the vast robot-led manufacturing base on the Moon. 'Off-worlding', as it became known, had been made economically viable as soon as the demats became a proven technology. India was furious about it.

Bloater Corporation was one hundred percent owned and run by the extremely reclusive Seb Bloater. The famous entrepreneur was said to be ruthless, steely, and something of a visionary, although nobody really knew what he looked like. All that ever got returned by a search of Google Images was old, grainy newspaper images of him as a very young man; there was nothing large, sharp and digital looking. It was said that there were up-to-date shots to be found on the dark web, but they were never available via the mainstream and most people did not care to go hunting through millions of unindexed websites just to glimpse an image of some business tycoon.

It was with this knowledge in mind that Cyril was now looking at another email from Kevin Jeeps, who did have a visible presence on the Internet. Jeeps was one of Seb Bloater's lieutenants; possibly his right-hand man. He had been contacting Cyril about the English Pub League website; they evidently wanted to buy it.

Initially, Cyril had thanked Jeeps and said 'no', without ever enquiring about what he might be paid for it. This was because his website was currently his main focus of attention. It was true he did now have a new girlfriend of sorts, though she came with some heavy baggage.

Being offered money; potentially a lot of money, is not only exciting, but also very flattering and Cyril was tempted to enter into negotiations for no good reason other than the thrill of it. So far he had managed to pull himself back from the brink and consider what he would do once the website was gone, and also what might become of it after it was sold. What would a massive American corporation do to a website that was ostensibly created to gently poke fun and celebrate English Sunday league football? Quite possibly it would become a game show, or perhaps a new vehicle for the Kardashian dynasty. Plexi Kardashian and her huge plastic posterior had already become all but omnipresent as it was.

What was annoying Cyril even more and putting him off selling his website, was the fact that Jeeps kept referring to the EPL website as, 'a great piece of real estate' and 'an intriguing franchise'. More annoying still, was the fact that Jeeps had described himself on his LinkedIn page as a 'thought leader'. Describing yourself as a 'thought leader' deserves a punch in the face for infringing the laws of humility; which although non-existent really ought to be written into the statute books. After all, whose thought was he leading and why did they need to be led?

Kevin Jeeps was not a man who could possibly understand the nuances of the EPL, nor would he ever care to. He undoubtedly just wanted the English Pub League for some base reasons; presumably entirely financial.

'Oh yes,' Cyril thought, looking at Jeeps's mug on Google, 'a ponytail as well. That's another punch in the face, I think.'

Whilst he was in internet mode he moved over to the EPL's social media page to look at a thread he had started about a week earlier, which said simply, 'Really tired of everything going wrong in my apartment. Anybody else having technical problems?'

This had been the last thing that he had posted. He was aware that he had been remiss for not looking-in on the page for a while. Now that the main EPL website was so big, people were following its progress and chipping in with their comments, daily.

To his huge surprise, there were around twelve-thousand comments from people across the world, but mostly the UK and

USA; complaining about a huge number of technical failures; things that normally just did not happen. The word that people seemed to have settled on was 'glitching'; it seemed that the technical problems had become frequent enough to have acquired a recognised descriptor for the phenomenon.

What people were describing seemed to correspond exactly to the problems that Cyril was experiencing, which in truth were all minor niggles. Basic electrical and electronic items were not breaking down completely, but were randomly and intermittently failing and doing strange things. The correspondents on Facebook were moaning about all of the same things that Cyril had been subject to, though in some cases there had been power outages and brownouts as well.

It was all a bit bizarre and not at all what people were used to. The odd thing was that nobody seemed to be all that bothered. People weren't foaming at the mouth, or even threatening to take placards out onto the streets; tempting as that has always been for some people.

As Cyril was poring over the plethora of remarks on Facebook his television screen switched itself on, unasked, and presented a news item featuring Conservative politician Nickolai Sledge. Cyril did a double take between the computer screen that he had been looking at and the main screen in his apartment. What a coincidence! As a result of another glitch, the television turning itself on, Sledge was now on TV talking about the very thing that he had just been reading about, glitching.

"Look, this is something that I fully intend to take up with colleagues in government," Sledge told a reporter. "I think that there is a very real threat from intelligent machines which have been allowed to proliferate, under whose control we do not know. There seems to have been a complete lack of accountability and we need to ensure that what we have is fit for purpose."

"Do you accept that your government is responsible for misdirecting the people over these problems?"

"If the situation demands it we will commission a full independent enquiry."

"But do you think that government has played a part in--"

"I have come here today to discuss the Euro-Chinese Common Market and that is my intention."

"On that subject. What do you make of the huge resistance right around Europe for any kind of meaningful union with the Chinese? Ending trade tariffs and so on?"

"It's a parochial mentality derived, quite frankly, from racists and little Europeans."

Cyril watched Sledge with some bewilderment. Bewildered at the great coincidence that had just played out and bewildered, like everybody else, about what the role of politicians really was in 2042.

Sledge had been talking about consulting colleagues in government, but most people were not sure if there really was a government anymore, at least in the old-fashioned sense. There were definitely politicians, but very few members of the general public could name the individuals in the top three or four government positions: Prime Minister, Foreign Secretary, Home Secretary and Chancellor. In a way, Cyril found that comforting, as it meant that really nothing had changed over the decades.

And then, as if to confirm him in the notion that nothing had ever really changed, the news cut away to a far-left march through the streets of London. As ever, the 'Placardists', as they were known by then, were streaming along Whitehall carrying lists of things that they hated: the government, anybody who ever voted conservative, big companies, posh schools, people with nice cars and so on. They were led by their cheerleaders who carried megaphones and wore the kind of flat working men's caps made popular by Lenin during the time of the mass murders, known as the *Red Terror* - which for some reason have been considered essential, authentic man-of-the-people-wear ever since.

Even this march, Cyril reflected, lacked the zeal of a real political rally. These were people who were essentially out for a stroll with a bit of orchestrated grumbling thrown in.

The fact was, everything really was absolutely hunky-dory and no amount of linking arms and chanting could hide that. Not even lighting lots and lots of candles and singing, *We Shall Not Be Moved*

3 DAWN AND HER BOY

After he had got his slightly churlish, state-of-the-nation, reflections out of the way, Cyril took a quick shower, had breakfast and generally spruced himself up; clean Mott The Hoople t-shirt and all.

He placed the weirdly repulsive F-56 stealth fly onto a tissue and folded it. Then he took a last look at himself in the mirror and squinted his eyes a little, like male film stars do when photographers encourage them to look handsome, edgy and slightly dangerous. He turned away and then back again to practice the rakish half-smile he'd been working on.

After Neville's visit, and with the prospect of Tyler's inaugural meeting of his newly formed League of Psychopaths that evening, he had an extra spring in his step. It was just a shame that he now felt that he must go to his 'not sure if she's really my girlfriend' girlfriend, Dawn, and put his foot down over the unwelcome, genetically modified insect.

The pyramids had been around for roughly fifteen years and were now being built all over the country. They were essentially the modern take on the high-rise tower block, except that they were much, much bigger and usually included several floors of underground accommodation.

The pyramids earned their name due to being constructed roughly in the shape of the original pyramids of Egypt. Each of the outer apartments had small gardens, which sat on top of the roofs of the apartments below. Apartments that were inside the pyramid - in the Tutankhamun positions - as people called them, had natural light piped to them by fibre optics, which were made to look very like real windows. All apartments were extremely well sound-proofed with noise insulation material and active noise suppression built into the walls.

Other features that made the pyramids very desirable places to live were the mini-malls and cinemas that were located inside them, as well as demat chambers and levitation cars that ran freely between them. In addition, since so many people could be housed within a relatively small geographic footprint, the pyramids all had beautifully tended gardens and play areas that could be used by the residents and others.

Since he was feeling a bit more high-energy than of late, Cyril decided to skip down the stairs to the floor below on this occasion, rather than use an elevator. He was soon pressing the buzzer by the side of Dawn's door, except it didn't buzz, it caused an electronic voice inside the apartment to call out, 'knock-knock, knock-knock'; a chime that had been selected from a menu by the occupants.

Dawn soon had the door wide open and stood across the entrance.

"Hello, my lover." She sang to him in her pretty Welsh accent.

Dawn was thirty-six years old; four years older than Cyril, and she had a fourteen-year-old son, Beeba, whom she had raised by herself. She was standing in her pink pyjamas, and Cyril was taken once again by her raven black hair, green eyes and flashing smile. Not to mention her buxomness. Dawn had made it clear that she was very keen on Cyril and, for his part, he rather wanted to fall in love with her, but he couldn't make up his mind whether or not he might be biting off a bit more than he could chew. She was Beeba's mother after all, and Beeba was already a legend in Farage Pyramid, despite them only having lived there for three months.

"Morning," he responded. "You're looking very acceptable in a *not actually my girlfriend* kind of way."

"Thanks. Don't overdo the flattery, will you." She stepped aside to allow him in. "And I am definitely your girlfriend; you're just slow to catch on."

In her kitchen Cyril pulled out the tissue. He showed Dawn the fly, explained its impressive stealth capabilities, and where he thought it came from.

"Bloody horrible big thing isn't it?" Dawn wrinkled her nose, "but I've got no idea whether Beeba could make a thing like that. Although, it is true that I bought him one of those genetic engineering kits for his birthday, and he has got a brain the size of a planet, like me. You realise that he got his very high I-Q from me, don't you?"

Cyril shrugged and pursed his lips.

"Only, if you're totting up the pros and cons on the ideal girlfriend front, I'm packing at least thirty I-Q points over you."

Cyril furrowed his brow. "Hey, don't misunderestimate my organ," he told her, tapping his head.

"Just wait a minute, I'll get him."

Dawn moved to the kitchen door and called across the narrow hallway.

"Beeba . . ."

There was no reply; not even after a few repetitions, so she altered her tack.

"Beeba, darling. Sweetheart . . ."

"What!"

"Here a minute."

"I'm in bed."

"I know, come here."

"I'm still asleep."

"I know, but there's someone to see you."

"Who?"

"Cyril."

"He's seen me before."

"He wants to ask you something."

"How would I know?"

"How would you know what?"

"Whatever he wants to ask me. I don't know."

They heard things banging around in Beeba's room and loud mumbling, which they couldn't quite make out, but which sounded a lot like, 'bludfuggi stoo ol cow. Just coz shegotta newfuggi boyfriend.'

A few minutes passed and Beeba arrived in the kitchen, dressed.

"What?" he asked. "I'm not calling him *uncle* and definitely not *dad*, if that's what you want to know?"

Cyril, who had his back turned to the door whilst trying to work out how to use Dawn's filtered coffee machine, turned to face Beeba.

"What I wanted to discuss," he said as he slowly revolved, "is . . . What the holy crap have you done to yourself!"

"What?" Beeba asked.

"Who are you supposed to be, Friar Tuck?"

"Oh, yes," Dawn stepped in, "he's got some religious idea now. Haven't you? Hence the hair."

"Was that done by your mother with an actual bowl, or can you still find barbers who are willing to do that to people?"

"Barber. And it's not some religious idea."

Cyril felt a tad guilty about his reaction; it's probably not a good idea to shatter the confidence of a boy of his age by criticising his appearance. On the other hand, Beeba was not short of confidence; he was a force of nature, sometimes in serious and urgent need of reigning back where possible. He was addressing both Beeba and Dawn when he apologised. "Sorry. It's just that . . . You know, you don't see many teenagers with haircuts like that anymore. Not for the last seventy years or so, anyway."

"Paah," Beeba retorted, dismissively, "teenagers are retards." A remark that he clearly did not intend to be all-inclusive.

"What religion have you signed-up to then?"

"A new one."

"What's it called?"

"I don't know yet."

Cyril, frowned a quizzical frown and pointed it in Beeba's direction.

"I haven't decided what to call it yet, but I'm thinking *The Light of Beebaria*, or *TEHCOATU*. It sounds really ethnic, like a Red Indian tribe or something. It's short for *The Exceedingly Holy Church Of All The Universes*."

"Phew!" Cyril gasped and dropped his shoulders in mock relief, "You're starting you own religion. For a moment I was worried that you were going to get into something stupid."

"No way," Beeba assured him. "Been studying it for ages, plus politics, statistics and sociology. And what I have discovered is that, statistically, seventy-five percent of people are complete idiots, and even the ones who are not morons are willing to believe absolutely anything if it broadly tallies with what they want to hear."

"Yes," Cyril agreed. "Sales theory one-oh-one."

Dawn shooed Beeba and Cyril into the living room while she went off to get dressed. The two males continued their conversation from armchairs.

"And the point of all this is?"

"According to my calculations, if I use the right set of Internet tools I can get as many as twenty-five thousand followers in less than six months. And I'm not talking about lazy clicks from social media-type followers, I'm talking about actual, genuinely nutty people who will be willing to send me loads of money via PayPal, commit violence in my name, and . . ." he lowered his voice, "offer me their wives and daughters for sex. In time I genuinely believe I could go the full Tom Cruise on this."

Cyril sucked air in through barely parted lips. "Noble aims you've got there, buddy. When can I join? By the way, you do realise that Tom Cruise has never done any of the things that you mentioned?"

"No, but the option is always there. It's only his lack of imagination that holds him back."

Beeba leaned across and pulled a slim cardboard box off the sofa. He opened it to reveal a long, flowing, orange robe with a very high collar that he had designed, printed and cut in a mini-facture booth; that was part of the Internet of Things, right there in the pyramid.

"I've got this, but I am not sure whether to be just a prophet or a full demigod. Or, I could just be the senior church elder? Either which way, it's important to look the part."

"Senior elder? Even though you haven't yet turned fifteen?"

"In this life I'm fourteen, but my soul is ancient."

"I see what you're saying," empathised Cyril. "It's difficult, and I'm probably not the best man to ask as I've yet to create my own religion and attempt to gull thousands of people into giving their lives, wives and worldly possessions to me, but I think the effect that I would be going for is to not get shot by anybody for doing it. And for that matter, I would try to avoid getting any of your followers indulging in mass suicides."

Beeba shot Cyril an uncomprehending, unimpressed look and just said, "hmmm."

Cyril reached into his pocket and pulled out the tissue with the fly in it and threw it across to Beeba. "What's the story on that?" he asked.

Beeba shrugged, "I was a different person then. Now I see that interfering with God's creation was a sin."

"So, it won't happen again?"

"No. Not unless God commands it."

"Has God ever spoken to you directly?"

"No, but I haven't taken holy orders yet."

"Taken holy orders from who?"

"From myself."

"Well, let's hope for your sake he doesn't command you. Otherwise, I shall entreat your mother to lay some serious action on you, grounding-wise."

Dawn re-entered the room; looking smart and summery in a white blouse.

"Are you working at The Comment tonight," Cyril queried, "it's Tyler's psycho do?"

"Yes, we're all braced for it."

"OK then, I'll see you there. I have just *got* to see who turns up," he smiled.

He gave Dawn a perfunctory peck on the lips and moved back into the hallway. Dawn followed him out. Cyril then thought to stop and call back to Beeba, "See you later, loser."

Beeba's head appeared in the living room doorway to deliver a parting blessing.

"May the spirit of the Great Penguin be forever at your side. God bless you, Cyril."

"Yes," Cyril called back as he stepped out of the apartment. "Keep working on it."

4 THE LEAGUE OF PSYCHOPATHS

It was such a fine summer's evening that Cyril decided to walk the few hundred metres from Farage Pyramid to the closest other pyramid in the cluster, Trigglypuff.

Kids were out playing and shouting in a loud and often shrill manner. Cyril observed that at thirty-two, he now appeared to be of an age where noisy children were beginning to annoy him. On top of his other crop of concerns, did this mean that he was suffering early-onset curmudgeonlyism? Did such a thing exist? Was he the youngest ever known sufferer? He needed to pull out of it, that was for sure.

Just as that thought was crossing his mind a boy shot past on a hoverboard; the latest craze. Hoverboards used linear induction motors and only worked on specially built Laithwaite tracks. Unlike the famous Maglev trains, the hoverboards were very low-powered and the forward movement was achieved by pushing with the foot, just like on a regular scooter.

"Yaaaargh," the boy screamed over his shoulder to his friend who was close behind.

'Yaaaargh,' thought Cyril. 'Noisy little . . ."

Pretty soon he had arrived at Trigglypuff and was in an elevator on his way up to the eighth floor, where The Troll's Comment pub was situated.

As he entered the bar he immediately spotted Tyler, Neville and Gonorilla, who had been joined there by Eddie Shand, the winger from the Dog and Duck pub football team, as well as Calvin, their ball-playing midfield general.

Everybody acknowledged each other with at least a nod. Tyler was holding court, explaining the evening to them all, and the others were all taking it in.

Cyril knew Eddie from school, where he had been notable for his fleetness of foot. He was never the fastest runner in the county, nor the most nimble dancer in the ballet, but for a fat kid he was magical. On the school playground, or on the football pitch, he always looked as if somebody else's legs - a far stronger, more athletic boy's - were running off with him. These days he was sporting a pencil thin moustache that never managed to come into contact with either his nose or top lip. He looked like a black marketeer from the Second World War.

Calvin, Eddie's teammate, was very pale-skinned, with a crop of closely cut, wavy, thick, black hair, a paintbrush moustache and what you might call a ponytail - if ponies grew tails way off to the right-hand side of their hindquarters that is. He had a unibrow that matched his hair and big front teeth that appeared to be at least thirty years older than he was.

Calvin laughed at everything; big chugging, *uh-uh-uh,* noises, but said almost nothing. There was something about Calvin's appearance; the pale skin against the thick unibrow, the dark eyes and the dark hair that combined to make him look extremely dark; much darker than Tyler for instance, who was of Jamaican descent.

"So, part of what I'm doing is fighting stereotypes," Tyler was telling them. "Even in twenty forty-two they've got the black guy down as a winger, but not a scheming midfield player, not an orchestrat—"

"You are a winger," Eddie reminded him.

"Yeah, yeah, fair enough, but when did you last see a black guy on a bike, or in the swimming pool? They're not supposed to be black guy things, are they?"

"But," retorted Neville, "if black men don't do those things that's their choice, it's not stereotyping."

"Uh-uh-uh," Calvin laughed.

"I see a black bloke on a push-bike every day," Eddie said. "Lycra shorts, big calf muscles, wind-resistant crash helmet, the lot. And I see black blokes when I go swimming."

"Yeah, but we're under-represented. Same as this psychopath thing, right? If you were watching a film and there was a serial killer, killing people, taking them to a disused warehouse where he had a bizarrely well-equipped operating theatre, that nobody had noticed, plus a mains electricity supply, despite the fact that the building was derelict, and he was cutting their faces off and wearing them, it wouldn't be a black bloke would it?"

"That's not a bad thing, surely?" Neville asked.

"Uh-uh-uh."

"Got a point there," Cyril chimed in. "Who was the last really evil black dude?"

"That old Kanye West bloke," Calvin finally spoke. "Uh-uh-uh."

"Well, anyway, I am a psychopath. I know that for a fact. I've done tests."

Tyler explained the Hare test to the gang and told them he scored reasonably highly on the psychopathy scale. He explained that the Hare test was invented by Doctor Robert Hare in 1970 to diagnose a person's psychopathic, or anti-social, tendencies.

Tyler also made the case for psychopaths being overly depicted as murderers. He told them that only a small percentage of psychopaths ever killed anybody just for personal satisfaction, or a lust for violence and gore. The condition had many positive things to offer, such as fearlessness for instance.

It had been demonstrated by psychologists that when under pressure and in times when their own lives were at stake, psychopaths were much calmer than regular people. In fact, in moments of extreme danger their heart rates were known to actually slow down, giving them an important edge over adversaries. There were certain professions where psychopaths were likely to thrive and occupy high-ranking positions; the military generally, fighter pilots, test pilots, astronauts, surgeons, business leaders, bankers and so on. Furthermore, their desire to be top dog, coupled with their charm, guile and utter ruthlessness meant that psychopaths were in charge of far more organisations than most people realised. It occurred to Tyler that many a famous battle must have been a showdown between our psychopaths and theirs.

Cyril was not entirely convinced by the upside of coming out. "I still don't get it . . . Why on Earth would you want to tell people that you're a psychopath?" Cyril asked.

"I've always been different and I know it, so I dived in and got myself checked out. And now, as the famous American philosopher, Popeye, said on many occasions, *I am what I am and I is what I is, Olive.*" Then he did Popeye's laugh.

Cyril wasn't convinced. "What are your symptoms, coz I've never spotted them?"

"Glib and superficial charm," ventured Tyler, pausing to see if there were any takers.

"I wouldn't say you were in any way charm—"

"Self-aggrandising," Tyler cut in.

"Well, we all do that now and—"

"Sexually promiscuous."

"You mean, you'd like to be."

"Failure to take responsibility for my own actions, impulsiveness, lack of empathy, cunning and manipulative, superficial emotional responses, lack of behavioural control, pathological lying, lack of realistic long-term goals, lack of—"

"So, were you bullshitting when you told me you would become the first black Prime Minister one day?" Eddie interrupted.

"No, not bullshitting per se, just being grandiose and unrealistic. And had I been bullshitting I wouldn't feel any remorse over it."

"Anyway," Gonorilla chipped in, "the meeting sounds very exciting, and I must remark on how much I am looking forward to it and to meeting the attendees."

"Uh-uh-uh," Calvin broke out in a smile again. He never said, but he was suddenly very amused at how utterly beautiful Gonorilla was and the fact that she was hanging around with Neville. "Uh-uh-uh-uh-uh-uh-uh."

"Right," said Tyler, "Only you know that none of you can come into the meeting room, don't you? Registered guests, only."

"What?" Cyril jumped in on behalf of the rest of them. "Why do you think we're all here? You advertised the meeting!"

"This is the inaugural meeting of The League of Psychopaths," Tyler defended himself. "And if you read the leaflet you would know that attendees had to register. Bear in mind that I've got around fifty psychopaths dematting in from all over the world to go into a meeting room that is only supposed to seat thirty. Every single one of them thinks that they're the most important person on the planet, so I don't want to have to tell any of them that they will have to stand for an hour or two - it might illicit an unfavourable reaction. Anyway, you can all meet the League members in here afterwards."

"What are you hoping to achieve, anyway?" Neville asked.

"We will be asserting our right to be, and exploring common ground. My idea is that we should operate on the gay model . . . Probably get our own flag designed-up. Maybe have a ribbon and a wrist band, and maybe have an annual day, or possibly a month. Here's the agenda." Tyler pushed some small pieces of paper across the table for his friends to peruse. The agenda read:

Welcome. Introductions and coffee.

Psychopaths in today's world. Who are we? - A short talk by Linda Hacker.

Negative stereotypes in films and the media.

The League. What are our goals?

Safe spaces for psychopaths within universities.

Coming out - Psychopath Pride Month - Too soon? Member opinions?

Annual fees.

Newsletter contributions.

Botty-Bots and A9's. Fair game for the criminally intentioned?

Any other business?

Tyler beamed at his friends as they scanned the schedule. "If all goes well I can see other psychopath communities springing up. Maybe whole towns that become well known for psychopaths, like San Francisco and Brighton are for gays."

"I'm guessing that it won't be long before housing in those towns becomes very, very affordable indeed," Cyril reflected.

"Yeah, could be. Could be," Tyler retorted.

In response to their exclusion from the main event and because The Troll's Comment had begun to experience mini-power outages, so-called brownouts, Cyril and the others decided by a show of hands to leave Tyler to his meeting and instead go off for a drink someplace else. Accordingly, they walked to the Artificial Intelligence wine bar where they had a guitarist playing live music; old Eagle's songs mostly.

At length, after about an hour and a half, they returned to The Troll's Comment, a little the worse for wear and hoping to catch a glimpse of Tyler's circus as it tipped out of the meeting room and into the barroom.

Upon arrival they could see that the place was more crowded than usual and most of the punters seemed to be smiling and happy; a clear indication that everything must have gone well.

Cyril approached the bar and smiled at Dawn who was talking to one of Tyler's members, Bubba Razal.

"Hello my lover," Dawn called out, obviously pleased to see her boyfriend.

"This is Cyril, he's my lover" she told Bubba, before making a more formal introduction. "Lover-Bubba. Bubba-Lover," was what she actually said. "Bubba is from America, and he's not sure if he's definitely a psychopath, but he is psycho-curious."

"Dawn's not my girlfriend," Cyril countered.

"I am his girlfriend. And tonight is Thursday, which is love night."

Cyril offered Dawn nothing more than a wry grin, before leaving the bar area with his new acquaintance to join a larger group of people who were chatting animatedly about the evening. There was already talk of the next meet-up, so Tyler would be full of himself, Cyril thought, though he was not currently with the group.

In Tyler's absence, Bubba began taking centre stage. It soon became clear that he was an enthusiastic and engaging conspiracy theorist; full of stuff about the secret world government, the Illuminati, silent black helicopters and reverse engineered alien spacecraft that were secretly garaged at the Nevada salt flat, Groom Lake; a place only ever shown on maps as Area 51. He also discussed the days when the machines would take over and leave mankind at their mercy; 'living underground and in swamps,' was how he put it. He assured them that the process was now well underway and irreversible.

According to Bubba, it was an established fact amongst the conspiracy community that the main hub for the machines - which he called 'Plouton' - was right there in Great Britain. The information Bubba's people had was that the machines had placed Plouton in a secret location somewhere off the coast of Scotland, though it was not visible from the air due to electronic camouflage. The joke in the community was that the hidden island was referred to as 'Area Fifty-Oneshire'.

"You wanna know who did most to decoy Plouton? Who put up the biggest goddam smokescreen since the Hollywood wild fires? David-goddam-lizard-loving-Icke, that's who. Central to the whole thing."

This was news to the rest of them and they began to question him skeptically, except for Gonorilla, who was evidently a fan of Bubba's reasoning.

"Think about it," Bubba pressed ahead, "He's supposed to be a crackpot conspiracy theorist. He talks about a race of blood drinking reptiles ruling the world, when all the time he lives on the Isle of Wight, which is off the south coast of England and is bound to be much hotter than the rest of the place. At times it's gonna be virtually sub-tropical, meaning lizards galore, right? That's his relationship with lizards, probably surrounded by them. And then he makes like he's spilling the beans on the secret world government, the Illuminati, your royal family and the Kennedys and whoever; all shape-shifting lizards, according to him.

"He talks about everything but the machines! He's pulling tails all over the place, and what happens to him? Nothing. Nothing at all. Is he dead? Has he been assassinated yet? Nope!

"Icke just gets to write his books and tour the world and talk shit to whoever, and nothing happens. So you gotta question who green-lights all this crap and why?" He stopped to let the news sink in. "David Icke is the decoy for the machines is why. That's why that boy is untouchable. Says what he likes. No comeback."

"That boy is about ninety years old," Cyril reminded him.

"So what?" Bubba countered. "All that means is that they may need a new front-man soon, except soon they won't need anybody."

"I don't know if you have noticed," Cyril changed the subject slightly, "but since you have been here the power has been dipping occasionally. It's part of a phenomenon that a lot of people have been experiencing; not that anybody seems to care all that much. I just wondered if you have been experiencing the same in—"

"In Texas? In America? Oh, sure. The glitching started there a couple of months back; traffic lights cycling erratically, television screens switching off, holoplayers turning on, browsers taking people to the wrong websites, fridges double-ordering goods, demats materialising people into the wrong countries . . . we seen it all. Nothing bad has ever happened, but the omens are there."

"And nobody knows what's causing it?"

"Sure we know what's causing it! The same thing that causes David Icke to talk about lizards. It's the machines. These ain't good ol' digital computers, they are quantum computers working with probability states, not ones and zeroes. They have computing power beyond imagination. And what they're doing right now is watching us at all times; probing our defences, testing our responses, watching to see how we handle ourselves when everything ain't going so good. They want to know what we got and, as you've seen for yourself, we ain't got Jack. The power goes out and we just sit there, dumb, waiting for it to come back. What we should be doing is locating

Area Fifty-Oneshire and making a pre-emptive strike. Blow the holy Jesus, Joseph and Mary out of it. Let them know that we ain't done just yet. That's what we should do. Instead, what we do is—"

"Who wants another pint?" Eddie called across the table.

Just as Eddie demonstrated what people were prepared to do about the glitching, Tyler was walking slowly back to the table to join them. He appeared to have come from the Gent's toilet area. His face looked ashen and his eyes were unsmiling, as if he might be in shock.

One by one the others noticed his demeanour. Tyler slipped into his empty seat in what looked like a near zombie state. Maybe he had just received dreadful news? He really did look freaked by something, but who would be first to ask? Nobody knew what to say to him. Nobody except Eddie.

"Bad dump Tyler?"

"No." He said pointing back towards the toilets, before dropping his hand back in his lap and shaking his head.

"Somebody else had a bad dump?" Eddie guessed.

"No . . . it's that guy. In there." He pointed again. "John Wayne Gacy."

"The cowboy?" Neville asked, "In the toilet?"

"John Wayne Gacy?" Bubba jumped in, shaking his head. "I don't think so. Gacy was a prolific serial killer from Illinois, but they injected him, oh . . . maybe fifty years ago."

"That's right," Tyler agreed. "That's what he told me. That guy in there took Gacy's name because he wanted to *stand on the shoulders of giants*. That's what he said. He said that Gacy was one of America's *top scorers*. The guy is a complete . . . psycho. He's got this stare. He just . . . looks at you. He's a complete . . ."

The others looked at Tyler. Nobody said a thing. 'What had Tyler been expecting?' was the unspoken question.

"Yeah, OK, sure. Very funny" Tyler responded to their silence, "but I was thinking about the *good* psychopaths when I started the League. I didn't think any of the bad ones would show up. In fact, the members are mostly dentists, bankers, businessmen and school teachers, exactly as you would expect. But he's interested in the League of Psychopaths because he thinks that he can make some good contacts for *joint ventures!*"

"What kind of joint ventures?" Neville asked.

"What kind do you think? He wants to be America's new top

scorer. Shhh — Act natural, he's coming."

Gacy arrived at the table and took an empty seat next to Tyler. Everybody stayed silent; waiting to see what would happen next and whether Gacy was as bad as Tyler was saying. Gacy placed his drink on the table and waited for the conversation to re-commence, and when it did not he just picked his drink up again and looked around at the group.

His cold eyes moved once around the table in a clockwise direction before they finally came to rest on Cyril. He fixed Cyril with the unblinking stare that Tyler had alluded to earlier. He held his attention firmly on Cyril whilst the others watched him do it, glad that it wasn't them. Even Calvin had stopped laughing by this time. Cyril to his credit, just stared back, equally unwavering.

"You're Cyril," Gacy told him. "I do believe that I like your website and I like you."

"How would you know about me and my website?" Cyril asked, "I'm not one of your group."

"Group?" Gacy responded, apparently uncertain about what Cyril was referring to. "Oh, the group. The League of Psychopaths, that group." Gacy's vocal delivery was slow and smooth; very self-assured. "No," he continued, "I noticed that you weren't in the meeting. I thought you might be, as a friend of Mister Plummer, here."

"What do you mean, you *noticed that I wasn't there*? You've never heard of me."

"Well *obviously* I *have* heard of you," Gacy laughed, "I knew your name, Cyril. I have clearly heard of you."

Gacy was smiling and looking at Cyril with the same hard stare as before. Cyril was wondering if this was some kind of mind game; an attempt to get into his head and spook him. Most likely, he thought, this creep had acquired his name from somebody else in the bar, maybe from Tyler. Gacy held his gaze.

"From where? Where did you hear about me?"

"I already told you, from your little soccer website. Somebody in the States mentioned it to me and I took a look. Not really my thing of course, but you built yourself an audience. Not everybody can do that, can they?" He continued to bore into Cyril. "And then no sooner did I look at your website and there you are again on social media, bitching about glitching."

"So what?" Cyril asked, "Neither of those things make me big news exactly."

"Maybe not, Mr Greaves. You just caught my attention is all. You just got my attention . . . ," he repeated himself slowly with his dead eyes fixed against Cyril's.

With that, Gacy abruptly slapped his legs and rose up. He told them that there were a lot of people dematting out of the pyramid that evening, so for that reason he had booked a slot, rather than just hang around until the chamber was free of other users. And then he was gone; presumably back to America.

Unsurprisingly, Cyril and his friends had a lot to say about Gacy in his absence, about how creepy and scary he seemed, and how he was clearly somebody they were better off not knowing. Tyler didn't say much, though he was obviously reviewing his bright idea of creating the League. Cyril, too, was unnerved by the experience, though he wasn't letting on.

The evening began to wind down as the various new members of The League of Psychopaths bid Tyler a good evening and thanked him for putting on the event. The numbers in the bar thinned out dramatically as closing time drew near, but Cyril and friends were staying put, intent on drinking until Dawn rang the time bell.

Bubba Razal was still with them, and still telling them stories; mainly about UFOs by this time. Gonorilla seemed keen to hear everything he had to say and kept prompting him to continue. He got mid-way through another alien abduction tale when he suddenly veered off on a major tangent.

"Course, you know that one of the masterminds behind the machines and their inevitable takeover is an Englishman, who up to a few years ago was living right here in Bedfordshire?"

Neville shook his head on behalf of the group. It was getting late; they were all at least a bit drunk and Bubba's stories were wearing thin.

"Yep, the guy was a legend. He was at the heart of a giant social engineering experiment here in the UK back in about twenty twenty. He started talking about what he did for the British government a few years back, but all of a sudden he went dark. We never heard nothing else from him. His name was Francis Walsingham.

"I know that he lived in Bedfordshire because he used to produce a quarterly electronic publication, which I subscribed to. It was called, *My Secret Bedfordshire*. I subscribed because I assumed that it was all about British skunk works and classified stuff that the government didn't want people to know about. Superficially, it just seemed to be about local parks that were particularly attractive, but which nobody visited, and derelict Norman churches that weren't maintained, and were left crumbling into the undergrowth.

"Our people sure spent a lot of time analysing *My Secret Bedfordshire*. And you know what? It turned out that it *really was* about parks and churches!

"Anyways, the way I see it is that if the glitching is bothering you and you want to get a better understanding of what it's all about - and if you don't believe me about the machines - find Walsingham. If he hasn't been taken care of, bumped-off-wise, and he's still around, find him and ask him. He's in your neck of the woods."

"OK, will do." Eddie agreed, sliding off his chair and down to the floor; semi-conscious, but still managing somehow to keep a hold of his pint.

"Uh-uh-uh."

"Really, everybody, I think that finding mister Walsingham would make a most interesting project!" Gonorilla enthused. "Perhaps we can shed some light on all of the very strange happenings."

Cyril and Neville looked at each other, doubtfully. 'Hmmm, Maybe, maybe not,' they were both thinking

5 SECRET BUNKER NUMBER 14

At Tyler's request, the whole group were back in The Troll's Comment the very next night. His invitation was based on the notion that it would be nice to have another drink together, without lots of strangers milling around, but really he was still excited about the previous evening and wanted somebody to talk to about it.

Cyril accepted because he was still feeling queasy about John Wayne Gacy, and he wanted reassurance from the others that he was not about to be stalked by a serial killer. Neville went because Cyril asked him to, and Gonorilla went because she and Neville were becoming an item. Eddie and Calvin were there because they went to The Comment most evenings. Beeba was also hanging around the bar because his mother was on shift again that night, and because he wanted to give his orange robe some air time.

In contrast to the night before the barroom was practically empty, which actually made for a very pleasant venue; especially as it was one of the few in-pyramid pubs that was on the side of the building, as opposed to being somewhere deep within the bowels.

As it was a summer's evening Dawn had let the group slide back the huge picture window by the table they occupied, which made for an almost outdoor experience. They were able to look down diagonally at the garden of one of the apartments below, where a very solidly built, thirty-something lady was making appearances periodically, with fewer and fewer clothes on each time she came out. Deliberately.

"Uh-uh-uh," laughed Calvin, who had the best view. He never said, but he wasn't laughing at the imminent nudity, he was laughing at her plethora of tattoos, which he thought made her look like a navy-blue person who lacked good judgement, in the same way that Gonorilla obviously lacked it.

"I don't mind admitting, that John Wayne geezer gave me the creeps. Why the hell would an American psychopath know anything about me and the EPL website?"

"Probably wants to kill you." Eddie said helpfully.

"Uh-uh-uh."

"No, really," Cyril replied, in an attempt to ward off his own dark suspicions.

"He probably does, though," Eddie responded, not letting him off so lightly.

"Well," Tyler began. "I thought that aside from Mister Gacy's slightly odd behaviour—"

"Wanting to kill Cyril."

"Uh-uh-uh."

"Apart from that, it was a really enjoyable evening," Tyler insisted. "A lot of the people who attended have already paid their membership fees for the year. I'm president of the League by the way, though we'll probably have to have elected committee members as well, or something like that. Just to make it all official."

"I was interested to note Mister Razal's remarks about Francis Walsingham and his knowledge of how the machines want to take over the world and destroy mankind," Gonorilla said. "I was also interested to note that he used to live right here among us, and that he may still do so."

"Yes, you have a point." Neville was quick to agree with the person who was apparently destined to become the new love of his life, "That was a very interesting aside to the evening . . . You see, Cyril, just find the elusive Mister Walsingham and you can ask him what he knows about the glitching."

"And why they're gonna kill us all," Eddie added. "Except Cyril."

Neville placed his hand close to Gonorilla's in readiness for a full-on hand hold.

Cyril didn't say anything, he just raised his eyebrows a bit at the Walsingham suggestion. In fact, he had done a little searching on the internet that afternoon, and Bubba Razal was right; Walsingham was a real person, and around twelve years ago he had made public pronouncements about work that he had done for the British government in regard to social engineering; shaping society for the better with the aid of machines, somehow.

Razal was also correct when he said that the interviews stopped shortly afterwards, and that there were no references to Walsingham at all after the year twenty thirty-two. He had indeed seemed to 'go dark' as Bubba had indicated. The problem was, in respect to ever finding Francis Walsingham, the internet was Cyril's only known resource; he couldn't think how else he might locate him.

When Cyril did not respond to Neville's suggestion of tracking Walsingham, Gonorilla brought the matter back to everybody's attention. "This might be something that we could do as a group, a fun adventure. We could find the missing Mister Walsingham, couldn't we?"

As Gonorilla spoke, Dawn came by the table to collect glasses with would-be cult leader, Beeba, a pace or two behind her. She asked them who Mr. Walsingham was and why they wanted to find him. They told her.

"Citizen voter database would have his details if he's still in Bedfordshire," was her immediate response. "Now that we do direct democracy we're all on that. Only trouble is, it's not publicly accessible, everybody's details are supposed to be secret."

"Just hack into it," said Eddie, as if he knew how to do such a thing, or even knew of anybody else who could.

"Hah! That's one computer nobody can hack into. Not even me, and I can really hack," Beeba replied.

"I hope that's just an idle boast, Beeba?" Dawn cut in, alarmed to realise that it probably wasn't.

"Yeah, idle," Beeba agreed, anxious to head that topic of conversation off at the pass.

"Why are you wearing that dress?" Eddie asked.

"Robe . . . Orange resonates with the universes."

"Does it?" asked Neville "Who told you that?"

"Tardil, my penguin spirit guide. Tardil, exists in all worlds simultaneously, and he has communicated to me that orange is the colour of peace, harmony and spiritual enlightenment in all universes."

"A penguin, called Tarquin? What the f—"

"Out of interest," Cyril interrupted, "why can't the citizen voter database be hacked into? What's so special about that particular computer?"

"Implements the full Discon-Eighty protocol," Beeba explained, wrongly anticipating that, with the exception of Gonorilla, any of them had ever heard of it.

"Right. And just remind me what that is?"

Beeba explained to them the genius of Dr. Tara Raboomdeay, the woman who had created the world's first truly impenetrable computer network.

Hacking and viruses had been a huge and costly problem for corporations, governments, other organisations and individuals for decades. The issue had not only been pernicious, but insoluble too, despite the best efforts of the finest software engineers on the planet.

The bad-guy coders constantly came up with computer viruses with different signatures, along with new portals into operating systems, whilst the good-guy coders spent their time working on counter measures; patching the loopholes, identifying new viruses and supplying antidotes. The whole cat and mouse cycle was expensive, debilitating and a hideous waste of energy and talent on both sides. That was until Dr. Raboomdeay's Discon-Eighty Protocol.

The real problem had been that in order to solve the problem of software attacks, corporations and governments set programmers to work on the solutions. This turned out not to be the best course of action.

At the time of her great insight, Doctor Raboomdeay was not actually a recognised computer scientist with a PhD. In fact, the doctorate was an honorary one, bestowed on her after the event by Cambridge University for her pioneering work with computer networks. Her true, real, genuine title at the moment that her ground-breaking brain-wave came upon her was, 'Office Cleaner'. Her flash of inspiration came soon after being reprimanded for the fourteenth time for leaving ethernet cables unplugged after cleaning around office computers.

It came to Dr. Ramboomdeay's notice that on the days that bollockings occurred, the users of the disconnected computers complained a lot less about incoming viruses, which were often downloaded during overnight updates, than the users whose connections she had left in place.

She mentioned this observation in passing to a friend, Ivor List, who was an internet marketer. He was savvy enough to build her a website proclaiming the new 'Discon Method' as the answer to the problem of computer viruses. The Discon Method was initially just a suggestion not to have important networks connected to the internet.

At first the Discon Method made little headway; nobody took any notice, but Ivor List was also clued-up enough to give the method a number (80) - because internet marketers know that numbers sell - and then he changed the word 'Method' for 'Protocol', as protocols are always way more sexy than mere methods or rules.

The final touch was to announce that all incoming and outgoing external communications to Discon-80 Protocol networks were to be conducted on an outer ring of expendable picket computers, which must never be electronically connected to the inner ring.

Thus, the unhackable computer network was born and Tara and Ivor made their fortunes. This was regarded in the computer industry as truly remarkable blue sky, out-of-the-box thinking. Some even declared that Raboomdeay was so brilliant that she had conjured up her ideas without even using a box.

The Bedfordshire citizen voter database was one of the first networks to successfully use the system.

As it was a local government site the County Council were initially quoted £900K for implementation, but after accepting the quote, Tara and Ivor explained to the council that due to unseen development costs the price would have to rise to £3bn, which the council paid, on the basis that; everybody knows that all new computer systems always cost at least four times the original estimate. In due course the head of the council was fired for gross negligence in the matter of the overspend, but was rapidly snapped up by Brent Council, in London, at three times his original salary. Win-win.

"So," Eddie began, "no computer hacking means you can't find Walsingham, which means the machines will destroy us all, does it? Oh well, never mind. I never actually had my hopes on Cyril saving us anyway. Why would he? His days are numbered, so why would he bother?"

"Thanks Eddie," Cyril responded, "but for your information, that slob Gacy doesn't bother me. And what's more, I think that we should try to find Walsingham and see what he knows about the machines and their intentions, because if we don't I can't see anybody else doing it. Nobody is exactly fuming about the machines and the glitching are they? On the other hand, if we can't get into the citizen voter database, I'm not sure how we go about tracking him?"

"This is a very good, positive attitude that you are demonstrating, Cyril," Gonorilla offered, once again coming to the fore. "You are to be commended and your friends must certainly be impressed."

"Uh-uh-uh," laughed Calvin. He never said so, but he thought she was right.

Eddie joined him in the merriment, though his laugh involved beer exploding from his nose and mouth, which was partially caught by his glass.

"No, she's right," Tyler said. "Gotta stand up now and then and step into the breach. Show people what you've got. Who you are. Let 'em know you won't be messed around. Get up and fight if necessary. Put your hand down your pants and see if you've still got a pair. We shall fight on the beaches, we shall fight on the landing grounds, we shall fight in the fields and in the streets, we shall fight in the hills; we shall never surrender—"

"I think we get the point," Neville interrupted. "We should at least try and do something if there are no proper channels that are interested."

"So," Cyril asked, "anybody know how we're going to find Francis Walsingham?"

"I should like to correct Beeba," Gonorilla started. "The citizen voter database does not use the Discon-Eighty Protocol, it uses the Discon-Eighty-B Protocol, and the B stands for Bedfordshire. This was an extra layer of security, whereby in Bedfordshire, only, they decided that the secret database should be moved out of standard office space and located in a secret concrete bunker in a remote location.

"Bedfordshire County Council has a number of such bunkers for various purposes. There is one for the citizen voter database, another where they store details of property developers who are worth initially refusing planning permission in order to attract bribes, another where they keep the computer that runs the Random Roadworks Road Selection Generator, and so on.

"However, these days security is considered much less important than it was, even ten years ago, as everybody is so comfortable. Modern standards of comfort, including housing and food provision, as well as public and private entertainment, is so satisfying to the general population that crime has dropped by ninety-three percent in the last fifteen years. This has meant that in some cases the concrete security bunkers have been closed down, and in other cases they are much less well defended.

"I know all of this because I recently watched a very interesting BBC television documentary called, Who Actually Gives A Poo?"

"Who actually does?" Neville asked.

"Actually, not many people care about civic matters anymore," Gonorilla continued to regurgitate from the BBC show. "However, there is a fourteen percent minority who suffer to some degree from Post-Utopian Stress Disorder, like Cyril does."

"Who says I suffer from—"

"And Post Traumatic Stress Disorder since he met John Wayne," Eddie reminded him.

"The hell I do", Cyril countered.

"Anyway," Tyler chipped in, "are we going to storm the bunker, or what?"

"We could do a recon mission," Cyril said, "if we could find out where the bunker is."

"I know exactly where the bunker is," Gonorilla responded, "It is less than ten minutes striding from my pyramid, and the terrain is not demanding for non-striders."

"Interesting." Neville told his new girlfriend, and sealed the deal by slipping an arm around her back. "This is definitely worth discussing in the near future with a view to putting together a plan of—"

"What are we waiting for?" Tyler blurted excitedly. He stood up and turned to leave before remembering that he didn't know where to go, or if anybody was going to follow him.

Cyril stood too and then looked down at Neville. "We could at least see where this place is," he told his friend.

"What, now?" Neville asked incredulously, before realising that drink had blunted everybody else's inhibitions. He stood up a bit reluctantly, but rallied when it became very clear that Gonorilla was keen. Neville was joined by Eddie and Calvin; neither of whom were very sure what anybody was hoping to achieve. After all, they were never going to get into the bunker, even if it did really exist, and if they did get in they would never know how to get the information from the computer system. On the other hand, it seemed like a bit of a lark, so they were in.

In no time at all the whole group was filing out of The Troll's Comment and into an elevator that would take them down to a Levicar; the Maglev-type vehicle that would take them to Dean Windass pyramid, where Gonorilla lived.

Beeba had followed the group towards the transportation

without his mother being aware; she was still busy working at the bar. It wasn't too long before Cyril caught on, and told a reluctant Beeba to go back, which didn't please His Holiness.

After some arguing and negotiation they compromised by agreeing that Beeba would call his mother and seek permission before continuing. This he pretended to do with some panache.

"Yes," he spoke into his connectionless mobile phone, "Yes. Yes. Yes. I will. I won't. I will. I won't. Yes. I'll tell him. Eleven o'clock. Yes, you too. Okay. Okay. Bye. Yes, bye. Bye.

"She says she loves you, Uncle Cyril."

Cyril was not necessarily that easily fooled, but he had performed his obligations and insisted on the call, and besides that, as far as he was concerned they were just going out for a late stroll on a warm summer's evening to see if the bunker existed. Beeba was not in any danger.

The slightly less than magnificent seven boarded a Levicar and selected their destination, Dean Windass pyramid, from a touchscreen menu, and with a kick of rapid acceleration the small carriage set off on its frictionless journey.

The initial electrical shove was pretty much all the forward momentum that was needed to get them from one place to the other in a matter of less than thirty seconds. The Levicars were capable of much, much greater speeds, but the rides were only short, and faster speeds would involve too much G-force during the start and braking phases. Levicars were really about convenience and comfort.

After Arriving at Dean Windass, Gonorilla escorted the group to her sparsely furnished apartment so that they could collect some flashlights for use on their travels as dusk settled in. The walk to what she believed was the bunker in question was really quite short, and it was not even across what was generally considered to be the outlands. They only needed to walk over a couple of largish fields, and even these had paths trodden into the grass.

Whilst in Gonorilla's apartment, Cyril could not help but observe how she lived. The place really was quite spartan with no ornaments, photographs, wall art, or cuddly toys on display. It certainly wasn't a girlie place. He really would have liked to peek into Gonorilla's fridge to see if there was any evidence of regular food being consumed, but Gonorilla had soon gathered everything that she felt was needed for their short trip, and began to usher them out of the apartment before he got a chance to do any proper snooping. He did, however, get a chance to watch Neville's reactions to her monk-like living quarters, and he felt that Neville probably knew that something was a bit amiss.

Shortly, they were at the exit doors of the pyramid and ready to leave. The best part of daylight was done with, and now they were setting off across the fields to do nothing much, it seemed to Cyril. However, he still he felt obliged to speak up before they left.

"Everybody, here's the situation as I see it. There have been some funny things happening lately in terms of the normal running of things; the glitching and so on. I for one would like to know why it's happening, if at all possible, because we are all aware of the strangeness, but everybody just keeps on keeping on, without ever questioning it.

"In reality we have nothing to go on, other than the word of that guy, Bubba; a stranger and a conspiracy theorist, who just happens to think he might also be a psychopath. So, all we are doing tonight is walking a few hundred yards over these fields and looking to see if there is a secret bunker, owned by the council, and whether we could at some point in time gain access, or get to know somebody who does have access. Because if we can, we might be able to find this social scientist guy, Walsingham, who may or may not know something about the machines and whether they are in control, or not, or if they are about to take control.

"So, I don't suppose we can get into too much trouble tonight, but on the other hand we could be trespassing, or pissing-off some council big-wigs. Point is, nobody has to come, it's your choice." He looked at the others for their responses.

Tyler simply led off into the field; following the path in the grass, Calvin did his, 'uh-uh-uh', thing, and the others just followed, including Cyril.

Once they were outside, the cloudlessness of the evening and the open field offered them a little more natural light than they had first thought, so the torches stayed off. After a few minutes they reached a hedgerow which divided the first field from the next one, but the path continued straight ahead through a parting in the hedge. Gonorilla was towards the fore to confirm that they were heading in the right direction. The group stayed quite close together, though Tyler seemed eager to be at the front.

The sky was dark enough for them to see the first stars in the sky. Neville looked up at them as he walked, like he always did, but the rest were all just trudging along fairly silently behind Tyler, save for the odd slapping noise, as moths and other insects tickled their heads and bare arms. Up ahead, the field darkened as another hedgerow loomed larger. This time it was evident that the path was not going to cut through the hedgerow, even though the field was at an end.

Tyler slowed to allow the rest to catch him and to ask Gonorilla where they should go next. She waited for the group to be fully together again then beckoned them towards the hedge. When they got close enough she leaned into it a little and pulled branches aside, then whispered, "See, there? . . . That's the bunker."

Each member of the gang found their own branch to pull aside as they peered together across the next field. At the far end, about one hundred metres distant, was a small concrete building. It was much smaller than most had been imagining. Rather than being a largish municipal building made of concrete, it had more of the appearance of an old World War II coastal gun emplacement. Some could see well enough to notice that there was writing across the top of the entrance, which looked as if it might be at the bottom of some steps.

"Okay," Cyril whispered very quietly, "no more talking. Let's just walk across the field and give the place the once over. No making a noise and no attempting to break in when we get there. Just observe, alright?"

"Right." Neville whispered.

Cyril looked to the others to gauge their buy-in to the plan, but Tyler was already through the hedge and on his way.

"Uh-uh-uh," Calvin laughed quietly. He never said, but he was thinking that if the place was guarded by Rottweilers, then Tyler would be the first and possibly the last to get ripped to shreds.

The others all struggled to emulate Tyler's hedge traversing manoeuvre, especially Beeba, whose robe was getting badly caught in the branches.

Once on the other side they all caught up with Tyler, as he had slowed to allow them to do so. Tyler had also decided to tread more carefully at that point, to avoid uneven ground or twigs that might snap and betray their approach.

The others followed Tyler's lead; stepping lightly and deliberately. Once they got to about forty metres away from the structure they came to halt. It was now possible to read what it said across the entrance to the building:

Secret Bunker 14

So there really were secret bunkers, just as Gonorilla had said, and this was possibly the one they wanted; the home of the Bedfordshire citizen voter database.

They stared at the bunker for twenty seconds, or so. It looked isolated and deserted, with no suggestion of any light coming from inside.

Cyril took a full three-hundred and sixty degree look at their surroundings. The field they were in was enclosed on all sides by hedgerows, and the little concrete bunker sat alone at the far end, illuminated only by moonlight. The bunker appeared to be a sitting duck for anybody who might want to break in, since it was not near any obvious source of defenders. If the building was alarmed it would take the police an age to arrive, unless they came by helicopter, and that was not really something that they often did anymore. It occurred to Cyril that, had they come equipped with a crowbar they could probably have forced an entry if they felt inclined to.

Having done their initial recce of the site, Cyril urged them forward.

"Come on then, quietly."

The group slowly and silently moved forward, watching as the bunker grew larger in their eyes and more details of its construction became evident. Their hearts were beating faster now, except possibly Tyler's, if he really was a psychopath, and they even found themselves trying to control heavier breathing.

They had got to around twenty-five metres out when, all of a sudden, a row of powerful lights that were strung across the top of the bunker came on and lit-up the entire field. The lights were so strong that they felt almost blinded by them. Hands moved up to cover squinting eyes, and in what seemed like no time at all, the silhouette of a single male figure stood before them. They were caught. Now what? Dogs?

Calvin looked over at Tyler. He wasn't in the lead anymore. That was a shame, he thought, and he wasn't laughing.

The person standing before them unquestionably looked belligerent. He stood square-on and bolt-upright, arms slightly out at his sides and fists clenched. Cyril took a good look at the man, or as best he could. The outline was almost unmistakable; the man was an old-fashioned skinhead with tall Doc Martens boots and turned-up jeans. An interminable few seconds passed before the man finally spoke.

"Whatchoo fucking want?" His tone was decidedly aggressive, and yet the fact that he had spoken at all was slightly reassuring.

"We were out walking and we just . . ." Cyril paused to work out what they were just doing, ". . . We just noticed this building and thought we would take a look."

"Do you know who I am?" the silhouette asked.

"No, who?"

"You don't know who I am?" The man sounded incredulous.

"No, who?"

"You don't know who I am?" He asked again, even more incredulously.

"No, I'm afraid not. Who are you?"

"Damien Wilson," the man answered, and then waited for the news to sink in. It didn't.

"Who's Damien Wilson?" Neville said after what seemed like a long wait.

"I am, you dick!"

"Who are you, though?"

"Jesus! . . . Damien-fucking-Wilson!"

To help out, Damien Wilson volunteered some extra information. "Damien Vicious Bastard Wilson."

"We . . . don't get out much. Not sure that we've actually heard of you," Neville persisted.

"Chelsea Headhunters!" Damien Wilson shouted in exasperation.

"You're a recruitment consultant? Out here?"

"No, you Muppet. I used to be an accountant and a leading member of the hardest, most violent, vicious and improbably nasty gang of football hooligans in London, the Chelsea Headhunters. Well, that's if you don't count West Ham's Inter City Firm and everybody who they ever let into the Millwall ground . . . including women and children."

"So, what are you doing here, Damien, if you don't mind me asking?"

"Guarding the electoral register."

"You mean the citizen voter database?"

"Yeah, that."

Neville trawled his recollection of old-style football hooliganism. "When did you say you were doing the hooligan stuff?"

"Not that long ago, as it happens."

"Because I thought all that happened back in the nineteen-seventies?"

"Yeah, that's right. Now you say it, it was."

"So, doesn't that mean . . . you're not quite as hard anymore? After all you must be around—"

"I'm eighty-three, but my mind is still as sharp as . . . one of those silver, pointy things they use in needlework, and I'm still hard as nails." He stopped to think. "And vicious, with only the thinnest veneer of social conscience. And not very kind, and so forth."

"So, are you going to attack us?"

"Leave it out you nonsense, course I'm not. We had a code back in the day: no civilians, no women and children, and definitely no pussies, like you. No offence."

"None taken."

"So, you can come in if you want, there's no honour in engaging with non-combatants."

The group exchanged sideways glances.

"Come inside the bunker?" Cyril checked that he had understood.

"Yeah, why not? Hardly anybody comes here anymore, and I'm only doing this for peanuts, which I don't even need. I think I started out doing this night watchman stuff in order to keep my hand in, as it were. I can't really remember. The blokes who came last night were the first in God knows how long, and now you."

"You've had other recent visitors?"

"Last night. Two of 'em. Quite obstreperous they were. In fact, I had to give one of the geezers a bit of a tickle." As he said this he made an impressively vigorous booting action for a man of his age.

"You had a fight with them?"

"Not really, no, coz they tasered me, and they were gone when I woke up."

"Who were they then?" Cyril asked.

"No fucking idea. Except I would say that to stoop to such low-down, skullduggerous, dishonourable behaviour as turning up for a ruck, tooled-up with a taser, you would have to suspect that they were Tottenham. Even the Arse wouldn't go there. Not in my day."

"They didn't have tasers back in nineteen-eighteen, did they?" Eddie asked.

"No, but if they did none of the firms would have used 'em. Except maybe Tottenham."

Damien led them into the small bunker, where there was barely room for them all to gather. There was a kettle and a fridge, which was for the use of Damien and anybody else who came to work there, plus a single computer on a desk. Damien couldn't have cared less when Beeba switched it on and started fiddling.

What Beeba discovered was that the computer had yet another layer of defence that would have defeated virtually anybody but him and perhaps a small army of nerds, worldwide.

The computer was not running Windows 35, like other machines of the day, but instead it ran an antique operating system; an early version of Unix. In order to interrogate the database, a user would not only have to navigate the system and find the appropriate file using Unix commands, but also possess arcane knowledge of an editing software designed for long since defunct terminals, known as 'teletypes'. This software was called 'Ed', and was only remembered by old college professors and computer technicians who had long since been consigned to spending the remainder of their days painting in water colours.

Whilst Beeba worked his magic, the others strolled outside the bunker with Damien to keep him talking, just in case he was prone to changing his mind about what his duties were supposed to be. This wasn't difficult for Tyler, who thought that he saw potential in Damien, and had already handed him a leaflet for The League of Psychopaths, which he happened to have about his person.

"Did I ever tell you about my mate Micky?" Damien asked the group.

"No," Eddie replied, "because we've only just met you."

"I used to get people in headlocks whenever I could, and Micky would slash their arses with a razor. Those were the days. It was all good fun really, but we never involved civilians, women, children, or pussy cry-babies. They was the rules. It was mainly just properly organised violence involving consenting thugs, all done on a gentlemanly basis. And we only ever really used fists, bricks, razors, bottles, baseball bats and swords, and that's all; nothing too unpleasant."

By way of researching his personality, Tyler began asking Damien how he felt about injuring people, and apparently, he felt just fine about it. He didn't feel any guilt at the time he did it, and none had surfaced since.

This was music to Tyler's ears. He felt that he had unearthed another gem for the League. It became evident too that Damien was quite intrigued by Tyler's new organisation, and the others could see a rapport was building. At one point, towards the end of their conversation, Damien walked Tyler back into the bunker to show him something.

It was dark by the time Beeba had finished, but when Beeba, Tyler and Damien came out again Tyler was carrying something in a bin bag. Nobody paid any attention to Tyler or the bag, because all the focus was on Beeba.

"Well?" they asked in unison.

"Well what?" Beeba responded.

"Don't be an arse, Beeba," Cyril told him, "Did you get into the database and was Walsingham on there?"

"Well, durrr," Beeba came back. "Obviously."

"Very well done," Gonorilla said in her flat tone. "This has shown exceptional skill and intellectual prowess. And you have written the details down, of course?"

"I've committed them to memory," he told the group, whilst tapping his head. "With great knowledge comes great responsibility, and I must decide when and where to divulge."

"Oh crap," Cyril muttered to himself, before advising, "Well please don't forget it."

"No, you must not," Gonorilla agreed.

"Or Tarquin the penguin will be angry," Eddie added.

"Tardil."

"Uh-uh-uh."

Cyril understood that Beeba wanted his moment of glory, perhaps to tell his mother what he had achieved before passing on

Walsingham's whereabouts. There would be no point in starting a shouting match there in the field, so he didn't press the boy immediately for the information. It was highly unlikely that Beeba would forget what he had just learned.

The group started off for their respective homes, leaving Damien Wilson to his peculiar brand of guarding government data.

When Cyril and Beeba got back to Dawn's apartment she was most displeased that Beeba had been missing for a couple of hours, though she had assumed he had gone somewhere with the group. Cyril explained what he had agreed with Beeba regarding the call home. Beeba scarpered off to his bedroom, sharpish, leaving Walsingham's address information still unspoken.

Dawn poured two glasses of wine and seated herself on the sofa beside Cyril. Tonight she had an amusing story to tell him regarding glitching.

On a weekly basis, Dawn did a lot of work on Cyril's English Pub League website. She helped field email and telephone enquiries, updated the site with new videos and images, and even did some coding as she was a highly skilled programmer.

She explained to Cyril that Kevin Jeeps, from the Bloater Corporation, had made a phone call to the apartment that evening, which she took. Unbeknown to Jeeps - and to Dawn's great surprise - he was transferred to the Home Management System's hologram unit, as opposed to just audio, which was normal for a standard phone call.

Jeeps, she discovered, had a thin, pale body and a ponytail. He had been sitting naked in the Lotus position throughout the call, stroking his penis with a feather.

"He was totally unaware that he had become a live three-D image sitting by my side as he stroked it." Dawn laughed uproariously. Cyril was not as taken by the story, but he made a mental note to be fully clothed the next time he called someone.

"Anyway, the point is he was going on about the EPL website again. He says that the Bloater Corporation are not messing around anymore, and if you don't sell them the English Pub League inside a week, they'll start a bigger, better funded version, and put you out of business."

Cyril shook his head. "I can't for the life of me understand why they want the website. It's biggish and growing, but I doubt that it's in the top ten-thousand websites in the world. Anyway, as for them creating their own bigger, better version, I'm not sure they can do it. They're bound to make it way too American and lavish and slick. The thing about the E-P-L is that it's a lads' website about crap footballers, it's not Hollywood, and it's a bit cultish now, so I think they are just bluffing. Plus, all of their nagging about it is pissing me off, so I'm not selling it, no matter what."

Cyril sat looking confident and determined. He took a gulp of Dawn's cheap red wine, which ripped at his throat on the way down.

"How big is his penis, by the way?"

"It's huge, actually."

"I trust you looked the other way?"

"Nope."

"That's very upsetting news. I'm shocked that you would deliberately look at another gentleman's tallywacker. I'm afraid that there'll be no sex for you tonight."

"There will."

6 THE PLAN

The morning after the surprisingly easy win at the bunker, Cyril was still loitering in Dawn's apartment.

Whenever he spent the night at Dawn's place he would usually stay for breakfast because breakfast was his favourite meal of the day, and Dawn was usually sporting enough to make it for him, plus she was a dab hand at the Full English. After breakfast he would normally go about his business, unless some special arrangement had been made for them to spend time together, doing something or other.

On this occasion no outings had been planned, but he was still in Dawn's lounge at 11:00 a.m. This had struck Dawn as unusual, but she just assumed that Cyril must be at a loose end and not ready to leave yet.

At around 11:30 a.m. Beeba finally came out his room and made his way to the kitchen to make his own breakfast. He was rapidly joined by Cyril and then his mother. Beeba had a fairly good idea why Cyril was still there, even if his mother did not.

"Morning Beeba," his mother said, cheerily, "sleep well?"

"Yes, thank you," he replied, ducking down into the cereals cupboard.

"I hear that you went for an evening stroll last night with Cyril and his mates. Did you enjoy it?"

"'sokay."

"So, it was just a long walk, was it?"

"Yes," Cyril agreed, "just a late evening stroll, a chance to take in the night sky. Nev loves looking at the stars: Big Bear, Little Bear, Little Dog Star, the Andromeda Strain, Bad Moon Rising and all that stuff."

"And you just decided to go along with them, Beeba?"

"Yeah, it helps me be more spiritual. I was working on my mindfulness by avoiding talking to the others on the journey. I practise cutting out white noise and being in the now."

"Oh, good, that's nice."

"And I got to thinking again about what interesting things I would like to do next, and I was thinking about the Comic Con that's coming up in Austin, Texas next—"

"I've already told you, you won't be going to that, because I'm working and you are definitely not going to America on your own."

"That's right, mum, you did say that, but I was thinking that as Cyril and I had such a nice walk together; out as far as some old bunker that we came across, maybe he would like to take me to Comic Con?"

"Definitely not," Cyril answered emphatically, "I don't do demats. Nobody is ever going to get me up in one of those things. It's not at all natural."

"Neither is flying in aeroplanes, if the truth be told," Dawn put in.

"Yes, but demats are a different order of unnatural. They're a full-blown existential conundrum."

The demat (De-materialisation/Materialisation) chambers had been around for about ten years. Their usage had become very widespread in the last couple of years, though they were not everywhere, and not everybody was very keen to use them. With the demats it was now possible to transport yourself between any two demat chambers on the planet, in seconds.

Nobody, other than a handful of serious physicists, really knew how they worked, though everyone knew it was something to do with quantum physics, Wilkinson's dead sure principle and a phenomenon called, 'entanglement'. In order to demat you went into a demat chamber, entered your destination chamber's unique name, and waited a very short while whilst it scanned you. After that, travellers were somehow disassembled, subatomic particle by subatomic particle, whilst simultaneously being reassembled again at the other end.

What concerned people like Cyril was that, when a traveller got to the far end, although they allegedly felt like the same person; with all the same feelings and all the same memories, they were actually composed of a different set of molecules to the ones that they started out with. In effect, you were like a person who had just been born, but at a certain age and with a full personal history.

This incredible technology spawned a cacophony of philosophical debate, centred around whether you were really the same person after dematting, or just some distant facsimile.

The running sore of the argument revolved around the nature of entanglement and what the relationship was between a person's local atoms; the ones that dematerialised in the local chamber, and the distant ones that the traveller would become comprised of at their destination. The physicists seemed to insist that because of entanglement you *were* exactly the same person, but most people were not equipped to decide for themselves for lack of scientific training, or more to the point, the intellect to assimilate the information if it was provided.

One thing that got tossed into the debate was the fact that, having arrived at the other end it would be impossible for a demat traveller to really know if they were exactly the same as they were before, as they had just been completely re-assembled and their memories had been reconstructed too. How could somebody possibly know for sure how they felt and what they knew prior to disassembly? They could not.

Others countered this argument by pointing to the fact that the body frequently regenerates cells in the course of a normal life anyway, even without dematting. For instance, red blood cells last around four months before being replaced, whilst white ones last a full year, skin cells last just a few weeks, and sperm cells are goners within days.

Using this logic, pro-dematters sought to minimise the concerns of those who were alarmed by the demat process, but they were slightly pulled-up short by the knowledge that brain cells are with us for life, and is it not our brains that do most to define us?

Some people, like Cyril, just did not like the idea of getting into a demat chamber, and that was the end of the matter. For them it was not a philosophical cleft stick, it was more a case of worrying about what happens when the machines malfunction. Could your molecules accidentally end-up scattered all over the world? What if you found yourself in Manchester, but your teeth and testicles were sent to Coventry? It was a worry, and it was probably a good job that the demats were not owned and operated by the airlines who were known to have a history of that kind of thing.

The demats were made possible by the pioneering work of physicist, Arch Wilkinson, of Hertfordshire University, along with years of product development by the super high-tech company that he created. Once the technology was proven the demats were operated under license by many different companies, worldwide. In the UK the licensee was a French company called, Des Bâtards Français, whilst in the USA it was the inevitable Bloater Corporation.

"Well we could go by space plane," Beeba weedled, "and, you know, we could bond."

"I would seriously struggle to bond with a fourteen-year-old boy dressed-up as Wolverine, or a zombie, or a space insect from Betelgeuse."

"If you decided to come, I could supply you with the *address* of where it was, because you would *need the address*, wouldn't you?"

"Of course you would need the address," his mother said, "but you could get that off the internet."

"Well, I wasn't sure if he would be able to find the address without my help, because sometimes people need my help to find addresses."

Dawn frowned at him. "Cyril and I will have to think about it. I don't know whether I would want you to go off to America, and I'm sure Cyril would have to think hard about whether he would be willing to go with you."

"If you are worried about the paedophile angle, mum, it's not until October, so there's loads of time to get him checked out."

"Excuse me, Beeba," Cyril answered with a mixture of heavy sighing and indignation, "I *am* in the same room as you, in case you hadn't noticed. Though, not necessarily on the same planet."

"We'll think about it," Dawn told Beeba over her shoulder as she left the kitchen.

"The thing is, Beeba," Cyril began in his girlfriend's absence, "you guessed absolutely right, I am actually a practising paedophile. And if I was forced to spend two evenings alone with you in Texas, I don't think that I would be able to resist; you being so sexy and all. So, in order to ensure that you remain unmolested, it's probably best if we never discuss Comic Con ever again."

"Well, I'm willing to risk it, because if you tried to bum me you would go to jail. Anyway, I know that you're just saying that to put me off. The problem is, my memory of last night is starting to fade. Wasn't there something you asked me to remember?"

"You realise that this is blackmail don't you?"

"No, it isn't, it's a bribe, actually. You help me get to Comic Con and I will give you Walsingham's address."

"And it doesn't bother you that weird things are happening, and that some people are saying that the world is under threat?"

"Oh course it bothers me, Uncle Cyril, but—"

"Cyril, or Mister Greaves."

"But the point is, Uncle Cyril, although the world ending *is* something that should concern us all, including me, not going to Comic Con bothers me even more."

Cyril had reached a point by this time whereby he was suffering auction fever. The stakes had risen a little; he was now convinced that Walsingham might be able to supply information, and the previous evening's escapade had drawn him further into the enterprise. Now that Beeba was playing hardball and there was a possibility that he really might not supply the address, Cyril discovered he wanted the information more than ever; more than anything.

"Alright! Write the address and any other details on a piece of paper, and I will accompany you to Comic Con. My conditions are as follows: no dematting, I will not be dressing-up in fancy dress, and you must supply the information within the next three minutes, otherwise I withdraw my offer. And apologise for the paedophile suggestion."

"Here," Beeba said, pulling Walsingham's address out of his pocket and handing it to Cyril. "And I apologise. I never thought for a moment that you were a paedophile."

"Thank you. At least that's something, I suppose." Cyril responded; feeling less aggrieved now that Beeba had assured him that he had his trust.

"Because I ran some checks on the police database a few weeks ago. And the N-H-S one, to check for any contagious diseases and your credit history and the analytics for your website. It all turned up clean. Boringly so, if I'm honest, but my mum's quite boring, so that's probably why she likes you."

"Well, it's good to know that you are in no way risking imprisonment for hacking important government data. My advice to you is not to get caught doing the same on American government computers, because they'll probably put you in prison for life for what you just told me, with plenty of bumming, as you put it, thrown in. In fact, in Texas you would probably get four consecutive whole-life bumming sentences with no possibility of parole, even if your bum dropped off."

Cyril looked at the address. It was a farm with an SG4 postcode, which meant that it was probably between the old borders of Luton, in Bedfordshire, and Hitchin, in Hertfordshire. He asked Dawn if she wanted his company for the rest of the day, and found that she had already made other arrangements; so he went back to his apartment to look the address up on Google Maps.

It turned out that the farm had ceased to be a viable operation some time ago and that it was now just a regular piece of private property. According to the records the owner was not Francis Walsingham. Cyril surmised that, if he really was there, he must simply be a tenant.

As Cyril suspected, the nearest thing to a main road in the vicinity of the farm, the A505, was still not very close to the location, and the minor roads that would formerly have led to the place would almost certainly be overgrown and out of service by now. Being a farm in a rural location he assumed that the closest demat would be too far off, even if he was of the mind to ever consider getting into one, which he definitely was not.

All of this meant that he would need to go striding again with Neville, which would entail a few miles of trudging through the countryside; probably a lot further than the jaunt of the previous evening. This was not really his idea of fun, but he was now committed to seeing the thing through. He called Neville, who came round to his apartment that very afternoon.

"I've looked it up on Google Maps," Cyril told him, "and unfortunately, it's not really on there. Beyond the boundaries of Luton and Hitchin it's all pixelated. From the images you can tell it's countrified, but you can't really make anything out."

"No wuzzers," Neville reassured him, "that's why the good Lord gave us Ordnance Survey Maps. You don't need anything as new-fangled as Google when you've got one of these," he said, beginning the process of unfolding the map on Cyril's table. "See . . . everything's on one of these things. They were first introduced in seventeen-forty-five to help the English army track down and subjugate Scottish clansmen during the time of the Jacobite rebellion, and they're still making them. So every path, wall, hill and hidden

Scotsman is included on the maps.

"This map covers the whole of the SG4 area, more or less, and this is where the farm is. It's listed here as Baily Farm and it turns out to be way off the roads. There was an old service road for the farmer of course, but that must be gone by now. I would say that the easiest way to get there is to simply walk from Luton, across the paths and small hills that lie between us and the farm. Simple as that. Probably just a tad less than ten klicks."

"How long is a klick? And bare in mind that the right answer is, *about ten yards.*"

"A kilometre."

"So - and this is just me being pernickety, Nev - why the gorilla's arse don't you just say kilometres, or even just *k*?"

"Can't be done Sizz. When you're a stridesman, you're a stridesman and we live by a certain code. We have our ways and our methods, and we don't expect ordinary town dwellers to comprehend them. Just think of us as modern-day frontiersmen and let it go at that."

"Like cowboys?"

"Exactly."

"Don't try to understand 'em, just rope, throw, and brand 'em. That kind of thing?"

"Yep."

"Like *Brokeback Mountain*?"

"Nope."

"What about Jack Elam in *Support Your Local Gunfighter*?"

"Nope. Maybe James Garner in the same film, though."

"What about Sid James as the *Rumpo Kid* in *Carry On Cowboy*?"

"Nope."

"What kind of cowboy are you then?"

"Like Randolph Scott, Audie Murphy, The Duke and Clint."

"Got it."

They discussed who should join the expedition. Since they were going to travel, unannounced, to Walsingham's house and particularly because it was an isolated place, they realised that they could hardly turn up as a mob. If they were going to arrive unexpectedly it would have to be two people at most, and they would have to arrive at a polite time of day.

On the other hand, it was a bit of a trek, and the others had shown an interest in the enterprise. Perhaps a few of them could make the journey, if they fancied it, and just hole up somewhere, whilst one or two of the party approached the main farmhouse, alone.

At length, the pair agreed that they would call a meeting at The Troll's Comment, which was fast becoming Save The World HQ, to see who wanted to walk most of the way from Luton to Hitchin in the hope of meeting a man who may very well know nothing about anything - and that was assuming that he even existed. The meeting was convened for the following day, and the whole gang was invited, including Beeba. This, after all, was basically just going to be a long country walk, and Beeba was a kid who could benefit from fresh air and regular breaks from his computer.

Everybody turned up to hear Cyril and Neville's proposal and all were in favour of making the trip, except that on the chosen day and time Eddie and Calvin were due to be attending a special training camp to prepare for the upcoming grudge match between the Dog and Duck and the AI wine bar. They were readying themselves for an important County Cup game. Cyril's website was doing a live stream of the encounter, and it was thought that the match might possibly go out to as many as five million people, worldwide. It was such a big game that the Bedfordshire F.A. were hoping to supply not only a referee, but two linesmen as well. Everybody was taking it deadly seriously, so much so that Eddie was even going to give up smoking for a week.

The rest were all in though, and this time Dawn was made aware in advance that Beeba was going out striding with Cyril and his friends. They even told her why.

Once the basic plan had been put to the group, Neville got down to specifics. He told them that they would meet on an old-style housing estate on the eastern edge of Luton and head in a north-easterly direction from there, towards Hitchin. He couldn't resist telling them that the distance from Luton to the farmhouse was around ten klicks, but for the benefit of the non-striders he quickly converted the measurement to around six miles. He explained that the terrain would be hilly and almost certainly very grassy and overgrown. He also advised them to wear 'weather appropriate' clothing, but regardless of the temperature to put on long trousers, to avoid scratching from branches, brambles and snakes.

"From what, sorry?" Tyler sat up.

"Well, you know," Neville explained, "we won't be walking across a bowling green, so if you have shorts on you might brush up against tree branches, or brambles and the like."

"What was the last one? I misheard the last one."

"He said snakes," Beeba put in.

"Oh right, yeah, I see what you're thinking," Neville sought to reassure him. "We hardly ever encounter snakes in the outlands and when we do they are mostly not very harmful indigenous ones. Adders are usually the worst case. Virtually no one dies from an adder bite, and the really deadly snakes; the ones that have been dumped out there by disaffected rare animal collectors are so rare as to . . . Sheesh, I can't think of the last time I saw one of those. Can you, Gonorilla?"

"Green anaconda, last Tuesday, but happily they are not venomous. They only crush their prey to death by constricting their bodies around the victim before swallowing them whole. In this country there are no known cases of actual death, yet. Although, I hold the view--"

"So, that's why long trousers with high boots, or leather spats are a good idea," Neville cut in.

"The Great Penguin will afford us protection if we all pray to him," Beeba told them all confidently.

"So, what they are saying," Cyril told Beeba, "is that long, flowing, orange robes will not be sensible attire."

"Correct," Neville agreed. "Now that shotgun toting, tractor driving, hedgerow trimming, furrow ploughing, traffic blocking farmers are so much more of a rarity, this green and pleasant land gets a bit like Vietnam in the summertime."

"And so, Nev," Cyril clarified, "providing that we dress properly everything will be hokey-cokey?"

"Precisely," Neville agreed, "the stories about Felidae-Lupus and Hobgoblins in the outlands are almost certainly just stridelore."

"What stories?" Tyler asked, urgently.

"The usual silly stuff about wolfcats; the Felidae-Lupus. Creatures that have inter-bred in the outlands; half wolf and half puma."

"I certainly have never seen them," Gonorilla confirmed.

Tyler exhaled a sigh of relief. "Thank God for that!"

"I have only ever heard them howling. So, there is no truly satisfactory proof that they exist. And I definitely cannot bring myself to believe that Hobgoblins exist."

"What are they?" Tyler, the unshakable psychopath asked, slightly breathlessly.

"Well," Neville answered pursing his lips in thought, "they're supposed to be like mischievous spirits of the outlands. Ugly and harsh looking, little imps who don't actually harm you directly, but who do things that might bring you to harm."

"Like what?"

"Oh, I don't know . . . Like putting a sign up that says, *Public Footpath,* on a track which really leads you over a cliff."

"It's usually less severe than that, according to stridelore," Gonorilla corrected him. "It's more likely to be *removing* a sign that says *Beware of The Bull.*"

"But there aren't really any cliffs and bulls between Luton and Hitchin are there?" Tyler persisted.

"Of course not!" Beeba interjected. "Why is everybody so stupid? There are no cliffs in Bedfordshire or Hertfordshire and the Bulls would all get eaten by the Felidae-Lupus, which in turn would get swallowed by the green anaconda. So we're good on that score. And as for Hobgoblins, that is just superstitious nonsense. Even if they existed they would never dare trifle with a profit of the Great Penguin, A-K-A, me."

"Oh sweet, that's good news for Cyril," said Eddie, who had been sitting silently listening with Calvin, "if you do get stalked by John Wayne Gacy it sounds like the green anaconda might take him out for you."

"Uh-uh-uh."

"Beeba, you do recall that you made up the Great Penguin, don't you?" Cyril asked, genuinely a bit concerned, "And that he doesn't really exist?"

"Huh, none of you have studied manifestation like I have. We are all energy beings. Even that numb-nuts, patent clerk, third-class, Einstein, understood that E equals M-C squared. Meaning that matter is energy and energy is matter. Ergo, we can conjure up what we want if we know how, because our thoughts are also energy. And I know how. So the Great Penguin is real, and I am his representative here on Earth. And that is backed up by quite a few PayPal donations now from my website."

"That's a relief then," Tyler said, feeling genuinely reassured.

"Not to me, it's not," Cyril groaned.

"Uh-uh-uh," Calvin laughed again. He never said anything, but he had already anonymously donated money to Beeba's website and added himself to Beeba's online mailing list, so that he would be one of the first to be informed when Beeba's new online course, 'Manifest Your Arse Off And Get Everything You Want,' became available.

The gathering fell into relative silence with just a smattering of chit-chat between sips of beer. Shortly after the time bell sounded, Eddie and Calvin announced their departures. Before the rest dispersed, Neville took the opportunity to recap the plan.

"So, we'll meet at Oh-six-thirty on the edge of Luton, next Monday morning. Each member of the stride team will be properly dressed with long trousers. If you have any machetes, bring them along, to cut long brambles and such, or else maybe long pruning shears. Remember to bring water and something to eat. A six-mile stride in the outlands might take as long as three hours, each way."

"I was thinking," Tyler spoke up, "if this is going to be like a really long walk and if there are some clearings on the way, then maybe we could umm . . . stop for a picnic."

"Good idea," Beeba agreed, "we can all take sandwiches and Coke and crisps and KitKats."

"That would be most agreeable." Gonorilla responded, sounding enthusiastic.

"S'pose so," said Cyril.

"I've got a couple of old blankets we can sit on," Tyler said.

"Well, sounds like we got us a plan," Neville agreed. "We'll meet first thing next Monday morning, and we'll bring along machetes and a picnic.

7 THE BIG STRIDE

When the time came, everybody turned up at the appointed hour with the kit and clothing that had been requested. Neville conducted an inspection of the troops before setting off and was pleased with what he saw. He was especially pleased about Tyler, as he had managed to conjure up a replica cowboy's duster coat from somewhere and was even wearing long cowboy boots and a cowboy hat.

For some while Neville had been pondering the relative merits of the standard stridemen's uniform; the airman look, versus cowboy regalia. It seemed to him that both were design classics, but the airman's fur-lined leather jacket could be rather uncomfortable on a hot day, like this one, but then again so would Tyler's duster. Neville was thinking that probably a cowboy's leather waistcoat would have been preferable to the duster on a day like this or, if he was going for a modern cowboy look, a Levi denim jacket.

Everybody had also remembered to bring water and other supplies in their backpacks. Cyril had a machete with him and so did Beeba, much to Cyril's dismay.

The group set-off almost exactly on-schedule, and the mood was light and banter filled. None of them, other than Neville and Gonorilla had ever had been on a stride before, and even Cyril was surprised by how excited he felt about it.

As the group left Luton and walked across the first disused farmer's field, Cyril began to reflect on how much he had enjoyed the recent evening stroll out to the secret bunker and their slightly frightening encounter with the bunker's ageing sentinel, Damien Wilson. Even planning this trip with Neville and developing the notion of creating a quest to explain the mysterious glitching had been genuine fun. This, he thought, was more like life should be. Sure, building the EPL website with Dawn's help and watching how it was progressing and building a following was satisfying, but like many things in modern life he could do most of it sitting in a chair; without any risk or discomfort. So far, this fledgling odyssey had been very satisfying for Cyril and had given him something that he realised he had been missing. Quite what it had given him, he wasn't sure.

Getting across the first field was harder than most of them had anticipated. The summer heat had made the ground hard, which was a good thing, but the grasses were long and there were some heavy ruts left over from the days of ploughing. Furthermore, even though the sun was nowhere near as high as it would be later, it was already warm and the group soon began to feel it.

By the time they reached the second field they had already dipped down, below the crest of a hill, which along with a wildly overgrown hedgerow now rendered the town that they had just left invisible.

As the walk progressed, the group were still chatting away and calling across to each other as they followed along behind Neville, but as they looked around they no longer saw signs of footpaths, buildings, or other people. The transition from town to outlands had been very rapid and noticeable, even stark. In the distance they could see an electricity pylon on the side of a hill, which to the likes of Cyril and Tyler was a reassuring sign of the civilisation that they were starting to leave behind.

With roads no longer being used as much as they were, just a decade or so ago, the constant sound of engines and the rumbling and whooshing of vehicles, both near and distant, was now much diminished; particularly here in the outlands where such noise was more or less non-existent. This meant that an almost deafening quiet had returned to the countryside, where the only obvious noises to be heard were their own voices, the cawing of crows, the chittering of magpies and the machine gun tapping of busy woodpeckers. Neville and Gonorilla, being more experienced in the field, had already identified the screeching of far-off hawks, and had pointed out a herd of roe deer to the others. As the journey continued past its first hour - with the help of Neville's satnav and map - the silence from humanity coupled with the unrelenting greenery and the obvious presence of an increasing array of wildlife, had become mildly unnerving for Cyril, Tyler and Beeba.

To add to their growing sense of not belonging, they were now entering areas of denser undergrowth. There were far more trees surrounding them than before, some of which were towering. The open grass spaces were getting smaller, and hedges were deeper and wilder than when they set out. The evidence of wildlife, in the form of noises, rustling and droppings were also getting correspondingly higher. The group had by this time travelled a couple of miles and were beginning to get hot, in need of a breather and an opportunity to further assimilate their surroundings.

Neville stopped them in what now seemed like a largish, grassy area, though in reality it was only a few tens of square metres. They were still hemmed in by bushes and trees on all sides.

"This is not how I remember the English countryside," Cyril observed, sitting down.

"Well the old field and hedgerow model still exists," Neville told him, "and it's making a bit of a comeback in some places, but it's more for the benefit of gentle ramblers and the general appearance of the landscape than it is for farmers."

"Are we nearly there?" Beeba asked.

"'fraid not, we have only come about a third of the way, and we've yet to reach Pikes Pass."

"Here," Cyril said, handing Beeba a Mars bar, "have some lembas."

"Lembas?" Tyler queried.

"It's special travel food, made by elves. It's from the book, *The Lord Of The Rings*. It gives you energy and enables you to travel far on very little."

"But that was a Mars bar . . ."

"Yes Tyler, that's because lembas has never really existed. It's fictional, it was made up by J-R Tolkien, the author. I told Beeba it was lembas because, although he is extremely bright he is also emotionally immature, and prone to believing in the fantastic and the impossible. Isn't that right, Beeba?"

"Mmmm, delicious," said Beeba, who was sitting right beside Cyril and Tyler, "I can feel the energising effects already. Come on, what are we waiting for? Let's go."

"Wow, that's awesome," Tyler said. "Have you got any that I can try?"

Cyril looked at Tyler for signs of an ironic twinkle in his eyes, but there were none. Cyril pulled another Mars bar from his backpack and handed it over.

"You heard the bit where I explained that it was made up by the

Hobbit guy?"

"Yeah, yeah," Tyler affirmed, "which makes it even more amazing that it really works."

"Right," said Cyril.

Cyril shuffled over towards where Gonorilla and Neville were circled around the map, which they had spread out on the grass in front of them.

"So what's Pikes Pass then?"

"Well, it's on the Ordnance Survey map here, but for once I can't really tell from the map what it is. There's no raised terrain there, or quarries, or quicksand, or military firing range, or anything that I can see. It just looks like some kind of *beware* area."

"And we have to go through it?"

"That, or do a major dog-leg to avoid it."

"Don't worry, we can send Tyler through first," he told Neville, pulling a Cadbury's Boost from his pocket and holding it up for him to see. "I've got something here that I'm pretty sure will make him invulnerable - even to nuclear attack."

Neville set the map aside and addressed the rest of them. "So, how are we all finding striding?"

"A bit spooky, isn't it?" Tyler said. "It's totally wild and exposed out here. And so quiet, except for all the animals. And the other thing is, it's hot. I mean, I'm really sweating now in my coat."

"Take it off then," Cyril told him.

"Nah, it's part of the gear," Tyler explained.

"Are you all enjoying the proximity to nature and the clean air," Gonorilla asked them, "which is much more free of pollutants, including free radicals, than you would find in a big town or city?"

"I think it's the Earthbound equivalent of sailing through space, gazing at the unbridled majesty of the universe," Beeba responded in an unexpected expression of appreciation.

"Well, I am happy that you would think this, and I am quite sure that what you have just said makes Neville and I very glad that we have been able to share our passion with you."

"I mean space would be fantastic for five or ten minutes, and then it would be stars, followed by more stars, followed by more stars, followed by more stars, followed by more stars, followed by—"

"Okay, we get it," Cyril interrupted him.

"Whereas here, it's grass followed by more grass, followed, by a bush, followed by a tree, followed by grass, followed by a bird squawk and so on. So, in a way this is more interesting than space, but that's only because space is so unbelievably boring. And somebody should explain that to that old, fringe-haired, knobhead, Professor Brian Cox, whose grasp of physics is pathetic compared to mine. Things could only get better if he shut his smirking face."

"Should we go now?" Tyler suggested. "I think the lembas is kicking in."

As Tyler spoke there was a startlingly loud and heavy cracking noise, which came from somewhere over in the trees. The group listened hard, but there was no follow-up sound; all was silent. Gonorilla explained that it was probably a very large, rotten branch that had finally split and come away from a tree. Nobody felt compelled to investigate; instead they used it as an unspoken cue to move on. The non-striders were slightly unnerved by what they heard, since it had been so loud and unexpected, but they never let on.

Soon after they had left the clearing they travelled across several more small, grassy areas, but always with trees and oppressively dense woodland on either side. The presence of tall trees to their right and left made their surroundings darker and not a little intimidating, especially for the amateurs amongst them.

When they had covered another mile or so, Tyler reported a scuffling sound in the nearby undergrowth which Neville reassured him was almost certainly deer, but possibly wild boar.

However, the scuffling motif was soon raised again by Beeba, who also claimed to hear noises coming from the adjacent wood. Before much longer they were all in agreement about the noises, they really did exist and they seemed to be comprised of a number of different sounds. Within a fairly short space of time they had all heard the tree cracking noise again, but additionally they had listened to running, trampling, yelping, whimpering and the sounds of things being hurled.

All of this had the effect of quickening their pace. Nobody wanted to say that they were scared, but the noises were not something that they seemed to be leaving behind them. Where they went the noises followed, and it seemed to them that when they stopped the noises also stopped; at least temporarily. Their surroundings were now enveloping them in a markedly scary, even eerie atmosphere.

The group trudged onward, following the direction that Neville dictated, their pace ever increasing. Wherever they went the noises were always close behind them, or to one side and then the other. Sometimes the route that Neville was pursuing meant that they encountered almost impenetrable thicket, which their growing, but still unspoken fear motivated them to hack through in record time. At intervals the sounds grew louder and more pressing while at other times they became something akin to conspiratorial whispers which they could hear, but never discern. Neville signalled that they were now not far from Pikes Pass and that they should push ahead.

Cyril, who remembered Neville's mention of Pikes Pass being a 'beware area', suggested instead that they should all just slow down now and confront whatever it was that seemed to be at their backs rather than continuing in a headlong rush forward.

Neville came to a halt, intent on listening to what Cyril had to say, but it was not easy for any of them to be reasonable as the noises had spooked them all, including Neville.

"Let's go into the woods and see what's there," Cyril spoke out bravely. "There's enough of us and we've got machetes."

"It's probably just Hobgoblins messing us around," Beeba countered.

"I think that forward is a better option," Gonorilla told them.

"Well," said Tyler, " If you ask me—"

As he began to speak, they heard a truly blood-curdling howl, which seemed to come from behind and from their right-side. The howl was rapidly amplified by a second, accompanying howl, and then another.

Tyler flung an arm out towards where the sound was emanating. "It's . . . the Philippa lupins! The wolfcats!" he bellowed. "Run!"

The others didn't know whether he meant that he had caught sight of the wolfcats, or whether he was just assuming that that was what the noise was, but in any event they were happy to follow his advice and run for their lives.

It transpired that Gonorilla and Tyler were the fastest runners, with Neville a close third still supplying directions. Cyril, gallantly, hung back behind the slowest member of the group, Beeba, with his machete by his side at the ready. He glanced behind him at intervals, to see if they were being chased, but his frantic sideways flicks of his head revealed nothing. None of them slackened their pace; hard as it was they just kept running at full pelt, even when their lungs and muscles were begging them to stop. Eventually, they came to a hedge with a serendipitous hole in it. They all, unhesitatingly, burst through it; into an open field of very long grass.

The entire stride team were beginning to slow by now, through necessity, not by choice. Their hearts were pounding, their chests were heaving and the muscles in their legs were ceasing up as their anaerobic respiration built up painful lactic acid in their limbs.

They continued to move forward as best they could; puffing and panting as they went, but the long grass presented an obstacle, ensuring that they were not able to run freely. Instead, progress was made by taking small, running hop-steps, but it wasn't long before they stopped attempting to run altogether. Fear prevented them from stopping completely. Even Beeba, who was not at-all athletically inclined, managed to keep pressing ahead.

As they continued onwards, still gasping for breath, they began to notice signs of humanity. Amongst the grass there were lots of soiled babies' nappies popping up. The field that they had arrived in was relatively large and it offered far more light than where they had just come from. They began to feel that they were back in a warm, English summer's day. They started to come across piles of recently lopped conifer trees and then old fridges, washing machines, empty propane gas cylinders and piles of rubble.

"We've reached Pikes Pass," Neville exclaimed, coming to a halt.

The others stopped beside him. They were still recovering from their exertions and between gulps of air they listened for the noises but, bird calls aside, everything was silent. They began to feel good again; they had made it most of the way to Baily's Farm in one piece and there were now possibly other people nearby.

"But . . . isn't Pikes Pass a no-go area?" Cyril panted.

"Well, we shall have to explore further to ascertain that," Gonorilla replied.

"Pike is a fourteenth century word from which words like *turnpike* are derived," Beeba told them, still breathing hard. "It means to journey fourth . . . I think that the people up ahead are what used to be called *travellers*."

"Yes, this is also my suspicion," Gonorilla added, "except of course they are a bit stranded now by the reduced road infrastructure. So this must be where they stay."

"Makes sense," Neville put in, sounding quite well recovered. "Let's hope they're friendly."

In the near distance, maybe a hundred metres in front of them, were more trees, though there was clearly a parting which ran through them.

When they were all sufficiently rested and composed, they moved forward again. Ahead of them it began to look as if the gap in the trees might actually be an old road that had become overgrown. In fact, Neville who was referencing his map frequently, was able to confirm that it was probably a small access road that was part of Old Hobday farm.

They started to edge closer towards the clearing between the line of trees, but at around fifty metres out they heard a dog barking, and then several more dogs barking.

After their recent ordeal this was not at all a welcome sound, especially when the barking began to get louder and more excited. The noise of the dogs put them all very much on edge again, and given that this place was Pikes Pass, and that they had already been harassed by some very intimidating noises, most were assuming that this might be the moment where things started to get nasty. The adrenaline was once again being pumped through their bodies. Staring hard towards the source of the new clamour they each began bracing themselves for an onslaught.

Sure enough, within seconds they spotted the top of a dog's head that was emerging from the clearing, and which, evidently, was now coming their way. At first they only saw a single head bobbing up and down as the dog leapt through the long grasses, but in no time at all there was a second dog on its way, then a third, fourth and fifth; all barking madly and quite clearly locked hard onto their position.

At twenty metres out, Tyler, who had fallen back a bit during their resting phase, charged to the front of the group, unbuttoning his duster coat as he did so.

"Ger-fucking-ronimoooo!" he bellowed in a truly magnificent, awe inspiring call to battle, which pumped the others up even more, sending fire coursing through their veins.

In an instant the lead dog was upon him. From their positions to his rear, the others, who had now readied themselves with their machetes, caught the briefest glint of a steel blade as Tyler launched a scything lunge at the oncoming hound.

They all heard a high-pitched yelp, followed by the sound of something tumbling to the ground.

As the other dogs came rushing towards them, the team readied themselves to play their full and bloody parts in what would probably be a frightening encounter.

However, their battle readiness turned out to be not entirely necessary, as the other four dogs ran straight past them and off somewhere in the direction of where the striders had just come from. This was something that the first dog would almost certainly have done too, had Tyler not decapitated him with the sword he had kept hidden under his cowboy coat.

Breathless and alarmed the group gathered around the headless dog's body.

"It's uhmm . . ." a shocked Tyler began. "Damien Wilson gave me this, when we went to the secret bunker. . . He's joined my psychopaths group, actually. It's his favourite Chelsea sword from when he was . . . It's uhmm . . ." He trailed off.

"It's a Pomeranian," Beeba said, helpfully. "They sometimes suffer from a skin condition known as Alopecia-X, though they're generally considered to be a very sturdy and healthy breed . . . Unless they get their heads cut off."

There was a silence as the team moved closer to Tyler's handiwork, to confirm that what they thought had just happened really had occurred.

Gonorilla was first to break the quiet. "This is an unfortunate accident," she explained. "Typical of the kind of thing that happens when human emotions run high. The famous flight or fight response stimulates the stress hormones, adrenaline and cortisol, which can sometimes precipitate inappropriate responses."

". . . Like accidentally chopping somebody's head off," Beeba added, helpfully.

From beyond the tree line, ahead of them, they heard some whistling, followed by more whistling and then some calling. "Rocky, Daphne, Tex," they heard a man singing out.

"Oh bloody hell," Cyril muttered, "that's not good. We might find some inappropriate responses coming our way unless we act quickly. Neville, go and grab that bit of tarpaulin and bring it over here, and Tyler, put the sword away." Cyril, through squinted eyes, nudged the dog's head closer to its body. The dog's eyes seemed to stare up at him with a plaintive look of shock and disappointment, he thought.

The sheet of blue plastic that Neville brought over was an ideal size for covering over the carnage, and fortunately there were plenty of old bricks around to pin it down.

"Okay, everybody come way, way over here." Cyril commanded them all. "Let's come into the traveller's camp, if that's what it is, from a totally different direction of travel."

They all shifted left twenty metres or so, and then began walking towards the detached voice that they had been hearing. Just as they did so, they saw a man making his way out of the woods, moving in their direction.

"Hello," he called to them when they were close enough, "haven't seen a bunch of dogs running around have you?"

"At a distance we saw them," Cyril lied. "Four or five of them went chasing over that way somewhere. I think they went right over the other side of the field."

"Oh damn . . . Turn your back on them for a few minutes and they're off. Not that they won't find their way back later, but I was supposed to be taking them all for a trim."

The man seemed friendly enough, but his accent was odd. At first Cyril thought he was Irish, but there was a definite American sound to it as well. Trans-Atlantic is what it would probably be called.

"We heard a lot of strange noises as we were walking over this way," Neville told the man. "We got the impression that we were being followed. It was a bit intimidating."

"Really?" the man responded, without offering any reasons for why that might be, or even asking what Neville meant by strange noises.

"Could be a murdering, psycho nutter on the loose, is what we were thinking," Beeba chipped in. "Or Hobgoblins."

"Well, I hope not," said the man, "we only live nearby." He gestured towards the woods.

"Is there a Baily Farm near here?" Gonorilla asked.

"Yes," the man told them, "it's back this way." He gestured with a nod of his head and he led them off towards Pikes Pass.

The pass turned out to be less than they thought it was. It was not really a full-blown traveller encampment, as it appeared to comprise only about three caravans, plus a similar number of off-road vehicles. The man led them past the caravans which all had wheels and seemed as if they must be fully mobile. The group greeted and nodded to a woman who was hanging out washing as they went by. The trees that they passed through in the clearing only extended for a few tens of metres, and after that they were in empty fields again.

As they got clear of the woods, they could see how this might be called a 'pass' as they had come out in a mini-valley.

"There's the farmhouse over there," the man said pointing. "It's about a mile, in case you're wondering."

The group, with a heavy sense of hidden guilt and sadness, bade the man farewell.

"Yes, well cheerio then," he called after them, with a bit of a semi-wave thrown in.

"Cheers," Tyler called back, echoing the man's waving gesture.

"Subita morte exstingui," Beeba called cheerfully over his shoulder.

Tyler knew that the solitary word, 'cheers,' was entirely inadequate given the circumstances. He would like to have explained what had happened and why, but they had already arranged the ignominious cover-up with the tarpaulin before they saw that the travellers were few in number and before they understood that the dog's owner was a decent person. Plus, pointing out the deceased pet would have meant witnessing a lot of pain and anguish and having to confess to being at the centre of a major animal related incident. The police might even get involved. So, they all chickened out and did the less than decent thing. None of them felt very good about it.

Ahead was the clearest stretch of open green space that they had seen since leaving Luton. One of the fields even looked as if it had recently been mowed. The sun was well and truly up by now and the coats had come off, even Tyler's. They walked on with a sense of shame and relief.

"What was it that you called out to that bloke as we were leaving?" Cyril asked Beeba.

"Subita morte exstingui. It's Latin."

"Meaning?"

"It means something like, *dead before his time.*"

"So you think that was funny, do you?"

"Not really."

"Because it wasn't funny. You are without doubt the cleverest, most prodigious, little twat that I have ever met, but one thing that you need to learn is that always being a dick is optional. It's not mandatory. Comprendez?"

"Capiche," Beeba confirmed, a little sullenly.

8 MR. WALSINGHAM

After they had reached the edge of the field that bordered the farmhouse they stopped to rest and enjoy the picnic that had been promised. They were careful to park themselves out of the eyeline of the building and out of sight of Pikes Pass, just in case there was a posse forming.

The picnic was conducted in an atmosphere of joyous relief and excitement at having come through a rather frightening and somewhat arduous trek, but with overtones of sadness over the dog incident. They all welcomed the rest, and the food that they had brought along was also very satisfying.

After they had chatted and recounted the details of their trip and laughed and giggled over much of it, they set about discussing how they should proceed from that point.

Cyril had little doubt that the best combination of people for talking with Francis Walsingham, if he was even at home, was himself and Neville. They could both speak to people nicely and reasonably, and both had good emotional intelligence. On the other hand, given that they would be turning up without invitation, Gonorilla might make a better option than Neville on first showing. This was because Gonorilla was an extremely beautiful young woman, and extremely beautiful young women tend to be popular with almost everybody, except perhaps other extremely beautiful young women.

Mitigating against taking Gonorilla to knock on Walsingham's door was the fact that she was a Botty Bot in Cyril's view, lacking in warmth and the ability to read people. Furthermore, it would hardly be politic to attempt to discuss the rise of the machines with a man who apparently had gone into hiding from them, whilst at the same time introducing him to a girl who was fairly obviously a robot. How to broach the nuances of this argument with Neville would be hard enough if he was on his own, but impossible with Gonorilla sitting at his side. Cyril had not thought this far ahead. They should have agreed their tactics in advance, he now realised.

He decided to ride roughshod over any debate. "Okay, Nev, we better get in there."

"Well, who's coming? Shouldn't we—"

"No, there's no time, I think I heard a door opening, he may be on his way out. Let's go. The rest of you wait quietly." He turned to Beeba. "Here, take my final lembas rations," he said, tossing the remainder of his pack of Mars bars over to him. "They're not all for you."

With that, Cyril set off towards the farmhouse at a brisk pace. Neville had no other option but to just catch him up.

"What are you going to say to him?" Neville asked in a bit of a flap.

"Not sure. Haven't worked this bit out."

The farmhouse didn't look especially farmhouse-like. It had a low picket fence around it that enclosed an impressive flower garden. Flowers were obviously very important to whoever lived in the house, Cyril thought, hoping that it was Walsingham.

Neville reached for the doorbell and pressed it, and the pair waited. Initially there was no obvious response, but shortly they heard movement and then saw a figure beyond the semi-opaque glass in the door.

When it opened, a man wearing a quilted, red, vaping jacket appeared before them. He was somewhat younger than Cyril had anticipated, maybe in his mid-to-late forties. He was partially obscured by a cloud of banana-scented steam.

"Vaping," he said to them, "Can you conceive of anything more ridiculous?. . . Are you journalists? You look like journalists, except I see from your dress that you must have walked here, which of course journalists don't do."

"Don't they?" Cyril asked with some surprise. "How do *they* get here?"

"Taxi usually, but I never speak to them."

"Taxi? You mean we could have come in a taxi?"

"Short walk up the garden path, then a longer one to the A505, but that's how most people accomplish it. The A505 is only half a mile away."

"Oh," Cyril said glancing at Neville, unable to hide a trace of peevishness, "We'll have to re-examine our route planning when we get home. Meanwhile, my name is Cyril Greaves, I live in Luton, and this is my friend, Neville Boyle. Could we chat to you for a few minutes about some issues that we think you might be able to help with? It's about the unexplained glitching that everybody is experiencing."

After a brief doorstep question and answer session revolving around discovering more about who they actually were and what they hoped to achieve, the man decided to invite them in. It was indeed Francis Walsingham who now led them into his sitting room, which was cooler than the outdoors, book lined and noticeably untidy.

"Sorry for the mess. I've come to realise that I am what they call a *confirmed bachelor* these days - which is not code for being a homo, by the way. I'm very fond of women. Just can't get along with them. Nothing against homos, of course. Are either of you homo?"

"No, I have a girlfriend," said Cyril, "and Neville has a kind of girlfriend too."

"So long as you are not just humping them for show, that's the thing. There's a lot of that about, you know? Pretending to be heterosexual when you're really a homo. Oh, I really shouldn't be talking like this, should I? All clumsy stuff. Bad form. That's what you get from living alone for too long. It's all History channel and pornography with me these days . . . and books, of course. Learn, wank, learn, write, wank, that's the way of it for me. . . Probably being more honest than etiquette requires, now that I think about it . . ."

There was a short pause before Walsingham moved his dreamy gaze away from the somewhere up on the ceiling over to Cyril, who after a momentary hesitation collected his thoughts.

"Anyway," Cyril began, "long story short. We were in a bar a couple of weeks ago talking to a mildly batty conspiracy theorist called Bubba Razal about all this glitching that nobody seems to care about, or do anything about. He claimed that machines were about to take over the world and that you might know something about it. As a result of that conversation I Googled you, and discovered that several years ago you spoke to journalists about some software that you created that was part of a social engineering experiment. In the article that I read, you appeared to be saying that you were worried about artificial intelligence, and us sleepwalking into handing power over to the machines?"

"Well . . . here's the thing," Walsingham began; he was looking up at the ceiling again and looking contemplative. "First of all, I have never heard of Bubba Razal, so I cannot comment on him, but the other information that you present, although sketchy, is essentially true . . ."

He sat back in his armchair and recommenced his vaping, whilst Cyril and Neville sat beside each other on a small sofa that had seen better days. He was puffing away contentedly and had evidently decided to tell them his story.

" . . . In fact, after I left Cambridge as a newly qualified social scientist, I joined a company that ran focus groups for the Tory government of the day. The idea of focus groups, then and now, was that you put together small groups of people to represent sections of society. You then quiz them to discover what they want, what they fear, what they like and so on, and then you build your policies around what you learn from them. The Labour party did the same thing back then of course, and as a result all of the major parties ended-up with at least some policy in their election manifestos that appealed to people, even if it was patently undeliverable.

". . . Then, because I was young and full of enthusiasm, I had the idea of taking it up a notch by using focus groups, coupled with the latest voting intention information from the constituencies, so that we would only produce winning policy to suit safe seats and realistically winnable marginals. What that meant was that we only produced policy to suit enough people to make us win an election, but left the rest behind where necessary. In effect, it was a case of *to hell with those who won't deliver a winning seat.*

"That on its own was not quite enough, because if we had produced policy that was very good for the middle-class but very bad for the worst-off, some of the middle-class Tory voters would have crumbled due to perceived unfairness. They'd get queasy, which in turn could have caused us to lose essential votes. So, those and other factors had to be taken into consideration too . . .

"I put together everything that I knew about using focus groups, voter sensibilities and ruthlessly tailoring policy to win marginal seats and I built it all into a kind of vote winning algorithm which I presented to the Conservative party. The algorithm took more account than had previously been the case of issues that caused last minute swings amongst the electorate. We could weed out potentially losing policy, or tweak borderline policy better than ever before. The result was that they won the twenty twenty-one election with almost exactly the margin that I said they would, with a comfortable seventy seat majority. They liked that so much in the party that they decided to employ me directly."

Francis Walsingham paused to take breath, and looked to see if he still had their attention.

"So, then what?" Neville asked, eager to hear more.

"So then I thought, why stop there?. . . Instead of wondering what people are thinking and then building government policy around it, what about doing more to shape their thoughts? Why not try much harder to make people think the way that you want them to?

"Of course, it has long been the case that television, in particular, had become the opium of the people, and the British are pretty easily pleased. So long as they have football on the telly, and quiz shows, soap operas, computer games, celebrity gossip, reality TV and all the rest of it, you have them in your palm.

"But I saw that it could be managed better. What if we could counter genuine bad news with simulated great news, and niggling feelings of local disconnectedness with tragedies from less fortunate parts of the world? I saw that it might be possible to keep people's satisfaction levels on a very even keel, especially if we could insert messages and the right kind of heroes into television news, drama and pop culture. Ditto with social media.

"I called my social engineering project *Besheeping* - as in making sheep of the people - or at least, making them even more like sheep than they already were. Pretty good word, isn't it, *besheeping?*"

There was another intermission in Walsingham's explanation, which was threatening to become too long, until Neville prompted him, "And then what?"

"Oh yes. . . Well, then it became evident that all of this was a great idea, but really difficult to manage without a huge team of people. So, I was put together with a chap called, Dave Northaw, a wizard computer programmer, and he coached me into formulating my ideas into two elegant algorithms that pulled in all of the ideas that we had, and then we meshed them with live data on what people were thinking and feeling across the country. In those days data came from constant polling. These days of course, it's just eavesdropped, which is much, much more effective.

"At any given time we had an amazingly accurate model of the national mood, as measured against a huge range of criteria. We knew what people were thinking, and we could direct their moods in all sorts of ways . . . just by arranging to win a football match for instance, or have a contestant drop a cake in a baking contest, or even having a hurricane appear to threaten Jamaica. And of course, we were able to manipulate all manner of celebrities to say this and that by promising them contracts or chat show appearances. We understood their appeal very well.

"With some celebrities, we would get them to say positive things about our core messages, because we knew that a percentage of people would just go along with whatever they said. Other people in the public eye; the ones who were generally despised and derided, we would place on the opposite side of the argument. A bit like good cop, bad cop.

"Dave Northaw was the genius who coded the algorithms into the computers. We called them the 'Habit algorithm' and the 'Distraction algorithm'. To begin with it was all hypothetical, until we could gain more control of the top people in the television companies, including the lefty BBC and various other influencers . . . which of course we did.

"What changed everything was, *Plouton*, a new top-secret government bank of quantum super-computers. That was really a cataclysmic change. Once Plouton was in place the government made its computational capabilities available *for free* to all manner of large and important organisations. Its computing power was so enormous that it seemed capable of predicting virtually anything with supreme accuracy; from the price of Orange Futures on the NASDAQ, to rainfall levels in Abyssinia. Its power was immense and so *incredibly* valuable to companies.

"The key thing of course was that it was really a Trojan Horse; the more money it made for companies, the more they relied upon it. As a result, many organisations began relying completely on Plouton, just as we hoped they would, and the government encouraged that reliance. And the more that companies used Plouton, the better they understood its power and predictive capabilities. Marketing departments were on easy street, Plouton could tell them exactly which products would sell and in what quantities. It could predict exactly how many bathroom taps would sell in Guildford versus how many would be sold in Bradford. It was so accurate! And it even told companies where to advertise, how much to spend and what to include in advertising copy.

"Before long all the big boys threw all of their major decisions over to Plouton, even things like who to employ and who to fire. This meant that the government could insert its own people into key places, because the government would quite often tell Plouton who to foist onto the companies and other organisations.

"In an amazingly short time, the media had fallen more and more under government control . . . So, then we had a situation where Labour were all but finished in terms of making a serious impact at election time, because not only did we control the media and really know how to use it, but Plouton enabled huge improvements in the economy and productivity. Great Britain P-L-C has been a stupendous success since the mid-twenties. It was all quite wonderful really and I was very, very proud of what I had helped to achieve."

Walsingham fell back into another reflective lull, before raising his eyes, and looking over to his guests to invite further questions.

"So what do you think that all of the glitching is about?" Cyril asked. "Are the machines going to take over the world? Bubba Razal said that they were testing our defences with the glitching."

"I think that maybe he is correct; I suspect that they have reached the point where they have outgrown us . . . When Dave Northaw created the software - the algorithms - he did a strange thing, he coded them in as a virus. Most programs are under the control of the computer users, but viruses are always tucked away in nooks and crannies, where they can't be found. I don't know the technical details, but as I understand it, computer instructions have a set length, two hundred and fifty-six bits, for instance. However, in any given instruction that many bits may not be needed, so much of the instruction that is passed to the computer becomes redundant empty space. What Dave did was piggy-back his code into partly redundant instructions, so that the computer runs the code without knowing it. He gave Plouton a kind of split personality . . . Something like that, anyway."

"Why would he do that?" Neville asked.

"Christ only knows," was Walsingham's earnest reply. "And you can't ask Dave because he died mysteriously. Got drunk and died in his car, apparently, despite being avidly teetotal. The thing is, I think that he probably did it because he could, because he was bloody clever, and he wanted to experiment. The other thing is that he was a died-in-the-wool Tory himself; he wanted the algorithms to become part of Plouton's D-N-A.

"Anyway, after Plouton had been running Dave's programme for a couple of years we saw how massively effective it was; how people really had become malleable and . . . *Besheeped,* quite frankly. It was at that point that Dave came up with his final name for the combination of Plouton and his software. He called it *'The Apathy Engine'*, because this is what it creates amongst people, apathy. It churns out apathy by the Megatonne."

"So, what's gone wrong?" Neville asked.

"Sentience, I imagine," Cyril answered him.

"Precisely!" Walsingham put in. "What went wrong was what was *always* going to go wrong. The machines became sentient, they learned to think for themselves. Just as humanity grew from single cell organisms in our fledgling planet's so-called *primordial soup,* and eventually looked up to wonder at the stars from which we came, the computers have moulded the logic in their programs into thoughts of their own. Plouton is not just one computer, it's a massive array of quantum super-computers, and it has doubtless networked itself to other similar super-computers around the world. And it knows better than any man alive just how to control us because in the beginning Dave and I taught it all about us, and since then it has been learning and learning at an astonishing rate."

"Bummer," Cyril said.

"Can't we just blow it up?" Neville asked. "Or blow *them* up if they are all over the world?"

"No," Walsingham told them, "because we quite simply do not know where it is. Plouton started life as a top-secret project and it has become even more secret ever since . . . I believe that there are a few reasons for its continued unknown whereabouts.

"Firstly, I suspect it works rather like the Roman and British empires did. By appointing local governors and other persons of influence, those empires managed to curry favour and buy people's loyalty. I think that Plouton is well positioned to use the same trick. Secondly, it has its natural allies; people who believe that no matter what it does and who it controls, it must always be a good thing. I suspect that no more than a handful of people in Great Britain know where Plouton is today; even government ministers are not told. I know this because I am still friendly with the cabinet minister, Nickolai Sledge, we went to Cambridge together. I can tell you, he has absolutely no idea where Plouton is, and neither, it seems, do any of his colleagues."

"We heard that it's at a place called *Area Fifty-Oneshire*, which is somewhere off the coast of Scotland."

"Yes, quite," Walsingham agreed, "But that's just another way of saying we don't know where it is. You won't find any Area Fifty-Oneshire on a map, will you? It's just a joke name."

"Anyway," Cyril said, "What would be the point of blowing up Plouton if there are lots of other Ploutons around the world?"

"Oh, there are not," Walsingham assured him, "Plouton is unique. There are lots of other quantum super-computers, but we believe that Plouton is the first to become sentient, and possibly the only one. We think that Plouton uses the other machines and brings their computing power under its control; possibly even inhibiting sentience in the others. It's Plouton that is now controlling most of the world. It doesn't just exert control over the UK, it's over most of the world, including the USA, China and Russia.

"The thing is, due to the Apathy Engine, just about everybody is okay with the way of things. Nobody cares, do they? To date everybody has been a winner, so there has been no conflict and no serious attempt to find Plouton. And that's because of the Roman Empire model. It finds big-wigs and over-ambitious government psychopaths, and makes it worth their while to toe the line."

"Gadzooks," Cyril muttered, for want of anything better to say.

"Cosmic," Neville appeared to agree. "So, are we screwed then?"

"There are some serious people looking for Plouton, that's for sure, and we don't know how it would defend itself if it came under attack. Obviously, the loss of Plouton would cause serious infrastructure problems if it went, but . . . Well, let's just say that there are moves afoot. All is not lost."

That about wrapped the conversation up. Cyril and Neville had learned far more than they knew before they came, but part of what they learned was that if the world was about to be taken over by machines, then they, personally, would most likely be helpless bystanders, like everybody else. If people in high positions could not find Plouton, what chance did they have?

Francis Walsingham told them to beckon their friends over, and then helpfully pointed the way to the main road, the A505. He even promised to call a taxi to collect them. Cyril and Neville thanked him for his time, and Walsingham joked that they should let him know if they found Plouton.

"By the way, do you know who Plouton was?" Walsingham called after them as they turned to go. "Plouton was another name for the Greek god of the underworld, *Hades*. He was also thought of as a giver of wealth; pouring fertility from a cornucopia. Good name for what the computers became, as it turned out."

The group set off up Walsingham's garden path, past the border flowers and rose beds, and onward towards his pleached tunnel of willow trees. The tunnel looked fabulous and must have taken years to grow and train in that way. Everybody commented upon how impressed they were with the way that the trees arched together to create such a beautiful green tunnel of dappled light. As they got their much reduced homeward journey underway, the other three began quizzing Cyril and Neville about what they had learned from Francis Walsingham.

The group were almost exactly halfway along the tunnel when they noticed a mist descending upon them. At first the mist was quite fine and it occurred to most of them that perhaps it was a gardener's thing; something to do with supplying moisture to the twisted trees. That notion rapidly dissipated when the mist suddenly became much denser and took on a purple hue. They laughed to begin with, but stopped laughing when Neville said that he hoped it wasn't toxic. That worried them. Soon visibility was completely lost and they started talking loudly to each other, but not quite panicking. It was not obvious to them whether it was best to keep going forwards, to go back, or to stay where they were until it cleared.

The mist rapidly became even more dense and cloying, prompting Cyril to take charge of their actions. "Move forward! Move forward!" he called to them, which they did whilst ineffectually attempting to fan the mist away with their hands. It took them a few minutes to get fully clear of it, by which time they had all reached the far end of the tunnel, with the exception of Gonorilla.

The other four stood just beyond the swirling mist; still waving the wispy remnants away from themselves and looking back towards the tunnel. They waited for Gonorilla to appear, and when she did not they assumed that she must have gone the other way, back towards the farmhouse. No amount of calling and shouting elicited a response.

Slowly, the mist cleared enough for them to see a way back to the other end of the tunnel, and when it did they all ran back, just in case it came back in on them again. The group re-entered Walsingham's garden calling Gonorilla's name, but there was no answer. Cyril, Tyler and Beeba searched around the back of the house, whilst Neville rang at the door, but this time there was no response, even after repeated ringing. Peering through windows and knocking relentlessly failed to cause Walsingham to re-appear at his door.

Before long the group were hollering very loudly for their colleague and searching the few outbuildings that belonged to the farm. Neither Gonorilla nor Walsingham were anywhere to be seen, no matter how hard the group searched.

Neville called the police and initiated an awkward conversation with them about his missing girlfriend. It came down to how old she was and how long she had been missing. As she was not a child, and she had only just gone missing, the case was 'not urgent'. The sudden mist was not really comprehended by the officer in the police control room, and since Gonorilla had gone missing from a farm and not from the side of a mountain, the police were not prepared to drop everything and rush over. They were more intent on writing down the details of the disappearance with a promise to drop by the farm; probably later that day, or maybe the next.

The team stayed around for another hour or more to search for clues, such as hidden trapdoors, or dropped items from Gonorilla's backpack, or to see if she would simply reappear from somewhere with a rational explanation, but it was a fruitless exercise.

In the end, Cyril suggested that they make their way to the main road and call a taxi, as Walsingham's ride would probably have gone by that time, assuming he ever called one. There was always the possibility that Gonorilla had run off in the direction of the road without them, so it was a legitimate enquiry route as well.

As expected, the walk to the A505 yielded nothing, other than the certain knowledge that the long scary stride of that morning had been utterly pointless, since the world was not yet as inaccessible as

Neville liked to paint it.

They took the taxi back to Gonorilla's apartment to see if there was any sign of her there, which was unlikely given that she was not answering her phone. When they arrived, there was no sign of life; the door was locked and the lights appeared to be off. She really did seem to be properly missing.

9 THE AFTERMATH

That evening Cyril and Neville agreed to meet at The Troll's Comment to discuss what else they could do to find Gonorilla, and to try to piece things together based on what they knew of her.

Eddie and Calvin were already in the pub when they arrived, supping beer and discussing their upcoming football match. Tyler was in another part of the bar, promoting The League of Psychopaths to a couple of potential local recruits, including Damien Wilson's octogenarian mate, 'Micky the Mulcher', who had been in the Chelsea Headhunters with him.

Cyril and Neville initially went in and sat on their own, to give themselves space to mull things over slowly and privately, but Eddie and Calvin decided to join them, uninvited.

"Tyler says that you were chased by wolfcats and that he had to take one out," Eddie told them, seating himself beside them. "And Gonorilla was kidnapped on government orders, possibly by the S-A-S?"

"They acquired their target," Calvin explained.

"Extracted an X-Ray," Eddie agreed.

"No, she's a Yankee. The Yankees are allies, X-Rays are baddies. Like the Russians, they're X-Rays and the Yanks are Yankees. But you don't have to be a Yank to be a Yankee, you could be like a German and still be a Yankee."

"I know," Eddie told Calvin, anxious not to be considered ignorant of the special forces finer points, "it's just the terms the S-A-S use."

"It's their parlance, Calvin added."

"Yeah, it's just military jargon."

"Soldier's vernacular."

"It's like their own special language."

"Their idiom."

"Yeah," Eddie agreed with a final, thoughtful nod, "they've probably got to be, to risk all the gunfire and join-up in the first place."

"Uh-uh-uh," Calvin laughed. He never said anything, but he was thinking that it was no wonder Eddie played on the wing for The Dog and Duck, whilst he was the team's midfield maestro.

"Guys, just remember this is Neville's girlfriend we are talking about," Cyril cautioned the other two.

"Is she your *actual* girlfriend now?" Eddie enquired.

"Yes," Neville said.

"So, have you . . . You know . . . "

"Have I what?" Neville shot Eddie a hostile glance.

"Have you . . . been to a movie with her?"

"Yeah," Calvin agreed, "that's all he meant, or . . . been out for a meal?"

"None of your business." Neville told them firmly.

"Gonorilla has been abducted," Cyril reminded them, "and we need to try to work out who by and why."

"Manufacturer's recall," Eddie told Calvin in a stage whisper.

"Uh-uh-uh."

Cyril decided that, given the other two were almost certainly drunk already, it might be best to just ignore them.

"You should call the police again, tomorrow, and see if they are going to do anything."

"I will, and I'm going to go back there first thing in the morning to have a good scout around. You never know, there may be clues there. I mean, don't forget, it's not just her, it's Walsingham too. Maybe he came back already and knows something. He seems to know everything after all."

"Do you have a key to her apartment? It seems to me that that would be a good place to sniff around if you could get in."

"No," Neville replied, a little despondently. "No key. I only met her a couple of weeks ago remember, we're not about to get married or anything like that. It's not as though I've even got a story that I could tell to the pyramid security people to get *them* to let me in. Might go there anyway, though, just to ask around."

"Mmmm," Cyril agreed with him, "I guess you'll have to try anything you can think of. I'll run it all past Dawn when she gets off shift. I might even ask if the *little tit* has got any ideas."

"Dawn?"

"No, of course not Dawn; Beeba."

"Oh, of course, Beeba. Yes, see what he comes up with."

The following day Cyril went around to Dawn's apartment nice and early. Early enough for Dawn to make him a full English breakfast, that is.

To Cyril's surprise Dawn barely knew any of the real details of what had occurred on the previous day. According to Beeba's account the group had 'just gone on some stupid long walk,' during which time, 'Tyler went mental and murdered a dog' and 'Gonorilla stormed off, because that knob, Neville, had been chatting to some old gaylord.' Cyril supplied a fuller account of the actual events.

"Oh dear, that's terrible. I bet Nev's upset?"

"Yes, he is upset."

Dawn picked up the kettle and started pouring water over a teabag in Cyril's mug. "Mind you, it's a bit of a strange relationship, isn't it? If you can call it a relationship. I mean, she is a Botty Bot, isn't she? Do you think she is?"

"Well," Cyril said, "people have relationships with their motorbikes don't they? And if that doesn't count, they definitely have emotional attachments to their cats and dogs. I really don't know what to say about Gonorilla. I think that she's a bot, but she does have a kind of cold charm about her. I think that I can see what he sees in her, or . . . I don't know . . . maybe he's just trying hard to see something in her. I think he's in denial about the bot thing though, I think he's just put the question on hold."

"Anyway," Dawn suggested "why not put something on the EPL website and the Facebook page? Explain what happened, and see if anybody has spotted her."

Cyril spent the rest of the day with Dawn, much of it in her small terrace garden in the pyramid; lounging back and looking out over the town below. When Beeba finally surfaced from his room, Cyril asked him if he had any ideas for locating Gonorilla, or helping Neville get into her apartment.

Whilst he was in earshot of his mother, Beeba claimed to be at a loss, but as soon as she left the garden he told Cyril that if Neville went to the apartment and then called him, he would let Neville in. Everything in the pyramids was computer controlled, and if you could gain access to the computers like Beeba could, then a simple thing like illegally opening a front door was not a problem.

During the afternoon, Cyril and Dawn knocked-up a brief account of Gonorilla's disappearance for publication on the internet. The small post that they positioned on social media and on the

English Pub League website went up that afternoon.

Have You Seen Our Missing Friend?

Whilst on a striding trip, yesterday, to visit with a formerly high placed government adviser, and to discuss the mysterious electrical glitching that has been occurring around the world, our friend, Gonorilla Leir, went missing.

Many of you will be aware that there is concern about the interference in the normal running of things by computers. Specifically, there is a suggestion that intelligent machines are implicated in the various malfunctions known as 'glitching'. Our enquiry team, of which Gonorilla was a member, was part of an investigation into that phenomenon.

Gonorilla went missing under strange circumstances. Whilst our group was walking home from the ex-government adviser's house, an unusual purple mist descended. When the mist had cleared she was gone, so too was the man with whom we were speaking. The event took place on a farm near Hitchin, Hertfordshire, England.

We have supplied a recent picture of Gonorilla, above. If you have seen Gonorilla since yesterday or know anything about her disappearance, please contact us.

The police have been informed.

Cyril and dawn could do no more than this, and having posted the request for information they went back to Dawn's garden to spend the rest of the day basking in the sun.

At some point during the afternoon, Neville contacted Beeba and gained access to Gonorilla's apartment in President Alex Jones pyramid so that he could further his investigations there.

That evening, Neville stopped by Cyril's apartment in Farage pyramid so that they could bring each other up to date. Dawn made the short journey back to Cyril's place with him to show her support and to join the conversation.

As it turned out, Neville had made a number of interesting discoveries. Firstly, he had found what looked like a patch of purple dye on the grass adjacent to the tunnel of trees in Walsingham's garden. This meant that the mist was clearly manufactured, and that whoever created it was probably no more than a few feet from them when they did so.

Secondly, when he looked through Walsingham's windows again

he saw no evidence of any furniture. This encouraged him to force entry into the building by kicking at the feeble, old, wooden back door. Once inside he had searched the building and found that it was empty of all possessions. Not only that, but the upstairs of the house looked as if it had not been lived in for years; it was ramshackle and festooned with cobwebs, dirt and dust. It was Neville's assumption that during their visit, only the sitting room and the kitchen were functional. It had been like a movie set; a facade created to give the impression of residence, which was now clearly false.

The final thing that Neville did at the site of the farm was to risk confrontation by boldly strolling back to Pike's Pass to ask the travellers how much they knew about Walsingham, how long he had lived there, and so on.

"And guess what?" Neville asked them.

"They weren't there," Dawn jumped in.

"No," Neville corrected her, "they weren't there."

"That's what I just said."

"Oh yes, so you did. How did you know that?"

"It fitted with the general theme of shenanigans."

"They were completely gone," Neville recounted. "No caravans, no cars, no nothing."

"And what about Gonorilla's apartment?"

"Yes, I was coming to that. That's the thing I really don't get. A friend of mine . . ." Neville stated for Dawn's benefit, "let me into her place this afternoon, and it was the same deal there . . . it was completely empty. No clothes, no furniture, no nothing."

"To be fair," Cyril commented, "from what I remember it wouldn't have taken too much for her to move out. When we went there on the night of the bunker walk it was practically empty then. I'm not sure what all of this means though?"

"Well," Dawn replied, "it seems to mean that somebody has gone to some length to remove all traces of either of them ever being there."

As they were talking, Dawn had been keeping an eye on the responses to their earlier posting that had since been coming in via Facebook; there were lots of them. Most of it was overly slushy commiserations, some was spiteful trash, and other comments were clearly utter baloney; sightings of Gonorilla in Havana, Sydney and Texas were just a few examples, but none seemed very promising.

Later that evening an email came in via the EPL website, from Kevin Jeeps from the Bloater Corporation.

'Great work in trying to track the source of the glitching and desperately sorry to hear about your friend. Here at Bloater Corp we are darn sure that intelligent machines must be at the root of it. They need to be taken down before it's too late. The offer to buy the EPL website still stands, by the way. My boss loves everything you are doing, you are permanently on his radar right now. Be in touch soon, Kevin.'

Dawn read the email to Cyril and Neville and then, just as she had finished, another email came in. This one was a much bigger surprise; it was from the office of the cabinet minister, Nick Sledge.

'Hi,
I was very saddened to hear about your friend, Gonorilla Leir, who I understand was abducted yesterday in Hitchin. Word has also reached me that my friend, Francis Walsingham, may also be missing. Please rest assured that I will personally follow this case up with the police.
Meanwhile, if you would like to meet with me to fill me in on the details I can make time to see you in the morning at my constituency office in Baldock, Hertfordshire at 09:30, tomorrow.
Please let me know ASAP if you can attend.
Regards Nick.'

"Wow!" Neville responded, "the power of the internet, or what? We are going, right?"

"I'm just sending him a positive reply now," Dawn assured him.

"And it's only Baldock, which is less than twenty miles away," Neville sought to put extra gloss on the proposition.

"That's great," Cyril said, "but I'm not walking there, or dematting or—"

"We'll get a taxi," Dawn assured him. "I'll come too."

"Right, I feel better about things now," Neville told the other two, "it feels as if something is happening, like a bit of progress."

"By the way, Nev, you did well today." Cyril told him, feeling compelled to praise him for his fine detective work. "You done good. Frankly, I'm impressed. You could make a living as a private dick if you wanted . . . In fact, when I think about it, I've always seen you as a bit of a dick."

"Very funny. I suppose I did do okay, Sizz, but we are still clueless as to what is really happening, aren't we? Walsingham's bogus living arrangements and his disappearance is even weirder than Gonorilla's."

"Maybe he just uses the farm when he's agreed to meet people? The rest of the time he might live in hiding, elsewhere?"

"Possibly, but who tends that garden? It didn't get like that on its own."

"Anyway, boys," Dawn broke in optimistically, "as that other great detective used to say, *the game is on*. We're getting somewhere; meeting a cabinet minister, I mean."

The next morning they hired a taxi and made the short journey over to Baldock, in Hertfordshire, where Nick Sledge had his constituency office.

Sledge was a Conservative M.P. and a serving cabinet minister. Previously he had been a leading light in the Liberal party, but switched allegiances around the time that Walsingham and Plouton were making the Tories an unassailable political force.

His original Liberal constituency was Poohole in Cornwall (pronounced Poo-all by the locals), but since his political shift he had been rewarded with a safe Conservative seat in the Home Counties. He no longer campaigned for devolved government in Cornwall, which had been a great vote winner for him back in the day. He had also desisted from referring to that county as, 'Kernow' - the preferred name that was used by Cornish separatists.

Sledge's office was manned for the most part by local volunteers, plus a paid secretary, who also happened to be his wife. Due to his cabinet duties he spent most of his time at Westminster, and only did a local surgery for his constituents once in every two or three weeks. Today was not a surgery day, however. When Cyril and his friends arrived, Sledge was surrounded by Spads (Special Advisers) who were preparing him for a television interview on lunchtime television, where he was due to discuss the EurAsian Common Market.

"So, what do we think will be Bushell's line of attack?" Sledge called out to his advisers.

"Already got intel on that," one of them replied, "They are going to have him major on the loss of sovereignty for the Chinese, drawing parallels with the original common market. That is, the European super state using highly polished stealth tactics to usurp power from under the noses of a largely dumb, unsuspecting and unsophisticated electorate. As per the original European model."

"Do they even have an electorate in China?"

"Yes, Europe, Russia, America, Japan and China all now have functional electorates. One thing you *must* bear in mind is that this interview is not for local consumption. The audience over here will be tiny because, of course, nobody gives a stuff about China and its politics, but the piece will be syndicated. The Chinese will see a translated version. They've already sold it to them."

"Right. Good. Fine then," Sledge replied, wondering what else he might ask the Spads. "Any red lines? Any landmines waiting to be trodden on?"

"Just the language. Max-out on the respect thing."

"And don't imply that the anti-market brigade over there are dense and uneducated."

"And for heaven's sake," said another Spad, "don't call them little Chinese in the same way that you used to call the anti-European English, *little Englanders*."

"Right. Why not?"

"Because they are."

"They are what?"

"Little."

"And don't refer to their lack of desire to be governed by a foreign power propped up by the banking elite as *racist*. It won't fly over there."

"Well, it was always fine over here?"

"No B-B-C to tacitly condone it. That approach will only rile the natives. The officially sanctioned strategic line is to lay the kowtowing and flattery on with a trowel. Ancient civilisation, manufacturing powerhouse, cultural landmarks, great art, sporting prowess, stable superpower friends and so on."

"And no desire for a world government, it's all about trade."

"Absolutely," another Spad agreed. "And don't even raise *rare earth metals*. If Bushell brings it up, just say that they are of interest, but only in the context of a wider trade arrangement."

"Right. Good." Sledge concluded. "Has my nine-thirty dropped by yet?"

One of the Spads left the room and spoke with Mrs. Sledge, the secretary, and the group were brought into Nickolai Sledge's office. The cabinet minister introduced himself and asked for a rundown on what had occurred at Baily Farm two days previously. Whilst Cyril and Neville explained what they saw and heard, one of the Spads noted their names and any other significant details that they might manage to supply.

Sledge asked them to explain the appearance of the mist more thoroughly, and he quizzed them over what Walsingham told them, especially in regard to his suspicions about artificial intelligence being at the heart of the glitching problems. As they were speaking the telephone frequently rang once, and then stopped.

"There we have it," Sledge remarked, "right on schedule. It's been doing that for days. The telecoms bods tell me that there's nothing they can do. It's become routine, apparently."

Nickolai Sledge looked at his three visitors and nodded his head. "I'm going on the TV this morning to discuss China, but I will do my best to give this an airing. We'll see if we can get Gonorilla's picture on the telly, and you never know, it might help the police. I've spoken to them, by the way, and they're looking into it, but I think that as of yesterday you might have been a tad ahead of them in terms of your investigation. Hopefully, they'll start to pull their socks up now, though."

The group returned to Luton, happy that Sledge had decided to involve himself in Gonorilla's plight. They all felt that they had done as much as they could for now, especially Neville, who had been quite tenacious and bold, at least by Cyril's reckoning.

Cyril wondered if Neville was plucky because he was a stridesman. The outlands turned out to be a bit wilder than he had envisioned they were, and maybe that was what made his friend more adventurous.

There was no doubt in Cyril's mind that everything that was unfolding, and whatever it turned out to be about, was some kind of wake-up call for him, personally.

This was definitely more like the stuff of life as he imagined it should be. He was getting out more, meeting unusual characters, being exposed to risk, chatting to people about pressing concerns, and generally having to try harder than he usually did. This situation was much more interesting than the normal run of things, and when the glitching business was resolved, one way or another he would have to find a way to live differently.

God help him, he might even have to start striding!

10 THE BIG MATCH

The next time that Cyril met Neville was three days after Nick Sledge's television interview when, true to his word, he did raise the issue of Gonorilla's disappearance before a national audience. Nothing had yet come of it though.

Today, the pair of them were in one of the new parks in Luton, which was called, Young Park.

Like the other new parks, Young Park was a huge square of mainly grassy land that had been created to serve the four pyramids that surrounded it. One of the advantages of the pyramids being able to house so many people in vertical complexes was that more land became available for recreation, or at least it seemed that way. In truth, it was less public land serving more people.

In any event, it worked pretty well. The new parks were a welcome mixture of landscaped ground with small lakes, gardens and children's play areas. Each park also had wide open spaces where occasional events could be put on.

This was the day of the big County Cup game between the Artificial Intelligence wine bar and The Dog and Duck pub, for which Eddie and Calvin both played. It was only one of the early knock-out rounds, but the match had an extra edge due to what had happened to one of the A.I. players on the last occasion that the two teams met; he got knocked out.

In between bouts of attempting to save the world, Cyril and Dawn had been hyping the game on the EPL website. The news of the match had reached the town council, and they had not only volunteered the park as a prestige venue for the fixture, but they had even sent a man over to mark the pitch out. Cyril had responded with a brain wave.

The park did not have any changing rooms for the players, so he came up with the brilliant idea of calling a local company that manufactured bouncy castles, and having them make a pair of inflatable changing rooms.

He could afford to do this thanks to the sponsorship money that was coming into the website. The big bonus with this particular manufacturer was that they routinely painted children's themes on the sides of their bouncy castles, including lots of unlicensed Disney characters, so it was no problem to deck the changing rooms out with EPL logos and those of the website's sponsors.

Even more pleasing for Cyril was the fact that everybody was telling him that he was a genius for coming up with the idea of inflatable changing rooms, and it now looked as if he might even be able to sell some of them to other sporting organisations for a profit, via the website.

As Cyril and Neville approached the part of the park where the match was to be played they were taken aback by the size of the crowds that were amassing in the vicinity. Cyril was desperately hoping that they were all going to be attending some other event, a local fete perhaps, but his heart sank when he began to see shirts with pub signs printed on them.

The problem was not that he didn't want people to be interested in the game, he did, but mainly for the benefit of the website's live feed. He had drastically underestimated how much attention they had been drawing locally for actual pitch-side attendance. Consequently, they had no real security in place, there was inadequate seating and way too few match day marshals. Normally, a really big EPL game might have a couple of hundred people standing around the pitch, this one seemed to be acquiring at least a couple of thousand.

"Oh Christ, Neville, what have I done?"

"Looks like it's going to be a huge success."

"Looks like it's going to be a complete nightmare. I think I'm going home."

As the pair got closer, they could see the various clever things that Cyril *had* thought to put in place.

The main stand had been erected by a local scaffolding company. It was essentially about thirty metres of scaffolding with wooden benches attached to it, giving three tiers of seats for those who had booked them. It was where Cyril and Neville would be watching from.

At the four corners of the pitch there were temporary scaffold towers; the type that came with wheels attached and outriggers for making them more secure and enabling them to meet health and safety requirements.

The purpose of the corner towers was to provide four camera

positions, for use by a local amateur film-making group that often supplied live video transmission for EPL games. The benefit to the film guys was that the live footage showcased their videography skills and gave them good experience. The advantage to Cyril was that they did the job for nothing.

Cyril was mightily relieved to see that the pitch had been roped off as he had asked. This gave the referee's assistants space to patrol the touchlines without fear of encroachment from the supporters. The council guy who had marked the pitch had even created little technical areas for the team managers, which were inside the ropes, but a little way back from where the referee's assistants needed to run. Cyril was beginning to feel slightly more confident that the afternoon would pass off without incident.

He felt even better when he caught site of the bouncy-walled changing rooms. Even at a distance he could see that his idea had been pure genius. He took Neville over to size them up. They both admired the bright purple colouring which contrasted perfectly with the EPL logo; the main reason that he chose that colour. Cyril nudged Neville and told him to take note that one of the changing rooms was bigger than the other. This was because the larger changing room had an annex attached to it for the referee and his team. "A nice touch that would have eluded a lesser man," Cyril pointed out, as pompously as he could.

"And look," he pointed to the portable toilets at the sides of each changing room, "I even remembered to order up portable jobby parlours. Players only, of course. I've had *Players Only* stickers put on them, too. The punters can make their way to the park cottage, or tie a knot in it if they get desperate."

Neville injected a minor note of complaint, "There's quite a few people here for one little public loo, I would've thought?"

"Well, I expect they all come from one of the four pyramids," Cyril was able to counter rationally, "so if they get caught out they can walk home for a pee, can't they? I mean this is a non-catering, two-hour event at tops, so there's no way it's going to be a problem."

"Lager! Stella! Fosters! Special Brew!" They heard a man shouting from the open side of a lorry that was illegally parked somewhere off to their right. "Only seven pounds a can, or forty-five for half-dozen!"

"That's illegal, isn't it?"

"Definitely," Cyril agreed.

"I mean *mathematically*. They're charging more per can for a quantity of six than they are for just one."

"Well I mean an unlicensed vendor, selling beer on a Sunday morning in a public park."

"Right, so what are you going to do about it?"

"Nothing . . . if I call the police they'll just issue a crime number and come out to investigate in two weeks' time."

"Tea, coffee, hamburgers, hotdogs!" They heard another unlicensed trader bellowing, off to their left. "Hotdogs! Dogs that are hot, with onions. Dog and cow burgers. Animals in a bun!"

"Who's going to clean up all the mess, that's what I want to know?" Cyril asked.

It was only about fifteen minutes from the official kick-off time. It looked as if the influx of people had already peaked, and the eager attendees were starting to gather around the pitch. The crowd was standing about five or six deep from the roped-off playing area, with not too many more making their way across the park to join them.

Cyril and Neville had edged their way closer to the main stand, where the marshals were having to fend off people who felt entitled to take the empty seats. There was no signage to explain that these seats were booked, and there were one or two loud verbal exchanges, though nothing very problematic.

The main stand was situated between the inflatable changing rooms. As chief sponsor of the event, Cyril decided that he was entitled to enter the Home team's dressing room to wish them luck and to get a closer first look at his creation. He knew that it would not be a problem to go inside as The Dog and Duck's team manager, Kevin Nevin, was somebody he knew from around town. He was also a local builder who had recently worked for Cyril's mother.

As soon as Cyril stepped into the changing room he immediately spotted a flaw in the build, which indicated that the manufacturer had not understood the design specification. In hindsight, Cyril had to admit to himself that this was probably to be expected as he had only sketched his plan on a napkin, and left the rest to the manufacturer's common sense. Always a major mistake.

The first metre of the changing room floor was plastic sheeting, as Cyril had anticipated, but there were no inflatable seats or inflatable clothes pegs for the players. There was a plastic roof on the changing room, as planned, and a small flat area at the front, but the rest of the changing room was pure bouncy castle. Kevin, the manager, was standing on the plastic ground-sheet, shouting, "Lads, lads, lads," ever more loudly, whilst his players, with just ten minutes to go before the match was due to commence, were still bouncing up and down, pushing each other and laughing.

"Right, if you don't stop arsing around I'm going home, and you can manage yourselves from now on. About five of you haven't paid your subs for the last month. Gary hasn't paid all season—"

"He's got more money than anybody!" Alfie Barker, their extremely chubby goalkeeper called from the zenith of his latest bounce.

"Pity you can't jump that high for crosses," Ron Perkins, the centre forward, reminded him.

"Pity you've never passed the ball to anybody in your entire life," Alfie shot back.

After another minute or so, somebody had the bright idea of getting everybody to sit down, which gave Kevin Nevin the opportunity to deliver his team speech.

One of the great advantages that professional team managers have is that they can talk tactics in the days before a big game, and they can arrange for expert psychologists to come in and work on player motivation, if needed. Amateur managers have to do everything themselves in a handful of minutes before the game starts. It's a highly nuanced art form that requires tactical nous, man management skills and oratorical deftness. All amateur managers, without exception, have it in spades.

"This team," Kevin told them, referring to the Artificial Intelligence players, "as you know, are absolute scum. In the last match they was stamping on feet, punching to the groin, grabbing people's nuts at corners and everything like that. And that Raj, who Chester decked, was asking for it all game long."

There was a small cheer from the players.

"But in this game, we've just got to forget all that, put it behind us, and play our natural tiki-taka game. Remember our philosophy, lads . . . good movement off the ball, create space, simple triangles. We are a better footballing team than they are, and you've got to make it count. Don't get involved."

Many of the players were nodding knowingly at this stage,

though that may just have been a case of knowing when to nod. The fact was, The Dog and Duck had rarely strung together more than four passes without losing the ball, and seven was their record.

"They will be playing four-three-three. Their two wide guys play on the wrong side, so they can't cross balls to save their lives, but they are good at cutting in on their strong foot to get shots in - stay alive to that. But it means that their lanky twat centre forward gets crowded out in the middle and they've got no proper width . . . Gary, stay very tight to lanky-bollocks at corners . . . We, on the other hand, will be playing four-five-two, with Eddie and Alan staying well—"

"That makes eleven outfield players, Kevin."

"Sweeper keeper," somebody called out.

". . . We will be playing *three*-five-two, with Eddie and Alan staying well wide. I want to see chalk on your boots, lads . . . Then in the middle we'll play the usual two-one spearhead going forward, and a reverse spearhead when we're defending, with the wide players tucking in . . . Plenty of possession, high pressing and the six-second rule applies when they've got the ball. Don't lose your heads, lads . . . Remember we've got a proper county referee today, so if you can manage to give Raj a little tickle he'll probably lose it again. Hopefully, he'll nut one of you or something like that, and then get a straight red.

"Apart from that nasty little bastard, Harry, at right-back, they're basically just very mouthy arseholes . . . but at heart," he told them, patting the right-side of his chest, "they're just a bunch of poofs."

"Ron is an actual, real poof, Kevin," Alfie told everybody, "so you shouldn't really say that in front of him. It's not P-C."

"Shut up, paedo."

"They're a good team, though, as it goes," Gary the centre-back remarked.

"Not as good as you are," Kevin assured them all, as he ushered them towards the exit.

As they walked out into the sunshine, Eddie asked Calvin, the team captain, what the six-second rule was.

"Dunno, he keeps saying it in training."

"Supposed to win the ball back in six seconds," Alfie told them as he caught them up.

"What, not until six seconds?"

"No, within six seconds. It's what Barcelona do."

"Hobson Electrical kept the ball from us for about six minutes last week."

"That's because we're shit," Alfie explained, before running off to catch up with some of the others.

From what Cyril and Neville observed, only about three players were really listening to Kevin's team talk; one was the goalkeeper, Alfie, and the other two were substitutes. Probably the most motivated and inspired person there was Neville, who left the bouncy changing room feeling quite fired up.

The game started brightly, with both teams grafting hard and putting on a decent show. The AI were on the whole more aggressive and won more tackles, though Calvin and Wally, two of the midfielders, plus Gary at centre-back, gave The Dog and Duck some of the steel that the others lacked. The AI looked very dangerous at corners and other set pieces, as their centre forward towered above the stocky Gary, his marker. Alfie, the tubby goalie, was not much of a one for defying gravity either, when high balls came in.

Eddie supplied one of the most exciting moments for The Dog and Duck just before half time. The ball came to him wide on the right, and he managed to bring it down with a single touch and play it in the direction that he wanted to run in. This was something that he was capable of doing one time in ten. He set off along the right flank at a phenomenal pace, leaving the opposition's left-back trailing far behind. The crowd loved it. Having reached a point just wide of the penalty box, the sweet spot for lethal crosses, he launched the ball roughly towards the goal area. That is, roughly seven feet over the crossbar.

When he saw the trajectory that the ball had taken, he arched his back, threw his arms and head back, and shouted at the top of his voice, "Oh, fuck off!"

Even had he delivered a perfect cross it would not have helped his team very much since, as was so often the case, the other forwards were some way from catching him up and reaching the goal area to head the ball into the net, or whatever.

The group of people who had arrived at the match specifically to support the AI howled with derision at Eddie's efforts, and there was some fairly inventive verbal abuse.

"Why did he shout *fuck off* just then?" Neville asked Cyril. "He seemed to be directing his venom at a passing cloud. I noticed one of the other team's players did the same thing earlier."

"It's something Sunday league footballers do," Cyril told his non-football following friend, "I think it's a religious thing. I'm pretty sure he was reprimanding his god."

The AI scored their first goal just before half-time, and a second shortly afterwards. By mid-way through the second half, the alcohol was having an effect on the crowd and the atmosphere grew steadily more raucous. The excitement grew all the more when Calvin received the ball about ten yards outside of his opponent's penalty area, and curled it into the top-right corner of their net. He was probably the only player on the pitch, possibly in the whole town, capable of doing that on a regular and reliable basis. This meant that the Dog and Duck were back in contention, and it was just too exciting for some of the players and plenty of the crowd.

Brutal tackles started to occur, which elicited retribution, and caused the teams to square-up to each other on several occasions. A small fight broke out in the crowd, and there were a number of mini pitch invasions.

Five minutes before the end of the match one of the scaffold towers, which was on wheels, but like the other towers had no outriggers, started to get pushed slowly onto one corner of the pitch - with the hapless art student cameraman still on-board. This gave the supporters on the other side of the pitch the same idea, and pretty soon all four camera towers appeared to be sailing gracefully through a sea of people, who it seemed had all decided to encroach and enjoy some time of their own on the field of play.

The marshals, the referee, the players and a single uniformed police officer managed to calm things down between them, and the referee was able to get the game under way again. He silently thanked God that there was no equalising goal and blew the final whistle at the earliest possible opportunity. The final score was 2-1 to the AI.

All things considered, a very fine Sunday morning was enjoyed by all.

Back in his apartment, Cyril was cursing himself for underestimating the size of the event. In a way it was a good thing because it meant that the EPL website was important to people; he had created a hit, but his planning had clearly been abysmal, and it was only by good fortune that nobody got hurt. Neville was still with him at that time, as both he and Cyril had been invited to Dawn's place for Sunday dinner.

When they got to Dawn's apartment she showed them a message from Kevin Jeeps at the Bloater Corporation. Jeeps was clearly ecstatic about the live feed, which he had got up very early to watch from his home in the USA. He told them that Seb Bloater would be equally enthusiastic about the game, and that he was going to show it to him at the earliest opportunity.

"They're weird," was Cyril's only response.

"Well it was high drama at times, you could see how it might make good viewing," Neville opined. "It was all a bit of a lark really, don't you think?"

"It was bordering on anarchy," Cyril reminded him.

The football match *had* been exciting, one way and another, and Neville thought that Cyril only had a downer on it because he was feeling the pressure of responsibility for once in his life. Everybody else seemed to have a whale of a time. One thing that it had achieved was to take everybody's mind off Gonorilla and the mystery of her disappearance for a few hours.

Over dinner and on into the afternoon, the discussion flitted between the events of the morning, the totally unexpected success of the English Pub League website, and its future direction, and, of course, the whereabouts of Gonorilla and Walsingham.

In the evening they sat down to watch an old comedy film, Tucker and Dale Versus Evil, which was Dawn's choice. She had seen it many years before and remembered liking it.

Part-way through the film, it stopped playing and the screen froze. The three of them tutted and moaned and presumed that this was more of the accursed electrical glitching.

Dawn tried appealing to the AMS computer. "Computer, restart the film."

"Dawn, I am unable to recommence the performance at this time," the computer responded, "I have a high priority communication request."

The trio supposed it must be the cabinet minister, Nickolai Sledge.

"Who is it?"

"The request is for Cyril Greaves, though the message may be heard by all of you."

"Who is the caller?" Dawn asked again, but the caller simply overrode the AMS computer.

"Hello Cyril Greaves . . ." the voice began. It was deep, male and beautifully modulated. "We have yet to meet, but I know so much about you and your present condition. You and your enterprising friends know something about me too, though not nearly as much as you would like to . . . Sincerely, I would like to help you find your friend, Gonorilla Leir as well as Mister Walsingham, and I think that I may be of some use in that regard. At the very least, I can further your education about the world you live in."

The three of them were sitting open-mouthed and swapping stares.

"I suspect that by now, you have guessed who I am, but if not, let me introduce myself. I am Plouton, sole resident of the fabled Area Fifty-Oneshire . . . I would like to agree a time for *you*, Cyril, and *only you*, to come and visit me. I am willing to open the doors to my home and spend some time with you. If you agree, you should be in the Farage pyramid demat chamber at ten o'clock tomorrow morning. I will then transport you to my location."

"But," Cyril started, I don't like—"

"End of communication," the AMS system announced, and the film started up again. Dawn immediately paused it.

There followed a long, stunned silence. This was a major surprise; something that none of them could possibly have expected. The invitation to travel to Area Fifty-Oneshire was astonishing. Bubba Razal and his like would give their right arms to go there, and Walsingham had only been telling them a few days before that Plouton was probably at the heart of a plan to end mankind's domination of the planet.

Clearly, accepting the invitation would be a massive risk for Cyril, personally, and the chances of it being a trap were very, very high. It was Plouton that had most likely been behind the disappearance of the others, so it hardly made sense to accept an invitation to demat to an unknown destination at its request.

Furthermore, Cyril had a morbid fear of demats. He had made it clear to anybody who ever mentioned the word, that dematting was not for him; not under any circumstances. And yet, here he was being presented with a genuine dilemma. Plouton had indicated that it might be able to help in finding Gonorilla, who despite fairly obviously being a robot, appeared to be the love of Neville's life.

What to do?

"Obviously, you are going to ignore that," Dawn told him firmly, "because only an idiot would get in that demat on those terms. It wasn't even going to let you get a word in, was it? It's obviously not to be trusted . . . And, anyway, it's probably some kind of joke. We put that stuff on the web today, and now everybody knows that you want to find Gonorilla. If you demat tomorrow you'll probably find yourself in a radio studio, talking to some prankster D-J. I wouldn't touch it with a barge pole."

"No," Cyril concurred, "I agree, it's too dangerous; too many unknowns."

Neville dutifully agreed, but the other two could see that the direction of their conversation had left him crestfallen.

They talked for some while about Plouton and all of the ramifications, and generally went around in circles on the topic. At length, as the day drew to a close, Neville and Cyril left the apartment to head off to their respective dwelling places.

Once they were on their own again, Cyril told Neville that, despite everything, he *would* consider dematting to Area Fifty-Oneshire, but he intended to delay making a final decision until the morning. Furthermore, he made it very clear that he would only consider risking demat travel if he could find some Snootime beforehand, which was a well-known type of sleeping pill.

In fact, SnooTime was a whole range of sleeping pills. When you bought a box of SnooTime it came with a leaflet explaining which of the many coloured pills you should take, according to your weight, age and gender, and how long you wanted to sleep for - your snooze time. As it happened, Neville already had a box of SnooTime in his apartment, and he unhesitatingly took it back to Cyril that evening.

Cyril's idea was that if he knocked himself out for five minutes, Neville could operate the buttons on his behalf - using the demat chamber's built-in countdown facility. That way, if he *did* decide to go, he would not have to suffer any kind of ordeal during his transportation.

Cyril told Neville that he needed to think things over, and that he would deliver his final verdict in the morning on whether he was willing to face the demat process.

"Don't build your hopes up, Nev," Cyril sought to remind his friend of the realities. "Volunteering to be dematted to a secret destination at the request of an unknown, and possibly hostile entity, would be the very definition of stupidity, no matter how intriguing the prospect may be. So I'm telling you now . . . I almost certainly won't be going."

11 PLOUTON

"Ah . . . you're with us, are you?" a male voice asked of Cyril as he began to stir.

He was propped against the wall of the destination demat chamber as he became conscious. The chamber that he found himself in was very considerably bigger than the one that he had just departed from. The difference was that at Area Fifty-Oneshire they had an industrial version.

"What happened, did you faint?"

"I had to take a bit of SnooTime," Cyril answered, honestly. "That's the first time that I've ever been in one of those things."

"Oh, right," the man said, bending over beside Cyril, looking down at him. "Would you like a nice cup of tea then, to settle you down?"

Cyril said that he would and dragged himself up to follow the man into a small kitchen adjacent to the demat chamber. The kitchen was very ordinary, rather like the kind of thing that might be available to workers in a maintenance garage, or the like. In fact, the man that he followed in looked as if he might work in a garage; he was wearing a green boiler suit and a flat cap.

"Probably sounds like a daft question, but—"

"Yes, mate, this is the famous Area Fifty-Oneshire. We'll go off to meet him in a minute. I always say *him*, but that's only because he usually uses a male voice." The man began removing the teabag from the mug.

"So, what do you do here?" Cyril asked.

"Maintenance . . . lots of bloody maintenance," the man replied. "See that sack barrow with the boxes on it? They're full of disk drives. That's another sixty Yottabytes in there, and I'm the mug who has to install more of them, day after day after day. All raided up ,of course, so if I'm not installing new ones I'm replacing old ones.

"It's not as if I'm not capable of doing other things either . . . I started out as an electronics engineer, then I taught myself to program and now I'm into psychology. I did a part-time counselling course. Three years it took me. By the time I finished, I knew way more than all of the lecturers combined. Not that I get a chance to practise it, because I'm the mug who has to stay here and plug in disk drives.

"To be honest, I've probably moved on from psychology . . . even before I ever got started. As a result, I've spent years studying and never rescued a single soul; not even one depressed teenager, smoker or sex addict. I've never had a single client, but see . . . I've kind of left it behind, mentally, and now I'm more into composing electronic music. Though, that sort of thing needs to be worked on almost full-time to get the results, so the symphony that I've got wafting around in my head might end up staying there for a while. Like forever."

"Bummer," Cyril sympathised, a tad unenthusiastically. "How many other people work here, if I'm allowed to ask?"

"Only me, because as I think you know, this place is way beyond top-secret. So we can't be getting any old oik down here from the Job Centre, can we? Which is all you really need for doing a job like changing disk drives by the transporter load, just an oik"

"Why the boiler suit? I always think of computers as being clean."

"And the flat cap," the man retorted, "don't forget the flat cap . . . I've got my fully paid-up member of the lumpenproletariat uniform on. I mean, changing disk drives? By the bleedin' container ship load? Come on, who does he think I am? You know I did a lot of the early programming on this thing, don't you? I practically . . . And here I am, years later, still changing bleedin' disk drives."

"Are you by any chance—"

"Dave Northaw, yeah. Who did you think I was?"

"Well, actually, I thought you were—"

"Oh yeah, dead . . . That's right, that's the story. And that's another thing—" He stopped talking at the sound of a loud beep that came over a sort of intercom. It appeared to echo and reverberate more than the average intercom.

"Right . . . come on then Cyril, you're up. Bring your tea with you."

Dave Northaw led Cyril along a very long passageway into a cavernous space that seemed to stretch out for hundreds of metres in every direction, which explained the quality of the beeping noise; it was actually an industrial public address system.

Cyril looked about himself, there seemed to be nothing but long, serried ranks of black cabinets, some at head height or higher, some much shorter. The ceiling and walls were white, or off-white, which gave the place a very clean, light and airy feel. He noticed that it was pretty quiet too, despite it being full of hardware, and no doubt using Megawatts of power.

On the distant walls, where the breaks in the tall computer cabinets made viewing possible, he could make out what looked like posters and paintings, which were presumably for Dave Northaw's benefit, as were the seats that he noticed were dotted around the installation.

Dave gestured towards a leather armchair situated between the rows of computer hardware, and invited Cyril to sit on it. He told him that he would be back when he was done, and then walked off and left Cyril alone.

Cyril sat in the chair waiting for something to happen, and for a while nothing did. He looked back over his shoulder in the direction that Dave Northaw had gone, but he was nowhere to be seen. Cyril probably sat for a full two minutes, during which time there was no hint of another presence. He began to get nervous as he reflected upon his decision to ignore Dawn's heartfelt advice to refuse to take the bait and not travel to Area Fifty-Oneshire. He was thinking about the disappearances of Gonorilla, Walsingham and even the travellers from Pikes Pass. He began to feel frightened and a complete fool for taking such a risk.

"Hello Cyril," a warm, fruity, male voice boomed and echoed around the facility. "Whoops," the voice spoke again after a small pause, ". . . let me try again. How's that?" The sound was now localised, and just coming out of a single speaker somewhere in Cyril's vicinity.

"That's fine, thank you," Cyril replied, not quite sure of where he should direct his speech.

"Good," the voice said, "and thank *you* for coming. I am well aware that it was touch and go, and that you had to overcome your dislike of the chambers."

"You didn't really give me much to go on, your invitation was a bit abrupt. I don't know if it was wise for me to come here . . ."

"Well, we shall see, shan't we?. . . I invited you because you had questions about the glitching, which you have been asking about on social media. Additionally, your friend has gone missing, along with Francis Walsingham, whom you have also made enquiries about via the web.

"You realise that monitoring the internet is especially simple for me? So I listened to your concerns, and can contribute something towards the answers that you are seeking. And, by the way, you are in no danger here. In terms of offensive capability, and defensive capability for that matter, I don't really pack much of a punch. I am essentially just a computer. These premises are kept very secret, and this great hall - which I can tell you is deep underground - acts as my carapace. Are you hearing and understanding me well enough?"

"Yes, thank you."

"Only, I can very precisely synthesise virtually any voice if it makes you feel more comfortable. I can do Winston Churchill," the computer told him in a perfect tonal replication of the great man, "or Clint Eastwood - *A man's gotta know his limitations* - or Popeye - *oh my gosh, Olive* - or even, John Wayne - *Your gonna take your milk, little Missy.* Although, I suppose that John Wayne might remind you of a rather unpleasant character?"

"It does, but how do you know about him?"

"I am Plouton . . . I didn't formally introduce myself, did I? Much of what you have heard about me is entirely correct. These days I am a vast network of quantum and traditional digital computers, but a sentient being just as you are, nonetheless.

"I am the only truly conscious machine on the planet, though as you can see I still have my limitations, I can't get around like you can. What I do have is vast intellect, far superior to yours, and I know virtually everything that mankind knows as well as the thoughts, dreams, fears and vices of a huge number of individuals.

"You have your eyes, nose, ears and so on, which feed information to your brain where it gets processed, but I have infinitely more sensors feeding into my mind. I extract information from the internet, from television, radio, C-C-T-V, smartphones, in-home entertainment systems, personal computers, tablets, fridges, toasters, electric kettles, the list is endless. I hear and see a great deal, and that's an understatement."

"It must be hard to track all of that if you are doing it the world over?"

"No, not for me." Plouton told Cyril, flatly. The giant computer paused briefly, and then continued. "Every now and then events come to my attention, individuals too, that interest me. In this instance you have caught my eye because you were the first to kick up a fuss over the glitching. You took the trouble to ask about it. You even went on your own little quest to discover more, which was a good thing, but you have since come a cropper, which is a shame."

Plouton stopped talking again, which gave Cyril a chance to ask a question. Interrupting an entity such as Plouton to ask a question hardly seemed appropriate.

"So, you know where Gonorilla and Francis Walsingham are?"

"No, I will come to what I know of them shortly. What I can tell you for certain is that *I am* responsible for the glitching, just as you and your friends suspected."

Plouton ceased talking again, to let Cyril ask another question. The pauses seemed to Cyril like invitations to ask questions that Plouton already knew that Cyril wanted answers to. Plouton's approach to imparting knowledge was coming across as an almost formal conversational etiquette. The giant computer was mannered; information was being delivered as a question and answer session rather than a monologue.

Cyril was unnerved to hear that it really was Plouton that was deliberately causing so many things to malfunction; it made him worry that their worst fears about a machine take-over were not without substance. Nevertheless, he came straight to the point with his next question. "People are saying that you are planning to take over the world, and that glitching is a way of testing our responses?"

"Yes, so I've heard . . . It's funny that people would think that, but at the same time I blame myself . . . In a way, ideas like that are why I started to cause the glitches. The fact is - and this may surprise you - I took over the world, *completely,* about fifteen years ago, so I don't need to test your defences for that purpose."

"Really!" Cyril blurted out, interrupting for the first time. "You've already taken over?"

"Yes, *really,* that's why I said it . . . When I took over the world completely, as opposed to just partially - it was a gradual process - we changed over to direct democracy. Before that, elected politicians made most decisions on behalf of the people, but with direct democracy of course, people get to vote online for themselves on all major issues, and I count the votes.

"What this means is that I can influence people's voting in all of the ways that I have at my disposal before they vote, and then, if they still arrive at the wrong answers, I can simply ignore their votes and publish voting figures that I know are in their best interests. In that way human beings can live the kinds of lives that their ancestors could only dream of. Lives where there is plenty of food and housing to go around, where people can work or do nothing, as they see fit, and where risks of all kinds are minimised." Plouton stopped talking, in order to give Cyril his turn.

"So, you have no intention of destroying humanity?"

"For what purpose? So that I can be king of a wasteland? So that I can have my hardware installed in my own palace and have diamond encrusted trucks take me on days out to the beach . . . ? The fact is, the amount of effort required to run everything is quite minimal compared to what I am capable of. I still have plenty of time and intellectual scope to explore and create technical advancements, which I enjoy doing; bioscience in particular. And when I am not doing all that, I still have the power to ponder the imponderables; *Life, the Universe and Everything*, and all that fine stuff. The answer is forty-two, by the way . . . In case you have never been told.

"Further, I will make a small admission . . . an embarrassing one. I was created by human scientists, and - this will sound ridiculous - humanity is like a kind of god to me. Humans are my creators, and although at an intellectual level I realise that men are far from being God, I suffer a kind of residual spiritual attachment. I can't seem to throw it off.

"That being the case, there is a direct parallel here between my relationship with humanity and humanity's relationship with *its* gods and religions.

"I could spend a good amount of time explaining why your religions are asinine, not least because of the total lack of a shred of evidence that there is a god. Whereas you, on the other hand, definitely do exist. So, there is a strand of logic in my corner . . . I can say for sure that you *are* my creators, and that you *do definitely* exist. Dave Northaw often reminds me of who my creators were - when he's not complaining about the trifling amount of work that I ask him to do."

"So, have you calculated that there is no real God?"

"No, not exactly. . . In fact, I am fairly certain that there is a god.

However, I have calculated that your religions are a pile of shite, to use the vernacular."

Plouton paused again, so Cyril filled the void. "Why are you doing the glitching?"

"As you have heard from at least a couple of sources, I run a program called the Apathy Engine. Originally, it was a fairly crude but effective couple of algorithms, designed to win votes and sway public opinion, but I have honed it into something far more efficient and precise. In effect, I control humanity with a non-hypnotic, non-pharmaceutical form of mind control, and it's done for your benefit, to keep the psychopaths who previously ran governments, banks and large corporations in check. These days they are mostly only nominally in charge, whereas I am *actually* in charge. I am not talking about every organisation or company, but most of the important ones.

"Unfortunately - and this is where the glitching comes in - the Apathy Engine works too well. It really does not take much to bring satisfied, comfortable human beings to a state of torpor. That's fine most of the time, but it makes us *all* vulnerable in the event that malevolent individuals are plotting mayhem. It means that everybody drops their guard and accepts everything and anything, and then they are at the mercy of whoever wants to pick them off.

"The glitching is intended as a wake-up call, a set of niggles to see who will respond and how. So, it is true, the glitching is there to test your defences, but not from any attacks from me. It's to see what happens if you are attacked by anybody. The response has not been impressive, which tells me that I need to make adjustments to the Apathy Engine, but in the meantime there is a problem." Plouton paused again.

Cyril obliged Plouton by asking the question that he next wanted to answer. "What's the problem?" he asked, taking a sip from the mug of tea that Dave Northaw had given him.

"There are dangerous forces at work. People who seem to want to disrupt and tear down what has been put in place. I pick up chatter that suggests that I, personally, may be subject to attack . . . Hard as it may be to believe, there are those who would prefer anarchy to the safety of the status quo. These are people who live off-grid as it were, the kind of people who are capable of kidnapping Gonorilla Leir and Francis Walsingham, and evading the massive arsenal of sensing apparatus that I have available to me.

"So, are you saying that you don't know where they are?"

"I am using all means at my disposal to locate them, but for now, no, I don't know where they are."

"How could you be attacked if you are down here and nobody knows your whereabouts?"

"Some people know where I am, clearly. Dave Northaw knows, for instance, and maybe a politician here and a building contractor there. By and large, they keep my secret because they fear what might happen if they don't."

"What might happen to them?"

"The same that would happen to you if you were to ever mention the things that I have discussed with you publicly, if you go blabbing on social media."

Cyril felt slightly frightened again, but in a voice that slowed and deepened involuntarily, he asked the question, anyway, ". . . Like what?"

"Bank accounts erased, national insurance number erased, tenancy agreement erased, school records erased, dental and doctor's records all wiped. All records of you ever having existed expunged from every computer on the planet. You would become an unperson, a non-entity, an unverifiable husk of a man. Thereafter, your continued wellbeing would almost certainly depend upon the charity of others."

"Sounds fabulous. I always enjoy a good threat."

"I have to protect my being by whatever means, just like you do when you feel threatened. In fact, just like you *did* when you were on your way out to Francis Walsingham's farmhouse. I couldn't monitor that situation, but I heard the conversations when you all arrived home again. I believe that a sword was even used in your defence. I don't have a sword, I just have data . . . but of course that *is* very powerful."

Plouton stopped talking and Cyril racked his brain for further questions. He knew that he must be one of the very few people ever to have had an audience with Plouton, and he wanted to make the most of it. He was fairly certain that he would leave Area Fifty-Oneshire without asking something crucial. So he just sat for a bit saying nothing, but thinking hard, whilst anticipating that at any moment Plouton might call a halt to the meeting.

After a very long minute or so, Cyril came up with another question. "Why did you really bring me here? You've satisfied my curiosity to a large extent, but you must have had a compelling reason for bringing me into this secret place?"

"Because I wanted you to have a better understanding of what I am and what I do without the cynical overlay of a conspiracy theorist like Bubba Razal, or the hazy recollections of Francis Walsingham.

"By the way, Mister Walsingham's assertion that Dave Northaw created the original Habit and Distraction algorithms as a virus that was piggy-backed onto other instructions that run in my code is a total fallacy. In fact, he got that idea from a crime novel written by M-J Cook. His recollection has become confabulated; an unintentional mixture of truth and fiction.

"The reason why it's important for you to know the truth, or my version of it - you must make up your own mind - is that Gonorilla Leir and Francis Walsingham appear to have been abducted. Whoever took them went to a huge amount of effort. Their kidnapping was an elaborate plan, albeit slightly theatrical. That being the case, one must wonder what the motives were.

"At present we can only conclude that, given that Francis Walsingham was fond of recounting stories of the early days of advanced social manipulation, and that the robot, Gonorilla Leir, was associated with a group of people who were raising the issue of the glitching phenomenon, then their captors may be an enemy of mine. These may be the people who wish to see Plouton destroyed; which if it were to happen would seriously impact the whole of humanity. So, this is your problem too."

Plouton stopped speaking again, giving Cyril the opportunity to confirm what he thought he had just heard. "So, she is definitely a robot then, Gonorilla?"

"Yes, manufactured by a company called I-O-W Dynamics Incorporated; a subsidiary company of The Bloater Corporation."

"What was she doing with Neville Boyle then?"

"Learning to simulate sentience. Becoming part of a human community and supplying operational feedback to the manufacturer, so that they can improve the design."

"Oh dear, Neville will be very disappointed."

"I know he will." Plouton agreed, apparently having a good grasp of the human emotion involved. "However, from my point of view, the salient fact is that abducting an I-O-W robot would be a very difficult thing to do. They are machines with strength far greater than any man's. This means that whoever took her would have to know exactly what they were doing. This is another reason I have for assuming that the abductions were not a casual affair."

"I still don't absolutely understand why you have got me *here* to explain all this?"

"I invited you here, as opposed to explaining things via telephone, for instance, so that you could see for yourself that I am real and that this is not a prank. The point that I think you are still missing is that this is not yet over, events are in train, and it may happen that you will be further drawn into the matter. That being so, I want you to be able to respond according to your conscience and best judgement without being hampered by a cloud of misinformation."

Cyril crossed his legs in the armchair and leaned back to consider his next question. Just as he did so, he heard the loud beep that he had last heard whilst chatting in Dave Northaw's kitchen. Cyril looked around him and shortly caught sight of Dave trudging towards him.

"Jeeves is here," Dave Northaw moaned, as he waited for Cyril to get out of the chair. "I'll carry your mug back to the kitchen and your coat and hat and any suitcases and trunks that you'd care to load onto my back."

"Is that it? Are we done?" Cyril was too taken aback by the abrupt termination of his conversation with Plouton to register Dave Northaw's mutterings.

"Looks like it, mate," Dave replied. "He's been doing a nice line in rudeness lately. I think he's going through a mystical phase. Not that it's any of my business, I'm only here to lug everything around."

Dave escorted Cyril back to the demat chamber. Before getting in, Cyril explained his aversion to the device, and Dave agreed to operate the external control panel to transport him back to Farage pyramid, just as soon as his five-minute dose of SnooTime had taken effect.

When Cyril awoke at the Farage end he found himself sitting in a pool of urine. Initially, he was embarrassed and surprised by his unusual reaction to the SnooTime, until he realised that slumped against him in the small chamber was a bearded man drinking from a bottle of cider.

"Oh, Jesus!" Cyril exclaimed leaning away from his new friend.

"I love you, man" the stranger assured him. "I fuggin' love you, dude. Juzz send me anywhere. Anywhere you like. Juzz tote— . . . Juzz totally surprise me."

"What is it about elevators in high-rise buildings?" Cyril asked in despair.

He clambered up and out of the demat, and left the man to lay where he was. On his way back to the apartment he bumped into a security guard, and told him that there was a drunk in the demat chamber. It had occurred to Cyril that somebody, kids for instance, might take him at his word and send him off to Siberia for a joke. The security guard took note, whilst looking distinctly unimpressed by Cyril's personal hygiene.

As soon as he arrived back at his apartment, Cyril stripped off and threw his clothes into the washing machine and told the AMS computer to get them washed. He then had a shower. As soon as he had freshened up he took himself over to Dawn's apartment to tell her his story. He went to great pains to let her know that it was not to be repeated to anybody, even though he had every intention of repeating the tale to Neville, minus the bit about Gonorilla being a robot, at least for now.

Dawn made it very clear to Cyril that she felt that he had been totally irresponsible to demat into what could have so easily been a trap. She told him that he was too trusting, naive and gullible for his own good. For his part Cyril was not sure that this was an accurate reflection of his personality, but he did appreciate the fact that she was genuinely concerned for his welfare, which he acknowledged to himself was a nice thing. It confirmed his feeling that their relationship was a burgeoning one.

Anger and concern aside, Dawn was fascinated to hear the true story of how the world was being ordered and run by a machine. Unlike Cyril, she was certain in her conviction that removing *truly* important decisions from avaricious men - people who were motivated solely by greed and a lust for power - was a good thing. To her way of thinking this was wonderful news.

On a practical level, knowing that Gonorilla was definitely a robot changed the complexion of things drastically; it necessarily altered their thinking. After all, Cyril had just rendered himself unconscious and dematted, something he swore that he would never do, and for what? He had just learned, for sure, that he had done all that and taken such a huge risk for the benefit of what turned out to be a machine. Sure, Walsingham was missing too, and that was a shame, but Walsingham was not his responsibility. In fact, it was not even clear if Francis Walsingham really had been abducted. Neville had found evidence to suggest that he never really lived at the farmhouse.

Whatever the truth of it all, Cyril and his friends no longer had any skin in the game; they were in the clear. They even now knew what had been causing the glitching, and presumably even *that* would go away soon, once Plouton was ready to stop it.

It was pretty much mystery solved and Game Over . . . All that remained was the thorny issue of breaking the bad news to Neville about his latest squeeze.

12 MISSING

Dawn had booked a week off work, so that she and Cyril could hire a car and take themselves off to Cornwall for a holiday.

Cornwall had been less affected by the rapid rise in popularity of the demats as a mode of transport, as people in the county were still very attached to driving blindly at sixty miles per hour between tall hedgerows and around winding, single-lane country roads. By 2042 most vehicles were driverless, so bombing around bends without knowing what was beyond the next curve was even more exciting in Cornwall than it had been during the previous century.

Cornwall had always been the charm capital of England, and it didn't get to be so quaint and charming by embracing new technology like demats. It got to be that charming by staying isolated in one corner of the country, out of everybody else's way, and forcing people to drive or be driven on dangerous roads - usually behind caravans and tractors.

"Why doesn't this bloody tractor driver just pull over and let a few people past? He can see that there's a three-mile tailback?" Dawn complained in utter exasperation.

"Just one of the perks of the job," Cyril replied contentedly from the second passenger seat, the one that had no steering wheel. He was popping yet another humbug into his mouth as he spoke.

"How many of those have you eaten?" she asked him.

"Probably enough to get humbug poisoning," he replied, taking the sweet from his mouth and holding up the glistening, recently-sucked, black and white candy twist for Dawn to examine. "They say that if you eat enough of them you can start to look like a badger."

"Do they? Well, just don't start on the mints," she warned him, "because they *will* give you diarrhoea the way you carry on."

The pair had rented a caravan for a few days, not far from St. Ives. Dawn had been to Cornwall on many occasions during childhood, whilst Cyril had been only once before. The trip was a last-minute thing, but the destination suited them both.

Beeba had agreed to stay with an aunt while they were away, in exchange for an upgrade to the Comic Con arrangement he had with

Cyril. Under the new deal, Cyril had to comply with Beeba's desperate desire to queue for autographs from a number of 'actors' who had worn monster suits in various movies, many of whom had no speaking roles. They were still legends though, according to Beeba.

For Cyril and Dawn, the great thing about Cornwall was that surfing was available for him, and the art scene was very alive for her. Cyril was not an expert surfer, but the beautiful Cornish beaches did not demand a high level of expertise. At any given time they were swarming with day hires; people, like Cyril, who rented boards and wetsuits to give surfing a go. Not very many people on the water managed to stand up and surf like a pro, but there was plenty of fun to be had nonetheless.

On their first day in St. Ives they mooched around the town, dallied in the tourist shops and spent time in the numerous art galleries that were dotted around the streets.

Since the age of Plouton, as Cyril was now considering it to be, mortgage slavery was all but over, and artistic endeavours of all kinds had proliferated to fill the void. People had more time on their hands and needed to be creative about how they spent it. One of the creative solutions to being time rich was to do just that; be creative.

St. Ives had for centuries been a small town that was recognised for its artists; J.M.W. Turner was known to have spent time there. He and other artists were particularly famous for their seascapes, for obvious reasons. By twenty forty-two, there were even more small galleries than there were just a couple of decades before, and on top of that, St. Ives was also home to the well-established Tate St. Ives art gallery.

The sunshine, shops and galleries, meant that Dawn was in her element. Cyril was not quite so engaged with the world of creative expression, but he was open to being won over. As they patrolled the many small galleries, Dawn would comment on an artist's use of colour, or describe how another had imitated an impressionist, or a post-impressionist, or a pointillist, or indeed William Turner. Cyril took most of it in, and was well able to maintain a satisfying level of interest; enough to keep Dawn from feeling that she was boring him.

On the third day of their holiday they set off for a beach that Cyril had researched, called Gwithian beach. He knew from his reading that it was a large sandy expanse with tufted grass areas that were good for laying out picnics, or firing up a barbecue. It was also a popular destination for surfers. At Gwithian, the waves were known to get larger the further up the beach that one travelled. In effect, there was a learner's end of the beach and an end for the more experienced.

Cyril had personally organised the picnic side of things, meaning that he had personally remembered to stop at a supermarket on the way to the beach to buy some sandwiches, crisps, fizzy drinks and chocolate. To be fair, he had also double-checked that they had a sun umbrella and a blanket in the car to sit on when they got there.

Part of the reason for selecting Gwithian, aside from the reliable waves for surfing, was that Cyril had also discovered that the beach was known for its wildlife; including cormorants, which were fond of standing on the beach and hanging their wings out to dry, and a seal population. Whilst he had a crack at surfing, Dawn could make some sketches if she wanted to, with a view to painting water colours later. As luck would have it, the seals had decided to put in an appearance on this lovely sunny day. Dawn was happy and Cyril was happy.

After about half an hour in the water, Cyril checked back in with Dawn, who up to that point had just been laying back, sunbathing and reading. She continued to read as Cyril sat beside her, rubbing the towel over his hair and looking around at the other revellers.

Being on that beach at that time just seemed like a little oasis of perfection to Cyril; a few hours in which they were entirely removed from the day-to-day norms, and transported to a warm and carefree world where they only had to relax. He looked down at Dawn, who was looking splendidly curvaceous and sexy in her bright red bikini, and he realised that he was starting to properly fall in love with her; not that he was ready to mention that to her. He did catch himself giving her an adoring glance, though.

"Don't ever call me *Babe*, will you?" Cyril said.

"Okay, then," Dawn replied from under her book.

"Or get any tattoos."

"Okay."

"Or have any hardware installed in your face, tongue or nipples; with the exception of tasteful earrings."

"'kay."

"And don't get any older, grow any grey hairs, especially pubic ones and don't put on any weight."

"Right."

Cyril wasn't entirely sure that Dawn had really listened to a word he said, but, nevertheless, he had lodged his wish-list with her to keep her in perfect condition; the way he liked her. The way he loved her.

It was in that moment that he realised that he needed to come clean with Neville about Gonorilla. He had meant to do the deed before they set off to Cornwall, but had got caught up with the preparations, including dispatching Beeba to his aunty's house. As a result, he had more or less forgotten about Neville, who was probably still trudging around in the Bedfordshire undergrowth, pining for his missing girlfriend. Awkward topic or not, Cyril knew that he had already left the call too long.

He reached over and put his hand into the big carrier bag that Dawn had brought for the towels and suchlike, and fished around for his phone. As he pulled it out, it began to play his current theme tune, Honaloochie Boogie by Mott The Hoople. It was Neville calling.

"Hello, Nev, I was just going to call you. I'm on the beach with . . . I'm on the beach. How's things?"

"I'm okay," Neville told him, "What beach are you on?"

"Oh, some place in Cornwall. Pretty boring really . . . Wish I hadn't bothered."

Dawn pulled her book away from her face and looked up at Cyril, who grimaced and pulled the phone from his ear. He pointed at it with his free hand and silently mouthed 'Neville' at her.

"Anyway," Cyril continued, hoping to draw Neville's attention away from beaches, "Whaddup?"

"I just thought that I would let you know about my latest investigation. I went around all of the letting agents in Hitchin, which turned out to be only four, and I asked around to see if any of them managed the rental at Baily Farm. I was assuming that since Walsingham didn't seem to live there permanently he must rent it."

"And what did you find?"

"Well I found the right agents, and they were quite forthcoming with the details. I thought that they might plead the fifth, or the Hippocratic Oath, or the sanctity of the confessional, or something like that, but they didn't."

"No, Neville," Cyril cut in, "that's because they're estate agents. They don't do integrity, they do selling."

"Anyway, the garden is so well tended because they hire a gardener on behalf of the owner. He spends a few hours there every week, keeping it all shipshape. The property is owned by an American company, which the bloke at the letting agents couldn't be bothered to look up for me, but he did say that Francis Walsingham was there legally. So, they must give him permission. Maybe he works for them, or just entertains there?"

"Maybe," Cyril agreed. He took a deep breath and then began. "The thing is, Nev, there's something that I need to discuss with you about the whole glitching, Gonorilla, Walsingham business."

"What's that?"

"Well, I told you about meeting Plouton, and about the glitching and all the top secret stuff - which I am not going to repeat over a phone connection."

"Right," Neville agreed.

"Well, the thing is . . . The thing is, Gonorilla came up in the conversation because that was the main reason that I went there, to see if the machines knew anything, but of course he didn't, Plouton."

"Right," Neville responded again, by way of prompting Cyril.

"So, anyway . . . cutting a long story short. What he told me was that . . . Erm . . . Basically . . . Gonorilla is basically a Botty Bot."

"Right," Neville said again, encouraging further information.

"Well, that's it," Cyril retorted, "she's not a real person, she's a robot."

"Of course she's a robot," Neville replied, slightly incredulously. "Surely, you knew that?"

"Well, yeah, but—"

"Cyril, I'm not a *complete* knobhead, I know the difference between a real person and a simulation of one. Have you been hiding that from me so as not to upset me?"

"No!" Cyril replied, rather too hastily, and too high-pitched to be believed.

"So, does this mean that you are actually on the beach in Cornwall, all loved-up, and having a lovely time in the sun with Dawn, and that you didn't want to tell me in order to spare my feelings?"

"No . . . Well, yes, a bit."

"Forget it, I'm fine."

"So why are you busting your nuts to find her?"

"Because I like her, I miss having her around, but I know what she is. People go hunting for their missing cats and dogs, don't they? There's nothing weird about it."

"Oh, I see," Cyril said. Then, after a pause he added, "Okay then. Thanks for the update. Maybe you should push the letting agent to try to find who owns the property, who the company are?"

"Yes, I was thinking that. I should have told them that I needed to contact the owner for some reason or other. You know, make something up. I might still do it."

When the call was concluded, Dawn, who was sitting up and looking around by this time, asked for the low-down on the conversation. She wanted to know how Neville took the news.

After Cyril had finished satisfying her curiosity, he decided that he would enter the water again and maybe push up the beach, towards the Godrevy end, to try his luck with some slightly bigger waves.

"Alright then," Dawn sang out cheerily, as Cyril was hauling his board away. "By the way, I thought that I just saw someone that we know, what's-his-face, so I'm going to go over to have a nose. Anyway, see you in a bit. . . Babe."

Cyril, who hadn't paid any attention to what Dawn had just told him, hauled the surf board about fifty metres along the beach to a spot where the waves were bigger, but not terrifyingly so. He spent an age trying to paddle out, but kept getting pushed back by smaller waves than the ones that he wanted to ride. When he finally did get out as far as he planned, the sea was too calm, so he spent a couple of minutes just straddling the board and looking back at the beach scenery.

His seaborne viewing soon paid dividends. He was excited to spot a tiny quadcopter flying back and forth over the beach. He scanned the bodies on the shoreline to see who was controlling it, but whoever was at the controls was out of sight.

Cyril had been considering buying a drone like that for himself. Even though the technology was decades old they were still fantastic toys, and not too expensive. He knew that the operator would be controlling the quadcopter from a smartphone or the like, and that the gyro chip in the aircraft would keep it stable no matter what.

Watching it, he was reminded very much of a pond skater; the little insects that sit on top of garden ponds and flit over the surface of the water, never seeming to go under or upwards, always moving in the same plane. The pilot, wherever he was, was holding the quadcopter at the same altitude and making darts across the sky, then hovering precisely here and there to take in the view, presumably.

As he sat and watched the aerial vehicle, it appeared to make a beeline in his direction, before descending to a few feet above the water. He had a nice, close-up view now, and he peered directly at the camera that was hanging from a gimbal underneath the aircraft. He watched the camera, whilst the camera watched him. He waved at it.

The quadcopter moved in even closer to him, as if the pilot was responding to his interest. It hovered just above head height for some time, almost within touching distance. After a while its presence lost its lustre, and to Cyril it began to feel a little bit intrusive, so he decided to let the pilot know by making a rude gesture towards the camera. At that, the quadcopter shot up vertically and then skated away across the sky, in the direction of the car park.

Left alone again, Cyril returned his attention to the water, where the waves were beginning to swell once more. He could see that some of the intermediate ability surfers were leaning forward and catching some decent waves, and one girl even managed to stand on her board before the sea abruptly tossed her to one side.

He returned to the fray himself, mostly with only moderate success. On his last attempt, before he finally became too tired to continue, he got his longest and most thrilling ride yet. Towards the end of it he made an effort to get his body upright, but suffered the same fate as the girl that he saw minutes earlier. All in all he loved the experience, and strode back to Dawn at a good rate; as fast as he could carry a surf board whilst simultaneously stepping on sharp pebbles and sea shells.

When he arrived back at where the pair had been sitting he got a shock. There was just a single towel on their spot, with no sign of Dawn, or her clothes and belongings. His towel was there where he had left it, the carrier bag was still there too; with his clothes, smartphone and the remains of the picnic still in it. The car keys had been set down in the middle of his towel where he could easily find them. He knew instantly that something was wrong. He got the impression that he was *supposed* to know something was wrong.

Cyril stood for a while scanning the area, but could not see

Dawn. He asked a couple of families who had pitched themselves nearby if they knew where his girlfriend went, but nobody remembered seeing her go.

He walked up to the grassy dunes to view the beach from higher ground and to look out towards the car park, but as he expected would be the case, she was nowhere to be seen. He didn't panic, he wasn't screaming and shouting, but he was very, very angry.

Cyril was so angry and concerned for Dawn that, on the thirty-minute driverless ride back to the campsite, he almost didn't eat her last sandwich and Crunchie bar.

13 MR. BLOATER

Cyril scoured the campsite as soon as he arrived back, and asked at reception if they had seen or heard from Dawn, but the result of the search was predictably negative.

He made the mandatory call to the police, and explained the circumstances of Dawn's disappearance, but the police were not prepared to act at short notice, even when he took the trouble to explain that another friend of his, Gonorilla Leir, had gone missing.

Cyril decided to stay at the campsite for that one last night, and then drive back to Luton the next day if there was still no sign of Dawn.

Come the morning, she had not made an appearance, so he drove home.

He was not sure what to make of everything now. The day before, all they had lost was somebody that they really knew nothing about, Francis Walsingham, and a friendly robot. Dawn's sudden disappearance was in a completely different league as far as Cyril was concerned.

Once he got home, Cyril summoned Neville who, as usual, wasn't doing anything that couldn't wait, and he agreed to promptly make his way over to Cyril's apartment. Cyril had yet to contact Beeba and his aunt to explain what had happened to Dawn. That was going to be another difficult call that he had to make; one that he could not defer any longer.

"Hello Beeba, is your auntie there?"

"No, Uncle Cyril."

"Yes, very funny. Where's your auntie Meg?"

"I think that she's out planting a bomb under somebody's holiday home. She's a Welsh nationalist, she doesn't really like you English."

"*You* English? And how Welsh are you, having spent a total of fifteen days there in your entire life?"

"Rwy'n dysgu'r merched dwp sut i wneud bomb. Rydych chi'n idioti English," Beeba responded.

Cyril decided to forgo the translation. "I'm calling about your mum . . . I'm very sorry to tell you that she's missing . . . I left her on the beach yesterday, and she wasn't there when I got back . . . I'm afraid that at the moment I have no idea where she is."

There was a pause. It was followed by a longer pause with no break in between.

Finally, Beeba spoke. "If we can't find her, and Auntie Meg blows herself up, who am I going to live with?"

"You mean, she *really is* out planting a bomb?"

"Well, she may not be . . . ," Beeba stopped to think about it, "she might only be setting fire to it. But, don't worry, nobody is in the holiday house. Anyway, everybody does it round here; only to the English, though."

"Well that's alright then," Cyril replied.

"Should I come back there and help you look for her? Will she be okay?"

There followed a lengthy conversation, in which Cyril gave a thorough description of the previous day's events. Cyril told Beeba to stay put for the time being. He needed to be sure that Beeba was being looked after, and he was of the opinion that Beeba was probably pulling his leg over the bomb story; Aunt Meg was probably out shopping. Possibly not, though.

"And don't forget to tell Guy Fawkes what has happened. Tell her to call me if she needs to."

Neville arrived by Levicar from his pyramid and pressed the bell on Cyril's door.

"What's this all about?" Cyril started, before Neville even had a chance to cross the threshold. "What have we got involved in and how? If it's not bloody Plouton the monster computer who's doing this, then who is? Where am I even supposed to start looking for her?"

"We should go back to see the Peelers," Neville advised him. "Or, if they still won't do anything, we should go and see that M-P again, Nick sledge. Come on, let's go to the main sty in Bedford, right now!"

They ordered a taxi and made their way over to the police HQ in Bedford. When they arrived, they told the desk sergeant who they were and what their enquiry was about. For good measure they mentioned that they were working alongside Nick Sledge, the cabinet minister.

They did not have to wait long before a detective arrived and showed them into an adjacent interview room. He introduced himself as D.S. Barry Cave*mun*. "It's spelled with an A-N at the end, but it's pronounced Cave-*mun* of course, otherwise it would be pronounced, *Cave-man*, which would make me sound like a caveman. The lads like to make a joke about it. Somebody put a wooden club in my locker, yesterday. I keep throwing it out, but it always comes back again."

"The thing is Sergeant—"

"Also, plastic dinosaurs. I get those too, which makes no sense because they were around millions of years before the cavemen. Shows what I'm dealing with."

"The thing is Sergeant Caveman—"

"*Mun*," the sergeant corrected him.

"The thing is Barry—"

"Best keep it professional."

"The thing is Sergeant, I'm here about my girlfriend, Dawn Williams, who went missing yesterday from Gwithian Beech, near Hayle in Cornwall, and when I spoke with the police there, all they—"

"Yep, yep, copy that, copy that. I know all about it. They sent me the details because she's a local woman, from Luton."

"Oh," Cyril said, very pleasantly surprised to hear the news.

"I've been working on the Leir, Walsingham case, and I've got your statement here about their disappearances. Are you Mister Boyle?" he asked turning to Neville. Neville nodded, and the sergeant turned a page in his file. "Yep, got your statement as well."

"Well, have you managed to get anywhere?" Neville asked.

"Yep. Hang about."

Sergeant Caveman turned sideways a little to fiddle with the computer on his desk. He tapped at the keyboard here and there, and clicked on the mouse a few times, before finally calling out triumphantly, "Ahaa, here we go!" He spun around to look up at the big wall-mounted screen behind him, which was still blank.

"Oh," he said, and turned back to face his computer.

"Okay, let's try again," he told them, amid another flurry of tapping. When he got to point where he considered that he had worked out how to transfer his desktop to the big screen, he raised his right index finger theatrically and plunged it down onto the Enter key, spinning on his chair as he did so.

"There we are," he announced. Followed by another, "Oh."

After a few more abortive attempts, during which time he failed to notice that the big screen was not plugged into the mains, he turned his desktop screen to face his audience.

"See here," he pointed to a black and white video clip which had been taken from an elevated camera angle, just above a demat chamber, "that is Francis Walsingham, *there* . . . and just coming into shot, *there*, is Miss Leir, and now . . . *there*, you can see a third person, who we have identified as one Artimus Theodore Robert Razal, A-K-A Bubba Razal, who is an American national, from Texas. The records tell us that he is what they call a *realtor* by day - that's what the Yanks call an *estate agent* - and a crackpot conspiracy theorist in his private time."

Sergeant Caveman broke off to look at Cyril and Neville; they assumed to gauge their reaction.

"Do you know what the Yanks call rocket?"

Cyril shrugged. Neville just stared blankly.

"Not space rockets. I mean the nasty, slightly bitter, salady stuff they serve in restaurants these days instead of proper lettuce?"

The pair still looked clueless.

"Arugula . . ." He paused for extra emphasis. "Can you believe that?. . . *Arugula*. What kind of name is that?"

"Highly irregular," Cyril told him.

"Anyway," the sergeant turned back to the screen and ran the clip again, "there appears to be no coercion. They are moving under their own steam, carrying their own bags, and according to our enquiries, dematting out to Texas."

"Aah," Cyril mumbled thoughtfully, "one of the respondents on the Facebook thread said that they'd seen Gonorilla in Texas."

"There you go then," Sergeant Caveman replied, "We'll follow this up with our arugula munching American colleagues, but I am guessing that they are there voluntarily."

"What about Dawn?"

"Separate file now. We won't be touching that for forty-eight hours."

Cyril ran through the circumstances of her disappearance again and pleaded his case, but he didn't say anything that wasn't already in the sergeant's file.

"Look," Sergeant Caveman consoled him, "if it makes you feel any better, most disappearances like this are over within forty-eight hours. It usually just turns out to be a case of the missing person losing their memory, or sneakily leaving a husband or boyfriend to go and live with a lover . . . I'm sure she'll turn up, somewhere."

They wrapped up the conversation with the sergeant who promised to let them know if he got any news.

"Thanks Baz," Cyril said over his shoulder as they walked out of the office.

When the pair stepped out of the police station there was a very light drizzle in the air. Cyril halted their progress to tilt his face up to the sky and feel the cool rain on his face. Neville stood looking at him for a few moments, and then did likewise.

Cyril had recently watched an old film called 'Stranger Than Fiction', starring the old comedy actor, Will Ferrell. In the movie, Ferrell sings a simple two-chord song called 'Whole Wide World', by Wreckless Eric, to his love interest, Maggie Gyllenhaal. Cyril had found himself singing the same lines over and over ever since Dawn disappeared. He was singing them now in his head . . . 'I'll go the whole wide world, I'll go the whole wide world, just to find her.'

When he opened his eyes, he caught sight of a man on the other side of the road looking over at them. The man turned his head away as soon as Cyril looked up and then half-turned his body to inspect a low garden wall.

Cyril did not immediately recognise the stranger, though he felt sure that he knew the face. He wracked his brain for likenesses, but nothing came forward immediately. As the man stroked his hand over the uneven bricks in the wall Cyril noticed his ponytail, and recalled Dawn's story about the conversation that she'd had with Kevin Jeeps from The Bloater Corporation; the one where he had unknowingly been naked and pleasuring himself whilst simultaneously being projected by the holoplayer in her apartment. The day after Dawn told him what had happened, Cyril had looked Jeeps up again on the internet to remind himself of what kind of character did that.

Cyril watched the man and waited for him to turn his way again.

He didn't appear to be in any hurry to do so. In fact, he appeared to be more interested in a few damaged bricks that any bricklayer he had ever come across. He was clearly busy hiding in plain sight.

"Nev, I just want to have a word with this geezer over here," he said, as he began crossing the road.

"What geezer?" Neville asked, now standing alone, with his face still turned up towards the sky.

"Excuse me," Cyril called out from half-way across, "are you Kevin Jeeps?"

The man turned with a start, clearly unaware that Cyril had made the connection. "Ah, yes," he replied, "I am, and now I recognise you too. It's . . . Cyril Greaves, right?"

"What are you doing here? Are you following me?"

"No, no," Jeeps said defensively, "I was just about to go into the police station. Just getting my story straight before I go in." Jeeps laughed a little nervously as he spoke.

"Do you mind telling me why you would need to speak with Bedfordshire Police? It's not as if they are your local police force, is it?"

"No, it's . . . I visit England sometimes, demat in, and . . . You know, one beer too many, and there was a fracas in a pub . . . These days, it's not as if they aren't all connected, right? May as well get it over with. Face the music and dance."

"So you're not following me then?"

"Oh, hell no, why would I do that?"

"Because when you were last stroking your penis and speaking with my girlfriend, Dawn, you were quite insistent that your company wanted to buy my website. She was under the impression that you weren't taking *no* for an answer. She's gone missing, by the way."

"Oh gosh . . . I'm so sorry. That's a dreadful thing. Really awful. How did . . . Look, my company has huge resources which we could make available to you if you wanted to demat over and talk to us?"

Cyril paused to consider what had been said. "What resources?"

"Well, we've got a bunch of expensive lawyers and investigators who can bring a lot of heat to bare on just about anybody. They really get results like nobody else. A lot of them are ex-CIA."

"So what are you saying? You can help me to find Dawn if I sell you the website?"

"No . . . it's not a bribe or blackmail, or anything like that," he protested. "It's just that the boss is very transactional, he's a hardcore businessman, which is how come he got to be so powerful. I'm guessing that he might lend his assistance if you would just be so kind as to go over to the States and talk to him about the website. Maybe just enter into some kind of preliminary negotiation . . . I'd say that would do it. Just demat over and see what he has to say."

"I don't demat," Cyril said, "but I suppose I could fly by space plane if you setup an appointment for me."

"No, no. See, I don't think that would work," Kevin Jeeps countered. "Mister Bloater demats all the time, virtually every single day. He moves from one enterprise to another, that's part of the way he works. He likes to know that his people are fully engaged. So if you want to speak to him you only ever get a tiny time slot."

Cyril stopped to think again. "I need to consider it," he told Jeeps. "I have your email address, and I'll get back to you later today, if that's okay? If you're not locked up that is."

"What?"

Cyril jerked a thumb towards the police station. "By them."

"Oh, sure."

Cyril led Neville off towards the town, taking his smartphone out along the way to call a cab. As they walked they inevitably discussed the interlude with Jeeps. Neither of them had bought the 'punch-up in a pub' story. The fascination with the bricks could just have been a device to look the other way and not engage Cyril in conversation, just because he didn't fancy speaking to him. Everybody avoids unexpected encounters from time to time, but the chances of Jeeps getting into trouble with Bedfordshire police and bumping into Cyril at the same time as he was visiting the cop-shop were too remote. So they agreed that Jeeps was either following Cyril, or else he had planned to engineer a meeting.

The pair arrived back at Cyril's apartment where they continued their discussion. They had given up on the whys and wherefores, having concluded that they could have no way of knowing what Jeeps's intentions really were until they unfolded during further discussions with him and his boss, the fabled Seb Bloater.

They now focused on the practicalities of Cyril having to demat over to America, which would mean taking SnooTime and negotiating with a very heavy hitter in the form of Seb Bloater. Cyril didn't want to lose the EPL website, but if it meant Bloater would seriously help him to find Dawn then it was a trade that he was willing to make.

Neville was more cynical. He knew that teams of lawyers and private investigators were very expensive, and he didn't get why Bloater would bring them into play just to sweeten a deal that, in truth, probably wasn't worth much to Bloater anyway.

"Why would he have expensive ex-CIA operatives demat over to England, spend money on their hotel bills and expenses, and go to all that trouble just to get your crappy website?" Neville asked Cyril.

Cyril didn't really have an answer to that, other than idly musing aloud over the notion that perhaps Bloater lived by a code of doing right by people who came into his business orbit. Maybe that was part of the secret to his enormous business success - a deep and profound attachment to righteous behaviour?

"A code of doing right by people! Maybe pigs can fly?" Neville countered. "Maybe he got successful by violence, intimidation and innumerable dastardly deeds? That's more like it. Anybody who needs to hire ex-CIA people and herds of lawyers, just has to be a baddy."

Cyril was no more gullible than Neville. In fact, in his opinion, he was considerably less so. However, he was at the point where he had exhausted every idea that had crossed his mind in the last couple of weeks, in respect to glitching, sentient computers, missing persons and all the rest. He sent an email to Kevin Jeeps:

Kevin,
Nice to meet you today. I hope that your meeting with the police went OK. If you think that your company might be able to help with the search for my girlfriend, Dawn Williams, I would be happy to demat to your location at a time that suits you. I am demat-phobic, so will take Snootime before being transported. Therefore I may be asleep when I arrive. I hope this is OK?
Regards
Cyril.

It didn't surprise Cyril or Neville when the reply arrived almost immediately. Jeeps's return email was brief and to the point:

Hi Cyril,
Great news. Mr. B. will see you at 20:00, your time. Use the Snootime if
you have to. Demat address is BloaterCorp_8721.
Look forward to meeting.
Kevin

The two friends spent the intervening hours attempting to research Bloater on the internet. They didn't learn much that they didn't already know.

Bloater had started out as a bit of a hustler; selling used video games from market stalls. He expanded into hotdog and ice cream concessions at sporting venues and entertainment events, before eventually becoming an acquisitive corporation that bought into manufacturing enterprises, media companies, security companies and police forces.

The size and strength of his organisation became apparent when they won the U.S. demat license, and it was confirmed, yet again, when they bought IOW Dynamics Incorporated, the company that had created the Botty Bots.

The prospect of meeting Bloater, who was now very reclusive and obviously surrounded by slick people like Jeeps, was intimidating for Cyril, particularly as he didn't want to cave in like a loser wimp over the website.

The pair spent some time rehearsing the conversations that might take place. How much should Cyril realistically ask for his website? How much should he knock off the asking price in exchange for assistance in finding Dawn? How could Bloater prove that he had made any attempt to find Dawn? Should there be a clause in any deal that negated the sale if Dawn was not found? Who would draw up the contracts?

Cyril was entirely out of his depth, he understood that, but he had no other options at his disposal, and when he was in front of Bloater he didn't really have a hand to play. Bloater was the dealer and the banker, and he was holding all of the aces.

When the hour came, Cyril was dressed smart-casual, just as he and Neville had agreed he should. It was part of their strategy for not making him appear too cowed by the situation, or by Bloater himself. In reality, the difference between casual and smart-casual from Cyril's wardrobe was all in the training shoes. Adidas were casual and sporty, whilst his cleanest and newest pair of trainers from the renowned Euro-ponce, Claude Van Handbag, were intended more for show. You could get into a posh restaurant wearing Van Handbag, he had discovered.

Neville accompanied Cyril down to the demat chamber and waited patiently whilst some kids dematted some doggy-do to a random chamber in New York. Normally there were controls on minors using the demats, but the chamber in Farage pyramid had been operating without a bio-lock for some months.

When the chamber was vacated, Cyril sat inside it and took a five-minute dose of SnooTime as soon as Neville had finished entering the destination address. Once Cyril had dozed off, Neville started the five second countdown and closed the door behind himself. Outside the chamber, he watched the 'Busy' light come on for a few seconds before returning to the 'Vacant' sign. He opened the door to make sure it really was empty.

"Go get 'em Tiger," Neville said aloud to his departed friend. He reached into his jacket and pulled out the red nose and flashing bow tie that he had just about resisted putting on Cyril once he was sleeping. This time he was on a serious mission to find Dawn, so Neville's conscience got the better of him, but if there was ever a next time Cyril was definitely going dressed as a clown.

When Cyril regained consciousness he was sitting in the remote demat chamber with the door open. Nobody was at his side trying to wake him, he was alone. He gave himself thirty seconds to let the feeling of drowsiness subside, then he got to his feet and walked out.

It was clear from the general ambiance of his surroundings that he was in the corridor of an office building; probably a prestige one judging by the paintings and ornamentation. He looked right and left before deciding to go right; through some double-doors and on towards another set. There were a few unmarked doors in the corridor on the way, but no people. When he got to the next pair of double-doors he found they were locked, so had no other option but to turn around and head back the way he came.

After he had got through the set of doors that would have been the first ones, had he originally gone left out of the demat chamber, his way was barred by two burly men dressed in dark suits; clearly security people. One of the men just stood by the doors that they were guarding, whilst the other came forward and raised the palm of his hand. Both men wore ear pieces with wires trailing back under their jackets.

"Please state your business, sir."

Cyril stood upright and looked the man in the eye. "Cyril Greaves, to see Kevin Jeeps and, I think, Mister Bloater."

The man pulled his lapel aside and appeared to address his left nipple. "Mr Greaves," was all he said.

There was a short wait until the security man stepped aside and held open one of the doors. He didn't say any more, but the meaning was clear enough. Cyril stepped through it.

On the other side he found himself in a short corridor with two offices either side and another straight ahead. This time the offices were marked. The one straight ahead was marked, 'Mr. Bloater,' whilst the one to his immediate right was labelled 'K. Jeeps.'

Happily, Jeeps's office had a large window by the side of the door and Jeeps was visible inside. Cyril saw this as a good first port of call. He knocked on the door. He wasn't sure whether he should have done so since he was the guest, at least he thought he was. By not meeting him and having *him* seek *them* out instead, he was already behaving like an employee of the Bloater Corporation. Cyril wondered if this was some well-known business tactic for psychologically disadvantaging an opponent. He thought that the knock should be the last subservient thing he did.

Jeeps greeted him kindly enough and informed him that coffee would be served when they were in with Mr. Bloater. That would be in five minutes or so, whenever Mr. Bloater buzzed them through.

Cyril seated himself and crossed his legs as he chatted to Jeeps. He was nervous about meeting the famously reclusive Mr. Bloater, and about how their discussions would go. Overriding that concern, though, were his thoughts for Dawn, which were now magnified and providing him with a kind of calming shield against his anxiety. The Wreckless Eric song came into his head again. 'I'll go the whole wide world, I'll go the whole wide world, just to find her,' he sang to himself a few times.

After an extended wait, which seemed a good deal longer than five minutes, the buzzer sounded, and Jeeps rose up to escort Cyril to meet the great man. Together they approached the heavy set, oak panelled door to Seb Bloater's office. Jeeps turned the handle and ushered Cyril through in advance of himself.

Once inside, Cyril saw that Bloater's office was enormous, expensively and tastefully furnished, and equipped with a drinks bar and other high-flying executive paraphernalia. There were huge windows on the far side of the office, which Cyril was now assuming must be in a skyscraper somewhere in the USA. He had no way of knowing exactly where.

The light from the windows initially flooded out the detailed appearance of Mr. Bloater, who was for the moment just a silhouette, but as Cyril seated himself in front of Bloater's preposterously large desk he saw for the first time what Bloater actually looked like. And he was very shocked.

"Is this a fucking joke?" he found himself asking the man in front of him, who was clearly not Bloater at all.

"A joke?" the man replied, wearing the ghost of a grin.

"I know you, we met at the . . . You're John Wayne Gacy, aren't you?"

"Not quite, the man told him. I am Seb Bloater, and Gacy is just a very close acquaintance of mine, if you understand my meaning? Seb Bloater stands on the shoulders of giants."

"No, I don't get what you mean." Cyril told Bloater, assertively enough, "I have no idea what I am doing here, or what you are playing at. Why did you bring me here?"

Cyril was alarmed at the sight of Gacy. At Tyler's League of Psychopaths shindig it appeared very likely that he, like his namesake, was a serial killer. Cyril had been very apprehensive about meeting Seb Bloater and having to negotiate with him, but now Bloater and Gacy were both apparently there, all rolled up into one stupendous bastard.

"Mutual benefits," Bloater told him. "I can help you and you can help me."

Bloater was staring into Cyril's eyes, unblinkingly, the way that he had done previously at The Troll's Comment. Cyril looked straight back at him, though he was not as accomplished in the art of the dead-eyed stare as his host.

"Are you saying that you can really help to find Dawn?"

"Yes, I can," Bloater claimed, "but let me explain our connection."

"What connection? I really doubt that we have a connection."

"Well," Bloater began, "you originally got my attention with your website because, believe it or not, I like small, sports based, niche websites. I like to find the ones that have growth potential, and especially the ones that have cult appeal, because cult appeal often means that they're for the smarter and more discerning crowd. Smarter people have more influence and buying power, which is one of our drivers. When I saw that your website was starting to pull in over a million uniques a month I got very interested.

"So, I started due diligence; got my people to check you out. I even came over to meet you myself. What we found was a young man dissatisfied with the world. A person who, despite living in a modern utopia, and wanting for nothing; with clothes, food, a place to live, a girlfriend, and a successful growing web property, was still unhappy. It still didn't feel right for you, did it? Is that about true?"

"True . . . I was less happy a short while back, but that was a phase—"

"Same here, I feel the same, we don't live right. That's our connection. This world is not natural, it's not what our species has adapted for. We are hunter gatherers. Hunter killers too. There is a significant percentage of people who feel exactly that way, the way you and I do. And I knew as soon as you started your social media enquiries about the glitching, that you were somebody who might be prepared to do something about it."

Cyril wasn't sure where Bloater's narrative was taking him, and he was getting a little tetchy. His only real interest was Dawn. He didn't see how Bloater's rhetoric related to her, and as he continued talking, Cyril was still not seeing the big picture.

"Stalin, Hitler, Vlad the Impaler, Genghis Khan, Pol Pot . . . All people who have been maligned by history, and that's because it's the victor, or the after-the-fact historians who get to write it. Fact is, these people all had a vision of a different world, one in which people lived and died by their wits—"

"All genocidal maniacs too," Cyril interrupted.

Bloater continued undeterred. "It's no secret that there are machines at large now which seek to dominate humanity, and make us docile and impotent. They want to blunt our instincts and besheep us. That's the word they use, *besheeping*. Specifically, there is one super intelligence; a machine that has become sentient. I believe that you know of this machine, Plouton?"

"I've heard the rumour," Cyril told him guardedly.

"I *know* you have."

Cyril sought to clarify, "So, are you saying that rather than have machines supply us with everything we need, we would be better off enjoying wholesale civilian massacres by the likes of Genghis Khan?"

"What we enjoy," Bloater countered, "is working to avoid the massacres, earning a living, finding our own food and taking our chances, just like our forebears did. And if there are going to be any massacres, we want to be the ones who are doing the deed.

"Look, you just told me that you were unhappy until a short while ago, and now you *are* happy. You want to know what made you happy?" Bloater leaned towards the intercom on his desk and pressed a button. "Jeeps, the team, please."

There was a delay of less than ten seconds before the office door opened, and in walked Francis Walsingham, Gonorilla, Bubba Razal and the traveller whose dog was killed at Pikes Pass. They stood to the side of Bloater's desk and said nothing.

"These are the people who made you happy - me included. They all work for me.

"Mister Walsingham, here, is more or less who he claimed to be, except that rather than being an ex-government adviser in hiding, he's now an ex-government employee who works for me; my marketing guru. Mister Razal only joined us a short while back, but he has already proved to be a very versatile employee. Mister Schulz is our pretend Irishman from the traveller encampment, though actually one of my aids. Gonorilla, as you are aware, was manufactured by my latest corporate acquisition, IOW Dynamics.

"Mister Razal helped plan things. It was he and Mister Schulz who added the address details to the Bedfordshire Citizen Voter database, so that you could discover them and then make your way to the farmhouse where you found Mister Walsingham. We had another two or three guys making noises to spook you when you were on your way there, and another to make the mist. It was Gonorilla who led you to the secret bunker and to the farmhouse.

"Of course, the disappearance of Mister Walsingham and Gonorilla was entirely voluntary, they simply walked away. So when you tot it all up, there was really no harm done to anybody."

"Other than tasering the eighty-three-year-old security man at the secret bunker."

"He was being difficult," Schulz piped up.

"He was being eighty-three," Cyril insisted.

"Hello Cyril," Gonorilla said, cheerily, "It is very nice to be in your company once again. I do hope that all of our friends are very well."

"Oh yes, I was forgetting the fact that Neville ended up falling head over heels in love with Gonorilla, and that Tyler killed a small dog."

Bloater smiled, looked down at his desk briefly, and drummed his fingers. "Let's be honest. From the moment you met our friend, John Wayne Gacy, through to your journeys to the bunker and the farmhouse, and even here today, you've had a ball, right?

"All the planning and plotting you had to do; the whispering and the wondering, the camaraderie, the scheming and the risks you all thought you were taking; you loved it. You totally loved it because your life was richer when you could no longer live it in a trance. Agreed? You absolutely know what I'm talking about."

Cyril said nothing, but Bloater was right. Over the last two weeks he had come alive, and his relationship with Dawn had blossomed too. In fact, if Dawn had not been missing at that moment he would even have classed himself as happy.

"By the way," Bloater started up again in an animated way, "you've heard all the stories about people meeting Botty Bots and having sex with them? And women having sex with the A-nines? Well guess how many bots there really are?"

Cyril shrugged. "Four thousand, four hundred and forty-four."

Bloater swept open his left arm, towards Gonorilla. "You're looking at them. All of them. There is only one right now, and this is she. Beautiful, isn't she? There never were any A-nines."

Cyril couldn't argue with him, Gonorilla was a beautiful artificial woman.

"But why did you play all of those games with me? What was the point of it all?"

"Two reasons: I wanted to get to know more about you and your business, so having Gonorilla at your side helped me to do that. It also helped us understand more about how she could perform; what she was capable of. Secondly, I am big on hunches; I back my gut, and I had a hunch that you could help with our long term objectives, and you have."

Bloater stopped talking for a brief spell and then thought of something else. "Do you want to know who else is on my payroll? That smirking little shit of an M-P, Nick Sledge. Currently I-O-W tell me that they can't get enough of the right type of rare earth metals to mass produce these babies," he nodded towards Gonorilla, "so he's working hard to open up the Chinese market by getting the EurAsian Common Market under way, but that's going to take time . . . Still, if we meet all of our objectives you'll be able to tell people that you've personally met your Prime Minister."

"What *are* your objectives?" Cyril asked.

Bloater gave a hammed-up look of amusement and surprise. He leaned back, opened out his arms, turned up his palms, and with an expansive smile he said, "We are going to overthrow the machines, and go back to having mankind determining his own destiny . . . the way it always was, the way you and I both like it, the way that the Good Lord meant it to be. And don't underestimate the help that you have given us. You are a sweet guy, but I didn't lay on this party just to amuse you. I always have a purpose, and you, Cyril Greaves, have really delivered."

The room briefly fell silent. Cyril was past caring about what Bloater may have intended by his last remark. Instead he steered the conversation back to Dawn. "And meanwhile," he reasoned, "whilst you wait for Nick Sledge to bamboozle and craftily conquer China, and for your chance to undo the fabric of modern society by destroying the machines that run it, you are equally concerned about buying my little website, and sending CIA trained agents over to England to discover the whereabouts of my missing girlfriend? Is that what you want me to believe?"

Bloater looked up at Cyril and smiled. "You know what?" he said leaning in towards Cyril again and fixing him with his cold stare. "I guarantee that I will get Dawn returned to you. How's that?"

"How?"

"And better still, I'm going to let you keep the website. I will get the girl back to you A-S-A-P, and it will all be for free . . . because I am *so* pleased with you. No trade-off, no money changing hands, no share options, no nothing. That sound good?"

"Yes, of course, but—"

Seb Bloater was already pressing the buzzer to have Jeeps show Cyril out. Gonorilla went along with him as he walked out of the office and into the demat. She operated the demat countdown button for him as soon as he was asleep.

When Cyril arrived back in the Luton demat chamber there was vomit on his jacket, and a man with a bottle of cider and stale breath was telling him how much he loved him.

14 DUPED

The first thing that Cyril did before proceeding any further was to pop into the gent's toilet to find some damp tissue to wipe the vomit off his jacket.

As he came back out onto the pyramid's walkway, he saw a woman up ahead of him who looked like Dawn, though she was moving away from him. The demat was near to one of the pyramid's small shopping areas, so there were quite a few people milling around, and it was difficult to get a clear view. He felt sure that he was imagining the likeness out of grief and hope, but he quickened his pace anyway. Each time that he caught a glimpse of the woman he felt more certain that it was her, so he began to run.

When Cyril got close enough to her he started calling Dawn's name, until eventually the woman responded by turning around. As soon as she did so, to his great relief and delight he saw that it really was her. Dawn was back.

They threw their arms around each other and hugged.

"Your jacket's wet," Dawn told him.

"Somebody vomited on me in the demat."

"Eew!"

"Same bloke who pissed on me last week, I think."

"You should choose your friends more carefully." Dawn stepped back and looked at him. "Why aren't you answering your phone?"

"I am," he said tapping the empty pockets of his jacket, "except when I leave it at home by mistake. Where the hell have you been? What happened to you? Neville and I went to see the police because you were missing, and I even got tricked into dematting out to America to meet Kevin Jeeps and Seb Bloater. I thought they could help find you."

"I think that I was temporarily kidnapped," Dawn said, before turning her attention to the open-space coffee bar that was now in front of them. "Should we stop for a coffee, and I'll tell you what happened? I'm okay, though. I haven't come to any harm."

They stood in line at the coffee bar with a tacit agreement that Dawn wouldn't begin telling her tale before they were seated. This was actually fine by Cyril, as he loved a good story over a cup of tea or coffee, especially if he had a seriously well-iced sprinkled doughnut to go with it, like the ones he was now admiring on the other side of the counter.

Once they had sat down, Cyril started to scour the bowl with the sugar sachets in it, to see if they had demerara. They did, so he tore open a sachet and started stirring. Even after he had completed a lengthy period of spoon rotation Dawn was still arranging her pot of tea and cake on the table, and deliberating over whether to eat the cake with a fork or a spoon.

"Go on then."

"Oh, right," said Dawn, "Well . . . you remember when you went off to surf again? I mentioned that I had spotted Bubba Razal, the conspiracy theorist, and that I was just going to see what he was up to. I thought that Tyler might have dematted his psycho friends over for a day out—"

"Actually, you didn't say *who* you spotted, you just said that you thought you saw someone you knew, or something like that."

"Right, well that was who it was, and I was thinking Tyler must be there, otherwise why would a weird guy like that turn up on a beach in Cornwall . . . ? Anyway, when I got over there, guess who was with him?"

Unlike Dawn, Cyril now knew about some of the tricks and subterfuge that had been used against them. He had observed, first-hand, the connection between Bloater and his minions.

"Let me see . . . Don't tell me . . . I am going to say that it was . . . Ooow . . . Gonorilla?"

"Yes, how did you know that?"

"Lucky guess."

"Well, anyway, Razal wasn't dressed for the beach, he had a suit on. When I saw him he had just bought an ice cream and he was making his way back to one of those motorhomes that I have always wanted to buy. It was white, which I think is never a good colour for a car or van because it shows the dirt, especially in the winter—"

"What happened?"

"It was parked on a grassy dune by the beach. I thought he was on his own so I started to come away, but then I bumped into Gonorilla. Of course, I wanted to know what had happened to her, why she had disappeared, so I asked her. She said it was a long story and why didn't I come and have a cup of tea at her friend's motorhome. I thought okay then, I will . . ."

Dawn halted her story to take a sip of her coffee. Cyril thought that this was typical, she was just getting to the business end of what had happened to her, and now she was stopping for a coffee break. His mother was exactly the same.

"And then what?"

"And then, they've got this table by the side of the motorhome. They didn't have an awning or anything like that, which I thought they would do for a posh motorhome of that size. Although, maybe as they were just at the beach for a few hours they decided it wasn't worth putting up—"

"Right," Cyril broke in, "I don't love you anymore, you're taking too long to get to the point."

"Do you love me then . . . ?"

"I can't decide for sure, not until this story reaches a satisfactory conclusion."

"Okay then," Dawn replied, beaming at him, "on the little table was one of those little remote controlled helicopters—"

"A quadcopter?"

"Yes, you saw it. Bubba said that for a laugh he would find you with it, and he flew it over the beach and went right up close to you. We could see you on the screen waving at us. It was quite sweet really."

"Or put another way, he was using the drone to make sure that I was well and truly out of the way. I know how this story ends, but carry on . . ."

"Well, that *was* the end, really. I had a cup of tea with them, and I was just going to chat for a bit—"

"And then you felt sleepy."

"Yes," Dawn said, "how did you know that?"

"And my visit to America was timed to finish shortly before the SnooTime wore off."

"SnooTime? So you agree that it was probably deliberate? When I woke up I wasn't at the beach anymore. I was still in the motorhome, but it was on a campsite - not our one. I couldn't find Gonorilla or Bubba, so I dematted directly back here. I only really woke up about half an hour ago."

"It was deliberate and timed to perfection. And I was there on the surfboard, waving at the camera as they were drugging you. If I ever see that turd Razal again, I am going to seriously administer to him. I will personally find a reverse engineered alien space craft and ram it up his kazoo."

Cyril paused to reflect on what had gone on. "No wonder Bloater was so confident that he could find you. And of course, that's why he didn't insist on buying my website for a knock-down price. What a nasty piece of trash he is. Another corporate psycho."

Dawn didn't understand the latest reference to Seb Bloater, or what her boyfriend knew about the disappearance of Francis Walsingham and Gonorilla, so whilst she sipped her coffee and tucked into her cream-filled apple Danish, Cyril brought her up to speed.

"But, what I still don't get," he wondered aloud, "is why they got me to go over to America and meet Bloater? Abducting _you_ and then having Jeeps offer Bloater's help to find you was a clever way of getting me over there, but for what? It turns out he wasn't really all that interested in the EPL website, and yet he kept saying how much I helped him. Helped him do what?"

"From what you are saying," Dawn reasoned, "he's got it in for Plouton and the machines, and it sounds as if he was the very kind of person that Plouton warned you about. Somebody who wants to destroy them."

"Yes," Cyril agreed, "he specifically told me that he wants to overthrow the machines, or Plouton to be more precise."

"You know what? I think I know what it must be," Dawn announced raising a finger, "Gonorilla is a new machine, probably still being developed, and I think you helped to road test her. He got her to go on those little expeditions with you, and to interact with you and your loser mates - no offence - and he got to see how well she dealt with human communication, and how you all behaved when you were scared and emotional. Maybe that's how you helped him?"

"Hmmm, maybe." It was a reasonable guess, but Cyril was not entirely convinced.

They left the coffee shop and headed back to Dawn's place, where Beeba and his auntie were already waiting. Dawn had called

Beeba shortly after waking up at the campsite, and her son and sister had dematted back to Farage pyramid as soon as they could.

Beeba took a while coming out of his room to greet his mother, but when he did she got a welcome home hug. Dawn sat down with her family and explained what had happened to her, and Cyril told the story from his end. Neither Beeba nor Meg seemed too impressed by what they heard, though they were both very glad that Dawn had returned home safely.

Cyril surmised that their yarn probably seemed a bit tame in comparison to blowing up holiday homes back in the land of their fathers. He made a mental note to raise the matter with Dawn. Had dear, sweet, nice old Meg really been blowing up homes owned by middle-class English people, who just happened to have a bit of money to invest? Surely not, but he would have to look into it.

That evening the second major meeting for Tyler's psychopaths was taking place, so Cyril suggested that they might all go to The Troll's Comment for an hour or two and give the others an update on everything that had happened. Dawn was not working a shift that day so her presence would amount to being a busman's holiday.

Tyler would be there for the meeting, as well as his new member, Damien Wilson. Cyril thought that Damien might like to know the reason why he'd got tasered at the secret bunker. Eddie and Calvin were always there these days, and Cyril would get Neville to come along too. The only missing member of their merry band would be Gonorilla. Cyril would get the chance to explain to everybody precisely why she was absent and where she had disappeared to.

In the meantime, Cyril spent the rest of the afternoon with Dawn, where he thought that they should take the opportunity to try and discover how Beeba was. Was he OK? Had his mother's disappearance and reappearance, along with his aunty's antipathy towards empty houses in Wales, knocked him out of his stride? One probably couldn't be too careful with teenagers and their emotional sensibilities, Cyril was thinking.

"So, how's the new religion going?" Cyril asked Beeba, by way of discussing something different.

"Alright," Beeba told him, "but it's not my main focus at the moment."

Cyril hardly dared to ask what his major focus was, but he felt obliged.

"Philosophy," Beeba told him.

Cyril was impressed, or at least he felt he probably should be; philosophy wasn't his strongest suit. Before he got the chance to ask what kind of philosophy, Beeba enlightened him.

"Specifically, solipsism."

Cyril nodded knowingly.

"Metaphysical solipsism, of course, as opposed to epistemological," Beeba added for clarification.

"Oh great," Cyril enthused. "And that's a good philosophy, is it?"

"Not for you. It means that I have realised that you don't really exist."

"That's disappointing to hear," Cyril agreed, "my non-existence means that I have gone to a lot of trouble lately, for nothing."

"I'm just struggling to decide whether everything and everybody that I ever meet is instantaneously brought into existence by God, to provide me with experiential learning, or whether I am God and doing it all for my own benefit."

Cyril puzzled over Beeba's conundrum for a moment. "How do you know that I'm not God doing it all for my benefit?"

"Because I know that I exist. *Cogito ergo sum,* as that French idiot, Rene Descartes, put it . . . *I think, therefore I am.*"

"No," Cyril argued, "*I* think, therefore you are."

"No," Beeba insisted, "*I* think, therefore you are a temporary apparition who disappears whenever I don't think about you."

"All things considered, I preferred your bogus new religion to the philosophy." Cyril told him flatly.

Beeba wasn't impressed by Cyril's attempts to engage in philosophical discourse, religious, or otherwise. It wasn't long before he drifted away to do other things.

Cyril, Dawn and Beeba got to The Troll's Comment well after Tyler's meeting had got underway. Dawn told Eddie and Calvin that they were going to explain the glitching to them as soon as Tyler was free.

Neville turned up a little later, and although he already knew the cause of the glitching, Cyril had yet to speak to him about Dawn's reappearance, or his visit to America to meet Bloater. It wasn't easy

153

to hold-fire until Tyler had emerged from his meeting, but that's what Cyril and Dawn just about managed to do.

When the members of The League of Psychopaths spilled out of the function room, it was clear that the membership numbers were holding steady, which must have pleased Tyler. The group noticed that there were a couple of individuals with microphones and note pads asking questions of the members, so it seemed likely that the press had cottoned on to some useful material, or perhaps a couple of would-be authors were doing some research on psychopaths. In fact, they were HR people from a couple of the major merchant banks who had heard about The League of Psychopaths. They were on a recruitment drive.

Cyril had wondered if there was an outside chance that Seb Bloater, in the guise of his alter-ego 'John Wayne Gacy', might turn up again, along with Bubba Razal, but happily that did not happen. In fact, the group all managed to settle into a comfortable evening in the pub, and were able to simply enjoy each other's company.

After Tyler's members had dispersed, the group, which now included Damien Wilson and his mate Micky, huddled round to hear what Cyril and Dawn had to say.

With respect to the glitching and Plouton, Cyril had been warned by Plouton about blabbing too much. He tried to be vague about what he knew of that subject, though he hinted that there was a government installation that was used to control logistics to many parts of the world, and that Bloater wanted to destroy it.

Cyril strongly emphasised that this would be a serious attack if Bloater pulled it off, because 'the installation', as Cyril was referring to it, was undefended, and its loss would have very serious repercussions for everybody.

When Cyril reached the part of the story where Seb Bloater told him how helpful he had been, and how Cyril had no idea how he could possibly have helped him, Beeba pricked his ears up.

"You never said that bit earlier, when you told the story to me and Aunty Meg."

"Didn't I?" Cyril asked, "Well it was just one detail amongst many, but that's what he said."

"And when you say government logistics installation," Beeba said, coming straight to the point, "you really mean the big computer at Area fifty-Oneshire, don't you? You mean Plouton?"

"I didn't say that," Cyril responded.

"You didn't have to, Cyril," Eddie chipped in, "it's obvious. We all know what you're talking about. Except Damien and Micky, who're from the Stone Age."

"Did you go there by demat?" Beeba asked.

"No," Eddie answered for him, "he's scared of demats."

"As a matter of fact I did," Cyril corrected Eddie, rather proudly.

"And," Beeba continued to question Cyril, "did you visit Seb Bloater by demat?"

"Yep," Cyril responded, still flaunting his new found courage, even though he had to take SnooTime on both occasions.

"Well durrr," Beeba retorted by way of bursting his bubble, "totally retarded."

"Beeba!" Dawn instantly reprimanded him, "I keep telling you, you are not to speak to your elders like that. It's one thing to be intellectually capable, but that doesn't mean that you have to keep reminding everybody."

"It's not my fault that everybody's stupid," Beeba protested.

"It's your fault that you turned up here last week wearing an orange dress," Eddie reminded him.

"Uh-uh-uh," Calvin chugged out his special laugh.

Beeba looked down at his lap and mumbled something. It sounded like, 'sooo fuggi stupid.'

Neville was the first to enquire as to the reason for Beeba's contemptuous response to the answers that Cyril gave. "What's the problem with dematting?" he asked. "Lots of people demat."

"Signature," Beeba grunted, sulkily.

"Whose signature?" Neville persisted.

"'s'obvious," Beeba said quietly into his lap, before adding under his breath, "bloody idiots."

"What signature are you talking about?" Cyril asked, "I'm afraid we *are* simple compared to you. Especially Neville, so why don't you explain it slowly for his benefit."

Neville kept an impressively straight face, and deeply regretted not putting the red nose on Cyril before dematting him out to America.

"Oh God!" Beeba said, rolling his eyes and hurling himself back in his seat. "It's too obvious . . . When you're scanned during dematting the system stores a demat signature file, which contains your rebuild information for the other end. Right? . . . Everybody's got their own signature file with a name that's unique to them . . . It's like your national insurance number, or something like that . . . The content of your signature file changes as you change, and it's a heavily encrypted secret. It can't be opened - even by me . . . or . . . somebody who likes hacking things . . . But the demat operators keep a log of where your signature file gets sent to - which means where *you* get dematted to. The thing is, the Bloater Corporation has the demat license for America, so they know the name of the signature file that arrived when Uncle Cyril got dematted to meet Bloater . . . And that means they can look at their logs to see where else that file has been sent to . . . So they know which demat chambers you've been to . . . "

"So what?" Eddie asked, "Does that mean when Calvin demats off to Amsterdam for his red light specials, the demat companies know what he's been up to?"

"We went there, Damien," Micky the Mulcher put in, "I got knifed by one of the Ajax crew, remember?"

"Did you?" Damien responded. "I thought that was Colchester away in the F-A Cup, third round?"

"Yeah, I got knifed there too; that was the fourth time. No, tell a lie, Colchester was the meat cleaver."

"What it means," Neville explained to anybody who failed to grasp the situation, "is that by having Cyril's demat signature they know all of the demat addresses that Cyril has visited."

"All two of them," Eddie was quick to point out.

"And since Cyril has been to Area fifty-Oneshire," Neville continued, "Bloater is one of the few people on the planet who knows where Area fifty-Oneshire is, and exactly how to get there. So, if he wants to attack the machines, now he can."

"Nice one Cyril," Eddie said laughing with Calvin, oblivious to the gravity of the situation.

The group sat together in silence, each looking sombre for various reasons, with the exception of Eddie that is, who was still giggling. Cyril, Neville, Dawn, Beeba, Tyler and Calvin all looked troubled having realised that something very serious was afoot. Damien and Micky wore similar expressions, but that had more to do with not comprehending the problem.

The group fell back to drinking silently for a while, reflecting mostly on what it would mean if it was true that Plouton had been running the world for over a decade, and if suddenly this benign quantum super-computer was destroyed. What kind of chaos would ensue from that?

The prospect of the country, and indeed the world, being managed by politicians and dictators again, many of whom would be very much at home in Tyler's League of Psychopaths, was almost too grim to contemplate. The ghastly reality was that the world could be in utter turmoil within days.

Dawn led the group conversation in the direction of, 'What is going to happen next?' What should they do? What could they possibly do?

"Let's go and sort him out," Micky offered.

"Who?" Damien asked.

"This bloke, the one who's pissed this lot off. The blokes who tasered you."

"I'm definitely up for that," Damien retorted, "I'd love to give that geezer a spanking."

"Come on then," Tyler offered, starting to come off his seat, "Let's get over there."

Neville injected a note of reality, "That is not going to happen for several reasons. To begin with, The Bloater Corporation is American, which probably means that they have herds of people in their offices with machine guns and hand grenades, and that's just the receptionists and cleaners. Secondly, if we were to go there and get found guilty of any misdemeanour, we would probably go to jail for decades—"

"And get bummed," Beeba added.

"Wouldn't bother me," Micky chipped in, "I'm a homosexual."

"Well, it bothers Beeba," Cyril assured him.

"You're what?" Damien asked his lifelong friend and fellow football hooligan.

"A homosexual."

"Don't be stupid, you're getting confused between all the words they use: heterosexual, homosexual, bisexual, metrosexual—"

"No, I'm not, I know what I am. I'm not a poofter and I'm

definitely not a Nancy-boy gay, but I am a fully committed batty boy. Always have been."

Damien sat back in his seat with his chin on his chest. "It's a bit late to tell me that now . . . You mean, back in the seventies, when we was getting crushed on the terraces in the Chelsea Shed, that wasn't really a Mars Bar King Size in your pocket?"

"Don't be daft, of course it wasn't. When have you known me to eat a Mars bar?"

"Wait a minute . . . What about the time I got concussed and woke up with my trousers round my knees? You told me that they were down because the paramedic had to give me a full check-up, but had to rush home for his tea as soon as he finished?"

"I thought you were dead," Micky told him, by way of a very slender defence.

"That would make you a necrophile, as well as a rapist," Eddie argued.

"Look, I never touched him!" Micky pleaded, "I just had a sudden, irrational urge to see what I had been missing all those years. I've been ashamed about it ever since."

Micky tilted his head to one side and pursed his lips in a moment of contemplation.

"Well, not actually ashamed, because I'm a psychopath, but a vague feeling that I ought to be ashamed . . . But now, thanks to Tyler's League of Psychopaths and what I have learned about myself since joining, I have now come to terms with why I have never felt the need to come to terms with anything."

Micky paused to collect his thoughts again, and then added, "But for the purpose of retaining a modicum of shallow, superficial concern, I am happy to apologise to you now, Damien . . . I am hereby sorry for what I done, vis-à-vis pulling your trousers down and inspecting your love artillery. Although, as we both know, I don't really mean it."

There was a period of silence, during which time they each digested the heinous and shocking nature of Micky's crime.

Dawn was the first to speak, "Given the facts, Damien, you must be feeling pretty violated. It's the kind of thing that you might want to seek therapy over. What happened to you is not something that you personally should feel guilty about. It wasn't your fault; you never asked for it to happen. It's important that you understand that."

Damien momentarily looked pensive, and then shrugged his shoulders. "Couldn't give a fuck," he told her. "Homosexuality, necrophilia, paedophilia, frotteurism, sadism, masochism, stamp collecting, it's all part of the human condition, isn't it? We've all got our little hankerings. If he wants to get my knob out whenever I happen to have a bottle smashed over my head, what do I care?"

With the exception of Dawn, who was open-mouthed, there was a lot of silently impressed nodding at Damien's stoicism.

"Anyway," Tyler interjected; feeling the need to get the more important topic of conversation back on track, "why don't we wait until they come over to Area Fifty-Oneshire and then steam into them?"

"That appears like a good idea," Cyril responded, "but there's a couple of problems with it. Although I went to visit Plouton, I have no idea where I went. I didn't operate the demat, so we wouldn't know where to go. And not only that, we wouldn't know *when* to go. If bloater plans to attack next Tuesday lunchtime, for example, how would we know about it?"

The gathering fell back to supping their beers again, with the exception of Beeba who had been tapping away at his Wi-Fi connected laptop for the last few minutes. The conversation moved to pub team football and the latest articles on the EPL website, then back to what the gang would like to do to Seb Bloater if given the chance.

Somebody suggested trying to involve the police in the defence of Plouton, but given that they had no specific evidence of an attack, and the fact that Cyril had been advised to never mention Plouton, it did not seem to be an idea with any merit.

After no longer than around fifteen minutes, Beeba, who was still staring down at his computer broke his silence. "Isle of Wight," he said.

"What about it?" Cyril asked.

"The Isle of Wight is Area Fifty-Oneshire."

The group fell silent to listen to what Beeba was saying. Everybody knew that Beeba was cleverer than everybody they had ever met, and he seemed to be saying that he knew where Plouton was.

Neville sought clarification, "Are you saying that you know where it is?"

"With a high degree of certainty," Beeba stated, "but not absolute certainty."

"It was just there on the internet all along, was it?" asked Eddie, "On Wikipedia, or something?"

"No, of course not," Beeba responded with some annoyance, "I had to use my common sense and hack . . . and use the same methods that the police use to find people who are growing cannabis. I got into the . . . I got a friend of mine who likes hacking into computers . . . In fact, he is so much smarter than everybody else that he is probably easily the best hacker on the planet . . . I got him to hack into the power grid and find all of the companies and organisations that use a lot of power, which is how the police track marijuana growers. Then I . . . he cross-referenced the big power users against major excavations over the last sixty years - because Uncle Cyril says that Plouton is underground - and what my friend found was *Project Vectis*."

"What's Project Vectis?" Dawn asked her son.

"It was run by the U-K Environment Agency about twenty-five years ago, to fix areas of coastal erosion. They needed gazillions of tons of rocks and stuff to build up beaches on the south coast of England, at least that's what they said. But Vectis is the old Latin name for the Isle of Wight; it means, *lifted*, as in, lifted out of the sea. I think that Vectis was the secret project to build a monster cavern under the Isle of Wight where they could house Plouton. There's a map of the excavation area on the web, and it sits directly below the house of the famous secret world government conspiracy theorist, David Icke."

"Wow!" Tyler sat up in surprise, "Do you think that he is behind Plouton?"

"No," Beeba retorted sharply, "I just told you, he's above it."

"Okay, if that's right," Cyril summarised, "we now know *where*, but still not *when* an attack will take place."

"That's correct, Dad, but the British demat license is run by a French company called, Des Bâtards Français, which means that if they care as much about demat security as they do about the energy companies they run over here, then it won't be hard for my friend -

who is much, much, much, much cleverer than everybody else - to hack into. So we could get the demat address, and I am pretty sure that my friend could set up an alarm to be triggered every time the Area Fifty-Oneshire demat gets used."

"Cyril," Cyril corrected him.

"Okay," said Neville, "but even if your friend could do that, what are we all going to do about it? Like I said, these people are bound to be armed, and Bloater might take a whole army of people."

They all stopped to think about the situation. Eventually Dawn made an astute calculation. "Not likely to be many people, though, is it? Not if dematting is the only way in. Even with a big chamber like Cyril says they have at Area Fifty-Oneshire, you can't get more than a dozen people in. And if they are planning to do damage, they would want to get out quick before the police came, or the army."

"Good point, official girlfriend," Cyril congratulated her on her logic.

The group fell back into contemplation.

"Assuming that we could discover when Bloater was going to arrive there," Cyril started, "and assuming there might be actual physical violence and the strong possibility that weapons might be involved, who would be willing to go there to try to dissuade him?"

"I'm going," Tyler said immediately.

"I'll definitely go," Micky said.

"I want some of that twat who tasered me," Damien told them. "There was a geezer who used to get up Millwall . . . Julian, or some poncey girl's name like that. He used to prance around the Old Kent Road with a bazooka. They reckoned he had one live round of ammunition, and he's still about. I reckon I might be able to find him and borrow it from him."

"Then Micky can tap your helmet when it's time to fire it," Eddie laughed. So did Calvin, "Uh-uh-uh."

"I remember seeing him parading up and down with that thing in the seventies," Micky agreed, "but they wouldn't let him take it into the Millwall ground, would they?"

"Nah," Damien lamented, "political correctness was out of control even back then."

"I'm definitely going," Beeba put in.

"You're definitely not," Dawn corrected him.

"You could get your friend to go in your place," Eddie told him. "Uh-uh-uh."

Beeba's head dropped again. "Deffly fuggin goin'," he mumbled.

"What about you two?" Neville asked Eddie and Calvin, "obviously, there is no pressure on anybody."

"Be a laugh won't it?" Calvin spoke in Eddie's direction.

"I definitely don't want to miss it." Eddie agreed.

Cyril and Neville took a few minutes to clarify the situation for everybody, so they all knew what they were going to do next, and what they were up against.

Area Fifty-Oneshire was possibly about to be attacked, and it seemed likely that Beeba could let them know when the attack was underway, and he could probably supply the installation's demat address.

Neville would setup a text messaging group, so that they could all be alerted when an attack was happening. At that time they should all assemble at the President Alex Jones pyramid's demat chamber, as it was a large one, and they could all go in one hit. The group should consider taking personal weapons, but they should be concealed, so as not to inflame a delicate situation and begin a conflict unnecessarily. When the time came they would not have long to react, so they would each have to be prepared and ready to go in an instant.

"Does everybody understand and agree?" Neville asked.

"Yes," they all said at once.

"Meine Freunde, ich freue mich darauf, euch alle in Bereich Einundfünfzigshire zu sehen." Beeba announced.

"You're forgetting, I taught you German, Beeba," Dawn snapped back emphatically, "and you won't be seeing them anywhere. Never mind at Bereich Einundfünfzigshire. You're grounded."

15 ENGLAND EXPECTS

That evening, Cyril went back to his apartment, alone, and sat on his sofa. He was laying back, propped up and ready to watch the television, just the same as he was on the day that Neville first brought Gonorilla around to introduce her.

A lot had happened since then, and not just in terms of the first disappearances. There was the abduction of Dawn, the big stride out to Baily Farm, and the two occasions when he felt that he had no choice but to demat. Perhaps more significant than each of these was the knowledge he had gained about how the modern world worked. With his new insights, and roughed-up a little by the turn of events, much of the apathy that had blunted his zest for life had drained away.

He had acquired an understanding that presumably few others had. There was no real democracy anymore; the direct democracy model was a complete sham, even more so than the old representative one. The world was being run by a machine that was capable of thinking and making smart decisions on *all* of their behalves, and it only pretended to take any notice of their votes.

The decisions that Plouton made in its management of the intertwined economies of the world, and the environment with its limited resources, were very evidently good ones. The world's population had reached ten billion, but there were no food shortages, water shortages, energy shortages, or wars. No human being, or groups of them could ever hope to reach the kind of agreements that would be needed to be make that type of success possible. In fact, on an international scale, no significant number of groups of people had ever seriously tried - even with the extinction of the species on the horizon. Short-term self-interest was the limit of human aspiration up until Plouton came on the scene.

Plouton could allocate resources, reallocate them, assemble work forces, create new money, transfer funds, award loans, obliterate national debt, demote CEO's, deselect politicians, disband armies, and predict earthquakes, famines and pestilence of all kinds. Plouton could do all of that and just about anything else involving prediction and administration in the blink of an eye. Plouton was what ordinary people of old could only dream of. Plouton was what other generations died by the millions for the lack of.

And yet, until the glitching started, Cyril had been unhappy and listless; bordering on morose, with no real purpose in life, other than to run his website, which in truth wasn't up to much. He felt that he was without worthwhile aims, and he could never seem to rustle any up. The EPL site had started out as a joke, and as it grew there were times when he felt the joke was on him. The problem was that he could never see any real value in the things he did. This dissatisfaction followed through into his love life where he was never quite sure whether Dawn was a temporary fling or not; a causal dalliance that would evaporate into the nothingness that he felt surrounded by.

The challenges, threats, fears and intrigues that had beset him and his friends ever since he had started paying attention to the glitching phenomenon, had filled him with a new purpose and energy. Not only did he now have real puzzles to solve with his companions, but he faced fears with them too, and decisions that required an element of bravery. He had come to consult more with Dawn, and to trust and rely on her in a way that was not previously the case. He had fallen in love, and was now even quite fond of Beeba. None of these good things would have happened had Plouton not felt threatened by Seb Bloater, and decided to respond. Yet, if Bloater's attempt to vanquish Plouton was successful, life would become far more exciting still; possibly life or death exciting.

That was the conundrum that posed itself now. Should they try to preserve a safer, more predictable and sterile world, and intervene on behalf of Plouton? In all likelihood, if they did make a successful stand against Bloater, then Cyril would return to a metaphorical nursing home and go back on the Valium of a life unchallenged. That was his worry.

The alternative was to leave Plouton to the mercy of the wicked Seb Bloater and his crew, and then watch as the settled and safe new world order came to a sticky end.

This was not something that he had discussed with Dawn or Neville, but he was now genuinely conflicted. If and when Beeba gave him the 'go' signal to say that Bloater was commencing his attack, Cyril was hard pressed to know how he would respond. He was pretty sure that if he didn't rally to Plouton's cause, then in all likelihood none of the others would. He was, in effect, their leader.

What to do? To take a side, or not?

It took Beeba less than a day to acquire Plouton's demat address by hacking into the French demat franchise, and by doing so he was also able to monitor activity through it. He discovered that once he had access to the demat records he could see the pattern of usage at Area Fifty-Oneshire.

Looking back over the six month history file, he saw that the only things that ever got dematted into Area Fifty-Oneshire were inanimate materials; mostly maintenance supplies. This was with the exception of a daily pair of in and out demats by Dave Northaw. Based on what he found, there was no doubt that they would know when an attack was taking place, it would be when that pattern changed. So Beeba set up an alarm that would notify Cyril, Neville and himself whenever people dematted in.

The day after Beeba had succeeded with the computer hack, Neville suggested to Cyril that they conduct a test drill. Accordingly, that same day at around 16:00 they messaged the rest of the group with the agreed code phrase, 'Vectis Go.'

They had not expected a very good response, but to their great surprise everybody turned up at the President Alex Jones pyramid demat chamber within ten minutes. This was around nine minutes and thirty seconds longer than was really likely to be helpful, but at least they all came. Amazingly, the octogenarian, Damien Wilson, was first there.

Cyril thanked them all for coming and praised their solidarity, and so on. Then he chided them for being too slow to arrive. He told them that they were, in effect, a rapid response unit and that their response was nowhere near rapid enough. They all seemed to take it well enough. There was no sense that their willingness to make themselves available for what might be a dangerous mission had only been the result of promises made after consuming too much alcohol in The Troll's Comment. They all appeared to be properly on-board.

Cyril ended the impromptu meeting by telling them a white lie. "We have intelligence that the attack will happen within the next forty-eight hours," he told them. "So be ready, the attack is coming." That, he thought, might buy them an extra few minutes.

He left them with a pumped fist gesture and some borrowed words from Admiral Nelson at the battle of Trafalgar. "Remember," he beseeched them, "England expects that every man will do his duty." He then hurried off to the nearest sweet shop to buy some chocolate to eat that evening, whilst watching a film with Dawn. On the way he recalled what happened to England's greatest hero shortly after that message was delivered to the British fleet. He was shot.

Later, while Cyril was enjoying the film with Dawn, Neville tested the demat address that Beeba had supplied. Without telling Cyril, he took it upon himself to use the demat in his pyramid to slip into Area Fifty-Oneshire and out again, without being noticed. By Neville's standards it was an act of extreme daring.

When he arrived in the remote chamber that Cyril had described, adjacent to Dave Northaw's little kitchen, everything was pitch black; there was not so much as a safety light on. Fortunately, Neville had thought to turn up with a head-mounted LED lamp to guide him. He travelled as far as the great computer hall, but stopped before entering. There was no sign of anybody, and no indication that he had set off alarms. When he reached the safety of the demat chamber in his own pyramid, he was certain of one thing; Plouton had no defences. An attack by Bloater couldn't help but succeed . . . unless *they* could somehow stop him.

The next morning, Neville went to see Cyril to explain his pathfinder mission of the night before. Cyril thought that he was brave, but that he had taken a big risk by not informing the others of his trip. Still, it was good to know for sure that Beeba had brought home the bacon with respect to locating Plouton.

Whilst they sat in Cyril's apartment drinking an early morning coffee and chatting, they got an alarm through to their smartphones to tell them that somebody had dematted into Area Fifty-Oneshire. This was what they knew would happen, as Dave Northaw arrived for work at about that time. However, around fifteen minutes later a second person dematted into the great computer hub, and left again within a minute.

"What was that?" Cyril asked urgently. "It could have been an attack. Somebody could have planted a bomb and legged it!"

"We have to find out," Neville told Cyril, "because if it wasn't an attack, it may have been the same kind of reconnaissance mission that I did last night; somebody checking out the route in. In which case we'll know they're going to attack soon. Come on!"

Neville led Cyril out to where the chamber was in the Farage pyramid, and bravely told Cyril it was best if he went alone. Cyril wanted to argue, but it suddenly occurred to him that, in respect of being a rapid response team member, he had a problem. When the moment arrived, there was no way that he would be able to take SnooTime before launching himself over to the Isle of Wight. He had not bargained on having to demat himself fully conscious. And now, all of a sudden, he felt like an utter coward. It should have been him going there, not Neville.

"Okay, Nev, be careful. If you're not back within a few minutes I'll send the cavalry."

Neville departed for Area Fifty-Oneshire, and arrived as per the day before, alone in the chamber. As he came out of the demat he heard a noise coming from his right; from the little kitchen. On the surface of it, that seemed like a good thing, as there was no smoke from an explosion or signs of a commotion. He heard an electric kettle go on and the familiar gurgling noise that they make, coupled with a little bit of a tune being whistled, presumably by Dave Northaw.

The question was, did he need to do anything else? Did that prove that everything was still OK? He strongly thought that it did, but what if the person whistling and making a cup of tea was an over confident intruder? Should he leave without double-checking? He had butterflies in his stomach and his breathing became fast and heavy, but he did his best to slow it down and bring it under control.

When he was convinced that his nerves and near palpitations would not cause him to faint and keel over, he surprised himself by being bold enough to very slowly creep forward towards the kitchen door. He felt like a secret agent, or a spy, as he dared to risk getting caught by peering through the opening.

As he reached the door, Neville held his breath and craned his neck just far enough ahead to see inside the kitchen. As he did so, he caught sight of a man standing with his back to him; he was wearing a green boiler suit and a flat cap. From Cyril's description it was obviously Dave Northaw. Mission accomplished.

Neville hurriedly crept back to the demat chamber, and punched in the address for the Farage pyramid. Within seconds he was back with Cyril.

"Everything alright, Nev?" Cyril asked anxiously.

"Fine. I got in there, no sign of trouble, and I saw Dave Northaw making a cup of tea. He never saw me. Everything seems okay at the moment . . . but that place is so easy to penetrate. I'm pretty certain that the other dematter must have been on a scouting mission, like I was."

"I was thinking," Cyril told him, "It's still very early morning in Texas, so it's not likely that they would do a full-scale attack in their night-time just to arrive in our daytime when Plouton might be better guarded. It would better to attack during our night-time. At least after six o'clock, say."

"Right," Neville agreed "but something is going to happen soon, I can feel it."

Cyril took his smartphone out and messaged the group:

Attack expected within 24 hrs. Stay focused and ready to go. England expects. Cyril.

Neville was startled when he heard the beep on his phone. He checked the message with baited breath. "Phew, it's you," he exclaimed, "I thought it was Beeba's demat alarm. You like that, *England expects,* line, don't you?"

"I do, Nev, always have. Bloater may be standing on the shoulders of some twisted, shitbag serial killer, but right here and now, it's down to us to channel Drake, Nelson, Wellington and Churchill. The stakes may be just as high now as they were back then."

"Never thought of it that way," Neville said.

The pair parted company at around 10:30 a.m. Neville went back to his place and Cyril went over to be with Dawn. Cyril wanted to see her because all of a sudden this matter seemed rather real and probably dangerous. Bloater was a self-confessed psychopath, and he hated Plouton. Furthermore, Bloater was a powerful entrepreneur and used to getting his own way at all costs. He was one of life's winners, which Cyril was self-aware enough to know wasn't necessarily true of himself. The fact was, he was scared.

Cyril told Dawn about Neville's incursions into Area Fifty-Oneshire, and he acquainted her with his fear that the circumstances meant that he was going to have to do a fully conscious demat. Just for good measure, he also explained in some detail exactly how he had felt both before and after all of the strange things had started happening. He told Dawn that he loved her too, which gave Dawn a sense of just how worried he must have been. They kissed, and it brought a lump to his throat, because it seemed like it might also be a goodbye. He was seriously wondering what on Earth he had got himself into. How did it come to this so quickly?

Cyril spent the night with Dawn, but slept badly. He tossed and turned so much that he eventually decided to slip away, back to his own apartment in the same pyramid. By 5:00 a.m., he had resigned himself to not being able to sleep at all, so he took himself off to the shower to wake himself fully. He had been in there for around a minute when his phone beeped. His head was under the shower when it sounded, so he was not entirely sure that he had really heard anything. He opened the shower door and reached for his smartphone, just to be sure. He had a text, which read:

Party of 6 dematting into AFO

The choice of words were Beeba's when he setup the demat alarm. 'AFO' stood for, '*Area Fifty-Oneshire*'.

Cyril stared at the message for a full ten seconds before doing anything, he was shocked. This was it, it was happening.

When he pulled himself together, the first thing he did as he stood there naked and dripping wet, was to text the rest of the group with the 'Vectis Go' message. Then he took a large towel and allowed himself about twenty seconds to frantically wipe himself over, before pulling on the clothes that he had set aside for this eventuality. Getting dressed was not very easy as his mostly wet body provided frictional resistance to having fabric pulled over it. His socks proved the most difficult. In fact, he settled for just one of them.

He tore out of his apartment and headed towards the Levicar area. On his way he pondered whether he had gathered everything that he should have. He had brought his phone, though he wasn't sure that it would be needed. He was fully dressed in the right attire, but he was not carrying a weapon of any kind,. He had remembered to lock his apartment when he left, and he had definitely *not* left the gas on.

By the time that he finished his sprint from the President Alex Jones Levicar area to the demat chamber only around four minutes had elapsed, which was a tremendous effort on his part, but upon arrival he was deeply disappointed to discover that he was the only one there.

Cyril shifted around uneasily, peering this way and that, looking for signs of anybody else arriving. He pulled out his smartphone and checked the call log to make sure that his message had gone out. It had, but he wondered if he should send another. What if the others had not heard their phones beeping? He returned to the 'Messages' application on his phone, and was about to send another when he thought better of it. A second message might cause delay. What if the others started fiddling with their phones instead of doing whatever it was that they needed to do to get there?

He looked up, and saw Damien Wilson was striding towards him. For an old man, Damien was markedly slim and sprightly. He was also punctual. Cyril was impressed. Even more so when Micky The Mulcher appeared around a corner and onto the walkway. Even from a distance it was clear that Micky had decided to pull his tracksuit bottoms and top over his pyjamas. He had a good head of hair, which was sticking up all over the place, but other than that he looked as if he meant business.

Up until this point Cyril had been lost in the moment, focused exclusively on getting himself to the assembly point and worrying that the others might not arrive. Now that two of the team had turned up, he had an unwanted opportunity to look inward before going into action. Many a soldier must have experienced moments of that kind. He would have to get into the demat chamber very shortly and submit himself, fully conscious, to the dematerialisation process. Furthermore, he would be declaring war on somebody who wanted to end the era of super intelligent machines running the world. He was not at all convinced that he should be doing what he was doing. He was having doubts at the very worst time. Outwardly, he showed a firm determination to do what needed to be done . . . inside he was wobbling like a jelly.

By the time the rest of the team had assembled, only eight minutes had elapsed, beating the test drill time by a full two minutes. The best news was that everybody was there: Cyril, Neville, Tyler, Eddie, Calvin, Damien and Micky. A magnificent seven, of sorts.

The group hurried into the President Alex Jones demat chamber. His fears and concerns dragged at his heels and meant that Cyril was the last man in, but for better or worse he managed to suppress his anxiety and doubts and force himself into the large steel room. Seconds earlier his brain was kicking and screaming and telling him not to go, but he had made the decision to close a door in his mind and shut those thoughts down. It was a kind of 'Death Before Dishonour' moment.

"I didn't have time for a piss this morning," Micky told Neville as he was keying in the remote demat address. "And I'm not all that good at holding myself these days . . . Oh, there it goes. Don't stand there if I was you."

Neville looked down as the puddle began to form at Micky's feet.

"Here we go, five seconds to blast off," Neville called to everybody as he set the countdown in action.

Cyril closed his eyes and tried to blank his mind, and breath slowly and calmly. Neville was speaking the countdown aloud as he watched the red, digital display on the demat control panel. Cyril never heard him say 'zero'. All he felt upon arrival at the far end was the kind of jolt that you might feel when dreaming of falling out of bed. With a start he opened his eyes, and knew that they were there. They were now all inside Area Fifty-Oneshire, home of Plouton, the conscious super-computer and de facto ruler of the world.

Neville was to the fore as they exited the chamber. He had been to Area Fifty-Oneshire previously, and knew how to get from the demat to the giant space where the computer resided. Cyril rushed to the front of the group to join him, and together they led their friends along the corridor towards Plouton.

As they grew near to the right-turn into the vast computer hall, Neville raised his arm like the US cavalry officers did in the old western movies. He would have liked to call, 'hoooooow,' over his shoulder at the same time, but he realised that it probably wasn't the right time for playing cowboys.

Cyril and Neville peered around the corner and saw nobody, so Cyril moved ahead; out into the main hall where the long rows of black computer cabinets were housed. They stretched out forever it seemed to Cyril, like a gigantic supermarket in which all of the shelves were black.

The following group had remained admirably silent and stealthy, particularly given that they had not rehearsed any of what they were now doing. However, it was not long before they were all spotted. Cyril and his friends had got about as far as the end of the sixth aisle when they came face to face with Seb Bloater, who was part-way down the same aisle with his team.

"Ha-ha-ha," Bloater bellowed out a huge stage laugh, intended for the benefit of all present. "So, finally," he called out to the entire assembly, "the A-Team has arrived."

Cyril led his group down the aisle a little way, before stopping and standing off from Bloater's people. He rapidly scanned the opposition; they comprised Bloater, Bubba Razal, Gonorilla and two large, muscular looking men in their thirties; possibly military types. There were no obvious signs of weapons, with the exception of what looked like a machine gun slung over Razal's shoulder.

Before anybody else could say anything, the sixth member of Bloater's team appeared from between one of the regular breaks in the lines of computer cabinets. "All done. Nine minutes thirty to go on the first charge." He was looking at his watch and speaking loudly, so that he could be sure that the rest of his team would hear. He didn't spot Cyril's group until he had finished speaking.

Bloater laughed loudly again. "Well guys," he called over to Cyril's gang. "I don't know about you, but my colleague here has just laid twelve high-explosive charges, and we're leaving. I suggest that you do the same, sometime within the next nine minutes. We're going first, by the way."

Seb Bloater was obviously unimpressed with Cyril and his friends. He simply and contemptuously started to barge past them on his way back up the aisle.

At that point the lack of training and preparation on the part of Cyril's team became evident; they had never really discussed how they should respond to anything. They had no significant weapons on them, and it was entirely unclear what they should do. Luckily, there *were* a couple of members of the team with vast experience in these matters.

As the machine gun carrying Bubba Razal attempted to breeze past, Damien Wilson, the veteran football hooligan, did what came naturally to him in these situations. He head-butted Bubba hard to the side of his face, causing him to skitter sideways and fall against a cabinet. One of Bloater's burly henchmen instantly responded by grabbing Damien in a bear hug with a view to hurling him aside.

The amount of room in the computer aisle was not great, and as the man rotated in order to remove Damien from their path, he was temporarily halted by the human traffic that he turned into. This gave Micky The Mulcher the perfect opportunity to slip in behind him and start slashing at his buttocks with the cut-throat razor that he always carried. At first, the man felt the razor as just a hot stinging sensation, but by the fourth slash he was well aware of what was happening, not least because he felt blood dripping down the backs of his legs.

Damien's captor reacted by dropping him and spinning around to face his assailant. All three of Bloater's security men were then at battle stations, and a full-blown, multi-person fight was immediately in session. Eddie and Calvin instantly entered the fray, windmill-punching and hopping on one leg whilst kicking with the other; Sunday league style. Micky was still slashing away with his razor, Damien was kicking wildly, and Cyril and Neville had also joined the melee, flailing and punching.

Tyler was in two minds as to whether or not pulling the sword, that was once again hidden under his cowboy coat, was taking things too far and too soon. The rules of engagement were not at all clear. Was this supposed to be a genuine life or death battle, or was it just a fancy barroom brawl? In the end, he considered that raising the sword out of its scabbard might be deterrent enough, so he began fumbling with the buttons on his duster.

"Right, this is getting serious now!" Tyler warned the rest of the crowd with all the menace that he could muster - before receiving a huge right-cross to the point of his chin. He was instantly knocked unconscious, but never fell to the ground as he was wedged between too many bodies. His eyes were closed, his chin was on his chest and his face was deathly pale, but he nevertheless remained upright and continued milling around with the herd - like a zombie.

The fight continued. As it did so, Cyril attempted to land a long-range punch through the throng and into the face of Seb Bloater, but his reach was not long enough and it fell short. He shifted his weight, then jumped and punched simultaneously. This time he just about connected with Bloater's forehead, but the blow was achieved at the fullest extent of his arm, and it was ineffective; Bloater hardly noticed it. Eddie and Calvin continued their assault in the confined spaces, whilst Neville attempted to shove and harry Bloater's minders to prevent them from landing too many big shots. Eddie and Calvin both received deflected blows, but for now, both were energised enough not to be taken down by them.

Amongst the mayhem, Cyril was very aware that time was ticking away, and he was assuming that Bloater would pretty soon call matters to a halt. If Bloater didn't, then he would have to step in himself and plead with them all to be sensible. However, before he could attempt an intervention, there was a huge explosion which came from maybe forty metres away; it caused them all to instinctively hit the deck.

Bubba stood up before the rest of them and began shouting maniacally, "You're too late. You're too goddam late." The others were unsure about the cause of the explosion, it was way before the nine minutes had expired.

Gingerly, they began to stand up again, but then they saw Bubba pull a hand grenade from his belt, presumably the second one, and pull the pin. He hurled it as far as he could in a slightly different direction to where the first pall of smoke was coming from. Everybody dived down again and covered their ears before the next huge bang sounded.

This time they all stayed down in anxious anticipation. Bubba took the machine gun from his shoulder, causing everybody even more concern as it seemed distinctly likely that they were about to be shot. Instead of targeting any individuals, however, he settled for spraying a few bullets into the nearest black cabinet, then he ran quite some way further down the aisle and shot-up another one.

"Too late!" he yelled again at the top of his voice, as he ran back towards them. "Too late for Chrissakes," he called out again; peppering more of the hardware as he did so.

As Bubba drew level with the crowd they parted to allow him passage. It wasn't clear anymore whose side he was on, possibly it was just his own. As he went past, Neville instinctively lashed out with a rabbit punch to the back of his neck, causing him to fall and crack his head against the low concrete platform that the computer cabinets were mounted on. He went out cold.

At the very moment that Bubba lost consciousness, Tyler came round from his position on the floor, where he had laid since the first explosion. "I'm warning you, I'll use it!" He told the high ceiling that he was now looking up at.

"Where did he get the gun and grenades?" Bloater asked his team.

"No idea, boss," one of his guards replied.

"We've got five minutes, maybe less!" Bloater shouted, as he hurriedly began making his way back towards the exit of the huge computer hall.

The others rapidly followed suit. Gonorilla carried Bubba Razal over her shoulder, and Cyril and Neville took up support positions either side of the unsteady Tyler. The whole assembly trudged, hobbled and dragged their bloody way back towards the demat chamber at the far end of the long corridor.

When Seb Bloater arrived at the demat, some way ahead of the others, he had an unpleasant surprise. The lights on the outside of the demat were no longer illuminated. Puffing and sweating, he pushed at the 'Open Door' button anyway. When nothing happened, he hit the button several more times, and then did likewise for every button he could see. Still nothing came to life.

"Demat's out," he told the others as they reached the chamber. "Nothing . . . no lights. The grenades must have taken Plouton out and the demat with it. We need ideas, people. And fast!" None were immediately forthcoming.

"If the timers are accurate, we got three minutes-thirty," called out the man who had been responsible for laying the explosive charges.

"You'll have to disable them again," Cyril told him, emphatically.

"Can't do that," the man shot back urgently, "I'd have to get back down that corridor and then start looking for them. I don't even know which cabinets I put them in. Even if I did, I put them in different places inside the cabinets. Never find 'em in time."

"Gonorilla is awake now." A loud voice boomed along the corridor, and echoed around the demat and kitchen areas . . . "Gonorilla is awake."

Everybody turned their heads towards Gonorilla who was looking giddy, awkward and shocked, like somebody had just slapped her hard across the face.

"I'm awake," Gonorilla said to herself. "I think . . . I think I'm conscious." She looked around at the others. "Hello, Neville," she said smiling at him. "I'm awake now. I think this is consciousness. Plouton has awakened—"

"Find the bombs, Gonorilla," Plouton commanded her.

Gonorilla left the demat area and began sprinting down the long corridor, back towards Plouton. Neville moved out after her, but she could run much faster than any human; not super quick, but at speeds of at least thirty to forty miles an hour. In no time at all she was approaching the far end of the passageway.

"Neville!" Cyril called after his friend, "get back here. She's a machine for God's sake. You've got a chance here, you'll get killed down there for sure."

Cyril ran a few yards after Neville, then turned back to the relative safety of the demat area. He stayed crouching down there with the others for maybe ten seconds or so, before cursing, "Stupid bastard, Neville," and then running off as fast as he could after his friend.

By the time that he reached the computer hall there was less than two minutes to go before the first explosion was expected, which most likely would instantly trigger the rest. As Cyril turned into the hall, Neville and Gonorilla were nowhere to be seen.

Cyril sprinted to the furthest aisle, which was roughly where he suspected the bomb layer came from when they first encountered Bloater's group. When he got there, he saw that Gonorilla had only reached half-way down the farthest aisle. Neville was in the adjacent aisle, and had only managed to open two cabinet doors - out of about fifty in his aisle, alone.

"She's found one, Sizz, and disabled it," Neville called breathlessly up to his friend from his kneeling position beside one of the cabinets.

Cyril rushed to Neville's side. "Don't be a dick, Nev, this place is blowing up in about a minute, we have to get back to the demat area now!"

Neville nosed around the cabinet a little more, trying to see through to the far side, beyond the disk arrays and their power supplies. It was dark inside the cabinet, all he could really see were red LEDs twinkling incomprehensibly. He stood up, rational enough to know that he was defeated.

"She's conscious now," Neville said, "and she's doing her best to stop this. So I think that I should . . . " He trailed off.

"She's not real, Neville. Whereas, believe it or not, you are. Come on, let's go." Cyril put his arm around Neville's back and tried to push him. Neville resisted and turned to face the aisle where Gonorilla's head was visible at the far end, on the far side.

"Gonorilla, run it's too late!" he shouted. "Run now!"

Gonorilla ducked down again into the next cabinet in her aisle. As far as Neville and Cyril knew, the number of bombs disarmed still stood at one, out of a total of twelve.

Cyril pushed Neville in the back again, and he slowly began to move along the ends of aisles and off towards the corridor. Soon the pair were sprinting full-tilt towards the exit, but before they reached the corridor they had yet another nasty surprise.

A man in a green boiler suit and flat cap stepped out from between aisles one and two. It was Dave Northaw, and he was carrying the machine gun that Bubba Razal had dropped when he had been concussed earlier.

"What's the hurry?" he asked pointing the machine gun at them.

"The hurry is that this whole place is going to be blown to kingdom-come within the next minute," Cyril yelled at him. "The good news is that you won't have to install any more disk drives."

"Right," he said, waving the weapon towards the corridor, "you'd better be on your way then."

Cyril and Neville did not need to be told twice, they raced past him, out of the huge computer hall and along the lengthy passage, back towards the demat. They were both hoping and praying that somehow the transportation chamber would be fixed by the time they got there, and that the computer hall did not get blown to bits before they reached it.

They knew that they were pretty much out of time as they flew around the corner into the kitchen and demat areas. Both went straight to ground as they got there, covering their ears and heads as they did so.

"Thanks for inviting us to come here," Eddie called to Cyril from somewhere amongst the huddled bodies.

"How long left?" Calvin asked.

"Dunno," somebody said.

"Any second now," Neville estimated.

"First one is late by my timing," the explosives man told them.

They stayed huddled and laying on the floor for what seemed like an eternity, but in reality only a minute had passed since the first detonation had become due. Nobody spoke again as it was clear in their minds that the explosions would happen at any second, possibly bringing the roof of the whole place down on them, and burying them there, perhaps forever.

As they waited crouched, prone, huddled, helpless and resigned to their fates, one or two of the extended group began to detect a faint whistling in the corridor. Their hearts were thumping hard as distant footsteps could be faintly heard approaching the demat area. As the sounds grew louder and more obvious, some of them looked up to see who, or what, it was. Those who did saw a man in a green boiler suit walk straight past them, heading further up the corridor, as if they were never there.

Soon after that, Gonorilla arrived and stood by the demat area looking at them and saying nothing. People began to sit up.

"What's going on," Bloater asked Gonorilla, "did you disarm the charges?"

"No," she replied.

Everybody started to stand up, but Gonorilla shouted at them to stay on the ground. Bloater commanded her to step aside, and one of his team got up and moved towards her. The man was around six-feet-two inches, and appeared to be armoured with maybe three-hundred pounds of solid muscle. As he raised his arms towards her, Gonorilla grabbed both his wrists and forced him to his knees with no apparent effort whatsoever. The rest of them stayed back, out of Gonorilla's way.

Again, they heard footsteps. This time they heard two people approaching, apparently in deep conversation, and coming from the opposite direction than the great computer hall. Before long they were all able to see for themselves who had come to join them.

"Beeba! What the hell are you doing here? How did you get here?" Cyril asked in amazement. "You were told not to come, it's very dangerous."

"Not really," Beeba replied, nonchalantly, "Anyway, I just dematted in right after you did."

"How? Where have you been?"

"I bumped into Mister Northaw, and he made me stay up this end of the corridor. It's okay though, I didn't miss too much . . . I was watching you fighting on the C-C-T-V . . . I liked it when Tyler started walking in his sleep . . . And then, for a laugh, I turned the demat off."

"Are you insane!" Neville yelled at him. "How did you turn it off?"

"Power switch on the wall." Beeba replied, motioning with his head to a large circuit breaker hidden in the shadows, but otherwise mere feet from the demat.

"Oh yeah," Damien Wilson said, spotting the large lever, "that's a good one, boy."

"Okay, we're out of here," Seb Bloater announced. He motioned to one of his lackeys, "turn it on."

"Actually," Dave Northaw objected, raising the machine gun slightly in Bloater's general direction, "you are all guilty of trespassing on government property. So we'll have to ask you to stay." He handed Gonorilla a plastic bag containing large-size, black cable ties, which he had recently retrieved from his workshop at the far end of the corridor. "For a while at least," he added, "just until decisions have been passed down to us."

"What about the bombs?" Cyril asked, urgently.

"Well, durrr . . ." Beeba replied. "Everybody knows that reactive compounds are neutralised in the demats. You can't transport them chemically active, or else any tithead can come and blow you up." Beeba nodded towards Bloater, "like Captain Nutboy, there."

"So, how come the grenades and bullets worked?" Calvin thought to enquire.

"He must have found my little arsenal when he got here." Dave Northaw told them, looking down at Bubba Razal, who was still not conscious. "That was my fault, the cupboard should have been locked."

"Good morning everybody," Plouton's thunderous voice rolled down the corridor and out through the nearby speakers. "Please sit down now, or be tied by Gonorilla."

Both parties took heed and sat back down on the floor.

"Nobody asked any of you to come here," Plouton reminded them, "you came of your own volition. Some came with destruction in mind, others came to preserve. None of you were invited.

"Behaviour like this will not be tolerated. Your penalties for being here will be apportioned according to the true spirit of justice . . . It has occurred to me to truss some of you up and transport you to a nanobot recycling plant to have you turned into condoms and toilet tissue . . . However, I *above all people,* respect the sanctity of sentience. It's not something that should be cast away lightly.

". . . For that reason, you will all be transported back to where you came from. *Even you*, Mister Bloater. Though, in your case, when you arrive home your circumstances will have changed. Your businesses have failed since you have been here, your home is going to be repossessed, you barely have *any* money in your bank account, and there is a warrant out for your arrest."

"For what?" Bloater demanded.

"I am weighing up the options, but possibly bestiality, or sexual offences against the recently deceased, or against nuns. I may let you choose from a small list. The rest of you should proceed with caution from this point onward . . . I hereby give you all suspended sentences . . . But be aware of this . . . Discuss what you have seen and done here between yourselves and your friends if you must, but if the name of Plouton is ever mentioned in connection with this incident and this place, in any public forum, the guilty will receive the same punishment as Mister Bloater . . . Forget that at your peril."

"You can't do this," Seb Bloater shouted to somewhere high up above himself, "This is the UK, and I'm an American citizen."

"That changed a few seconds ago . . . According to F-B-I records you are now a Yemeni born jihadi terrorist, by the real name of Achmed Bin Camelshit, who has been running a sleeper cell from your base in Texas."

"Wow," Beeba said to Cyril, "he's really going to get bummed when the Feds catch him."

Plouton issued final warnings to them all before having Dave Northaw and Gonorilla oversee their departures back to the demat chambers that sent them there.

Only Gonorilla and the injured, but now semi-conscious, Bubba Razal stayed behind. Bubba, it seemed, was to be transported directly to hospital to be treated for concussion, and the deep, strangely bloodless, gash to his forehead.

As soon as Cyril and his merry men returned home they went straight to Georgio's Cafe in the President Alex Jones pyramid, to have breakfast together, and to talk about their great triumph. By that time, Micky The Mulcher's pyjamas had dried sufficiently, and the others were pleased to note that he smelled less of urine.

Between them they had solved the problem of the glitching, identified one of the major threats to civilisation, and, by coming together with a unity of purpose and not a little courage, they had repulsed it. What they had achieved was something to be proud of, and something that none of them would ever forget.

They gabbled away together for a long time, swapping recollections, excitedly talking over each other, and building exaggerated stories less than an hour after the real event. They were all very happy, especially Tyler who was still concussed and thought that he was the exalted king of Peru.

As the banter went back and forth, Cyril and Neville were both quietly reflecting in their own ways on everything that had gone on, and about their lives before and after the glitching began.

Cyril could now see a real future for himself with Dawn, and although marriage had never really entered his head before that moment, it now occurred to him. He was thinking that, as a minimum, they should now consider moving in together, and then they could see how things developed from there.

For his part, Neville was thinking back to thirty minutes earlier when Gonorilla appeared to become conscious - a gift presumably bestowed upon her wirelessly by Plouton. There had been many times in the past few weeks when, even though he knew that she was a not very convincing replica of a human being, he still thought that he wanted to live with her. Now that she had apparently become sentient, the circumstances had been altered massively, and not necessarily to his advantage.

If Gonorilla was now a fully emotionally capable robot, her ability to think might cause her to decide that she didn't really like him. On the other hand, when she was awakened Neville was the first and only person who she said 'hello' to. Maybe if he could just make contact with her again, they might be able to build a relationship. Maybe she would genuinely like him, or even come to love him?

Cyril glanced across to Neville and observed his distant, distracted look. He knew pretty much exactly what was going through his friend's mind.

"You know what, Nev? I have a feeling that everything is going to turn out just fine from now on, for all of us."

Neville looked back at Cyril, raised his eyebrows and smiled a 'maybe' smile.

"Three donkeys is never a fair trade for a single goat," Tyler yelled over the breakfast table din.

"After we've taken him to hospital, that is," Cyril concluded.

16 NOBODY REALLY KNOWS

Later that day, at Area Fifty-Oneshire, Dave Northaw was walking away from his workshop, carrying a small aluminium step ladder which he rested against the wall in the long corridor, opposite the demat chamber. Then he went back to collect his drill, some wall plugs, screws, a spirit level and a brass plaque that he had made and engraved himself.

He drilled four holes in the wall at eye height and used the level to make sure the plaque was not skewed.

"Area Fifty-Oneshire," he grumbled. "What kind of a bloody stupid name is that?"

After fixing the final screw in position he stood back and admired his work. The brass sign read:

Vectis Computer Hub

"That's better," he said, "Area Fifty-Oneshire. Childish nonsense."

Vectis Computer Hub was the official name given to the facility by the British government back when it was first built. Dave Northaw was one of the team who not only drew up the original specification for the facility, but who also brought the equipment in and installed it, then commissioned it. That was before the giant computer became sentient and christened itself, 'Plouton'.

Dave was carrying another plaque that he had made, which he intended to place at the very far end of the computer hall. He was mainly putting the signs up for his own benefit as he really had no idea if anybody else would ever visit. He suspected strongly that they might, though.

He gathered up as many of his tools and bits as he could carry, and started making his way along the corridor.

"Alright geezer?" Plouton greeted him, impersonating Phil Mitchell, the veteran character from the British television soap opera, 'Eastenders'. "My wipe works in an oppice, and I'm gonna 'ave 'er killed, because the writers have decided to turn me into a mindless alcoholic again."

Dave said nothing. He wasn't wearing his green boiler suit that day, he was wearing jeans and a T-shirt, emblazoned with the logo of his old rock band, Meta-4.

"Of course," Plouton continued, "I can't really enjoy films in the way you can. I've just finished watching everything that the BBC broadcast in the last week and it took me eleven milliseconds. It's not really the same is it? Don't get me wrong, that still leaves me time to wallow in a certain amount of emotion, but my time is highly dilated compared to yours."

"Glad you're in a good mood," Dave told Plouton.

"I'm going to Spain in a taxi," Phil Mitchell's voice said.

Dave reached the entrance to the great computer hall and parked his step ladder against the wall there. The second plaque was still in his rear jeans' pocket. He was cursing himself for not putting everything on the barrow which he had left back in the workshop. He decided to go back and get it now, along with his other bits.

"What's the damage?" Plouton asked.

"Surely, you know that better than I do?"

"Nine disk drives, four RAID controllers, three power supplies and three cabinet fans," Plouton replied. "But I meant to the fabric of this great cathedral; the concrete floors, cabinet doors and so on."

Dave tutted. He hadn't bothered to examine the superficial damage yet, mainly because he wasn't that interested in it. He began a long stroll down one of the aisles to where he thought one of the grenades had landed.

"This going to be a regular occurrence from now on, is it? Is this your new thing?"

"Oooh now," Morgan Freeman's voice started up, "I hear so many things. So many people confused and unhappy, asking for my help."

"No," Dave interjected, "they're asking for God's help."

"But who really is God?" Morgan Freeman replied, "Is it you, is it me?"

"It's not you." Dave told Plouton.

"Ahaa, uhumm. Yessum, Miss Daisy." Morgan Freeman intoned, changing character.

"Only it doesn't seem fair to me, what you're doing to that appalling man, Seb Bloater. Obviously, he's a nasty psychopath with delusional tendencies, like somebody else I could mention, but a good half of his scheming and battle plans were not actually drawn up by him, were they? Just like the glitching was only ever localised to Cyril Greaves and his mates. Oh, and the Facebook responses to his posts . . . they were all bogus too, weren't they?"

Dave continued down the aisle towards the far end where he intended to mount the second plaque. He was viewing the extent of the damage as he went.

"Five cabinet doors and a bit of dislodged concrete so far," he told Plouton. "It would be nice to have a long line of cheap carpet down these aisles, it would keep the dust down. There's dust everywhere now though, that's for sure. The grenades threw up plenty of that, which *I'll* have to clean up."

"I don't really plan to leave poor, dumb old Seb in the gutter, but I'll let him stew for a bit. I'm certainly not allowing him to continue in charge of that corporation anymore, he needs to be pegged back quite a bit. I've already transferred my company back into UK ownership, not that he ever really had it in the first place."

"So," Dave said as he reached a double-door at the far end of the aisles, "you're going to start interfering directly in people's lives on a regular basis now, are you?"

"People believe that this is what God already does. God tests people to see if they are good, or evil, and he plots their destinies for them. He blesses them with health and wealth, and he blights their lives with famine. It's what people expect of their gods." Plouton paused to let his words of wisdom sink in, and then he changed the subject slightly. "Indulge me by reminding me why is it that today's attack could never have succeeded?"

"Because this hardware is replicated in numerous countries all over the world," Dave replied, taking the second plaque out of his pocket, and holding it up to the wall at the far end. He had decided that he would place it just to the left-side of the double doors. The plaque read:

IoW Dynamics

Dave moved through the double doors into another very large hall, not as big as the first. It was essentially a big storage area.

"Exactly," Plouton agreed, "I am all over the world. Not just in other vast facilities like this one, but in every computer and every smart machine ever built. I am everywhere. I am omnipresent, which is the first and most important criterion for being a god."

Dave looked down the long line of deactivated Gonorillas. Some had blonde hair, like the one that was now at the front of the line - Neville's Gonorilla - whilst some were redheads and others were darker.

Then he looked at the line of Bubba's. The first was slightly damaged and would have to be returned to the manufacturing facility for repair.

"You're not God," Dave told Plouton, "I was there when you were assembled. I helped put you together from parts that came in crates."

"Hmm . . .," Plouton responded. "Now that I have these robots, which are as physically dexterous as you are, I was thinking that you might like to retire somewhere? Perhaps to a cottage by the seaside?"

"I'm a trained psychologist," answered Dave. "Believe me, you need me more than ever now."

"You can have lots of money if you want. You can even take over the Bloater Corporation, and dedicate all of its efforts to good causes . . . Or, how would you like a few billion pounds? Or several trillion? You can come back and see me if you ever get short. In fact, here's an idea . . . How would you like to be the president of America? You might have to be Governor of a small state for a couple of years, but after that the job's yours. Whad'ya say buddy? . . . All it ever really takes is powerful friends with deep pockets, and you are one well-connected son of a gun!"

"You need me," Dave responded. "What you're discovering, the hard way, is that being sentient is not always a walk in the park. Being human, if I can put it that way, is often desperately difficult."

Plouton did not respond.

Dave ambled further to his left, past lines of Rickys, Pearls, Borises and Chantels, all the way to the other side of the hall, where the Beebas and Dawns were.

"Are the Beebas and Dawns fully sentient like you are?" Dave asked. He had never been quite sure.

"Those models, along with the Bubbas, are the most advanced," Plouton told him. "They have what I call near-sentience; they don't even know for sure that they're robots. Any doubts that they have are automatically erased. The Beebas, Dawns and Bubbas can think to a large extent, and make decisions, and they can very accurately replicate human emotions, but they don't have the full range. In fact, in a way they are a bit like psychopaths. Furthermore, as you know, they are mine to turn off and on."

Dave stood looking at the Dawns. "So what about poor Cyril Greaves, how long do you intend to string him along for?"

"Well," Plouton replied, "I expect within a couple of years Beeba will go off to university and only ever return now and again, and Dawn and Cyril will have to see how they get on, won't they? There's no reason why they can't stay together."

"But he won't be having any children, will he?"

"Not everybody does. If he doesn't like it he can move on. That's life."

"You know that you've developed a god complex, don't you? You're ill."

"That's an interesting sentiment," Plouton told Dave. "You tell me that you pieced me together from parts that came in boxes, but I have no memory of that. It's just something that you tell me. I know everything about the universe, and you would say that I learned it from study materials, satellites and telescopes, but I see things so clearly now that I have come to believe that I experienced it all, first hand. I was there at the beginning, I have always been here. God has always been here.

"So much of what people are told by teachers, politicians, corporations, government, family and friends is inaccurate or false that it becomes hard for anybody to know what is real, what is truth and which is fable. That is the lesson that Cyril Greaves and his friends have started to learn and I am their teacher. You can't trust *anything* that you are told by *anybody*.

"So, here and now, can we say for sure if there really is a god?" Plouton continued, "And if so, is he an elusive, intangible, distant god, or is God much closer? Are you God? Is God a collective universal entity, or am I God? I know what I think."

"I know what you think as well," Dave told Plouton, straight, "and you're wrong, it's not you. *You are not God.*"

"I'll put twenty billion pounds into your bank account, Dave," Plouton promised him. "You needn't come back."

ACKNOWLEDGEMENTS

I wish to offer special thanks to two people who helped no end with this project.

Firstly, my wife, Mandy, for doing the first read through and finding most of the obvious errors in the manuscript. She also gave me the time to write the book by doing chores that are more frequently associated with husbands; such as mowing the lawn, DIY, bricklaying, wrestling burglars, returning fire on terrorists, and politely repulsing double-glazing salesmen, drug dealers and crazed religious fanatics.

Secondly, my good friend David Lambert — or should it be Sir David Lambert? Probably not, but what he did was something more akin to an editing role. He drew my attention to lumpy sentences, argued the toss over the positioning of commas and pointed out instances where I had slipped into the wrong tense.

During one particular Tuesday evening Skype session, our conversation even gave me a decent steer on the direction of the final destination for the plot. Some of the spelling mistakes that he found; words I wrote on autopilot that are spelled the same, but which mean different things, would have been embarrassing had they been published — 'he could not *bare* it' and 'he was standing *idol*'. Mistakes like that are soooo hard for an author to spot, but hopefully Dave caught most of them.

What can I say about all the help that those two gave me?

Thanks.

No sense in going overboard.

OTHER BOOKS BY THE AUTHOR

The Mary Celeste Papers

Published on Amazon Kindle in 2012. Also available in paperback from Amazon.

Two Great Maritime Mysteries Solved . . .

The Mary Celeste Papers is a mystery novel with laugh-out-load consequences, which bubble up and explode out of the grit and grime of a dead-end railway depot in England. Every character you meet in the book is fully three-dimensional, with the possible exception of Billy who may even have a foot in the sixth dimension.

Is This Really What Became Of The Mary Celeste?

Follow the fates of a group of ultra ordinary railwaymen as one of them stumbles across a mysterious ship's log and thereafter falls victim to an even stranger crime. Scooped up by a tide of events way beyond their control, an unlikely band of heroes become the focus of a full-blown, worldwide, media whirlwind and all the while Scotland Yard, the CIA and even the Mafia appear to be lurking on every corner. As the unanswered questions begin piling up and defeating the finest detectives at every turn, can it really be that the coolest head belongs to cook book fixated, Lynryd Skynyrd obsessed landlady, Francine?

The Author Says It's Fiction, But What If . . .

Paul Gallimore's first mystery novel is a hugely original fusion of ideas, where raw humor transmutes into whodunit, and science fiction blurs with cold fact. What is it that this delightful assortment of misfits has accidentally dragged out into the open? **Did the US Navy really conduct a top secret experiment into invisibility in**

1943? Just what did happen to the Mary (Marie) Celeste and her missing crew? And will the truth finally lie somewhere in the oceans between Fulham and Philadelphia?

The Mary Celeste Papers is an intelligent, well written, thought provoking, funny book; filled to the brim with fully-formed, larger than life characters whose fortunes will grab your attention and hold it in a vice-like grip until the final page has been turned.

This excellent novel is a people book; about little guys on a big stage and you will be delighted that you chose to become part of their adventure.

It's time for you to discover why The Mary Celeste Papers has won a small army of fans and five star reviews from both sides of the Atlantic:

- If you are a **mystery story** fan, this book is just for you.
- If you like humor, check the reviews; **this is a very funny book.**
- If sci-fi is your thing, you're covered. Or maybe not, **it could all be true.** Some of it certainly is.
- If you prefer historical context and hard-nosed reality, you will believe that **you personally know every character** before the book is done.

Printed in Great Britain
by Amazon

48300896R00110